WHISPER
MURDER!

WHISPER MURDER!

VERA KELSEY

COACHWHIP PUBLICATIONS
Greenville, Ohio

Whisper Murder! by Vera Kelsey
© 2023 Coachwhip Publications edition

First published 1946
Audrey Vera Kelsey, 1892-1961
CoachwhipBooks.com

ISBN 1-61646-560-3
ISBN-13 978-1-61646-560-5

WEDNESDAY AFTERNOON, DECEMBER 24

Marcus P. Cumberland was not a large man. Less than five feet nine, he had the proportions of a lath. His triangular face, narrowing from a broad, high forehead to the point of a meticulously groomed goatee, suggested a scholar rather than the astute and successful publisher of the Clayton *News,* morning, evening, and Sunday editions.

He gave an impression of size, however, because on everyone and everything he turned the full power of a keen mind, penetrating brown eyes, and concentrated interest and energy. Under that battery, depending on whether Marcus P. approved or disapproved, individuals swelled or shriveled, things were done or never mentioned again.

Now, as he sat upright behind the massive desk in his private office, studying the photograph spread across five columns on page 1 of the evening's mail edition, anger made him appear to take on height and breadth.

"Well, Mr. City Editor," he demanded in the same moment the door opened to admit the long, lean body of his son, "what's the meaning of this?"

Dan Cumberland's smoky gray eyes met the brown ones steadily, but his slow-breaking grin softened their challenge. "I should ask you that question, sir. Thought the doctor ordered you to remain at home until after Christmas."

Marcus P. thrust the paper across the desk, jabbed a forefinger at the offensive photograph. "Don't you know this is Christmas Eve? Christmas Eve, and you run a shot like that!"

"Why not?" Dan moved forward to pick up the paper. "It's news." His tone implied, "It's dynamite."

His deep-set eyes warmed with appreciation for both the subject of the photograph and its quality. From left to right it pictured a continuing series of bleak, charred fragments of brick and concrete walls, all that remained of two of Clayton's three leading hotels. Made bleaker still by blackened mounds of snow and ice, the ruins divided to right and left of a short entrance drive on which both hotels had faced.

Those on the left represented all that remained of the six-story Claytonian, until a year ago the town's newest, most modern hotel. Those on the right, from which blurs of smoke still curled, represented the equally complete destruction of the Wayne River, until just three days ago a handsome seven-story structure, Clayton's finest hotel.

Above the photograph in boldface ran a noncommittal caption: Radisson Street, Clayton, Minnesota.

"Why not?" Marcus P. repeated. "Hell, Dan, Clayton isn't Prague! Five years as Balkans correspondent for the New York *Globe* have made you lose all perspective on normal American life. You've been so embedded in mass murder and destruction, in all the intrigue and corruption of those blasted little countries, you can't look at a couple of home-town fires without suspecting God knows what. . . ."

In his irritation he shoved his telephone perilously close to the edge of the desk. "Not only suspect! With that picture you suggest to our readers and advertisers all over Wayne River Valley that a firebug or worse is operating here. You know this town lives on its schools and colleges, that thousands of youngsters have gone home for the holidays. How many of them will come back if their parents get the idea Clayton isn't safe?"

"Is it?"

Marcus P.'s eyes crackled with anger; the small, rounded balls of his cheeks turned dark red. "Safe? Of course it's safe. What's got into you, boy, tonight of all nights? You're a born newspaperman. And born right here in Clayton. This town's in your blood. You know every inch of it, almost every man, woman, and child in it. You know their livelihood and mine—if not your own any longer—depend on Clayton maintaining its reputation for law and order, for friendliness and mutual respect and trust. And Christmas is the time to build, not destroy that reputation—"

As his phone buzzed he swung round but it was Dan who leaned over the desk, plucked the receiver from its cradle. "Yes," he said instantly into the mouthpiece. And at brief, almost rhythmic intervals: "Yes. . . . Yes. . . . Yes."

Marcus P. listened a moment, then rose to shrug himself into his overcoat, stand waiting. As his gaze traveled Dan from head to foot it softened, deepened with pride and feeling for this only son. But when Dan replaced the receiver the look vanished and his eyebrows rose in question.

Dan shook his head. "Just one of the pressmen. Nothing important."

"I'm seeing Dale, then going home," Marcus P. told him, his anger abated. "He'll work up a good Christmas layout for the morning paper. Perhaps no harm's been done, son. Not likely many people'll have time to read the *News* tonight."

"That's not the point, is it?"

"If the reaction of our readers and advertisers isn't the point, what is?" Marcus P. had a nice smile and he employed it now.

"When it comes to fires, I don't like coincidence. What's happened to my thirty thousand fellow citizens? Don't they—"

"Coincidence! It's no coincidence both hotels burned to the ground during twenty-below weather last December and this. Pre-Christmas cold waves aren't a coincidence in these parts. They're a habit."

He picked up his hat, turned for the door, turned back to look up into the grave, dark face almost six inches above his own. "Forget it, son. I guess I'm still a bit feverish. It's been good to have you home these past five months, to have you on the city desk for the last two. You've done a good job, a fine job. I wish you could see your way—"

With a stride Dan stood beside his father; placed a hand on the thin, narrow shoulder. "Not yet, Dad. Let's talk about my taking over the *News* when I come back from Europe. But thanks for the kind words. I appreciate them—from you."

Alike embarrassed by even this modest display of feeling, they stood silent and awkward a moment, then Dan opened the door and Marcus P. with a murmured, "Don't be late; Dora's counting on you," hurried away.

When he was alone Dan looked about the square little office. Save for the desk, chairs, and corner tables piled with newspapers, it was empty, even of atmosphere. His father seldom used it, certainly wouldn't return today. He could be sure of privacy here.

He needed it. That telephone call had been from Lisa! From a Lisa striving as hard as he had to be casual and noncommittal.

During the day Tina Johnson operated the telephone switchboard. And Tina, as all Clayton knew, listened in on calls not only with her ears but with assorted hypersensitive antennae that enabled her to add two and two with devastating accuracy. Marcus P. considered her one of the *News's* more valuable assets.

Lisa, however, had merely asked if he knew who was calling, how he was, if he remembered that tonight was Christmas Eve and that he had promised to be among those present at the annual party she and her husband felt essential to their social program. And he had replied with a string of yeses. Even Tina could make nothing of that conversation. He hoped.

But he could. For two reasons.

Primarily because in Lisa's voice this afternoon had been that same brittle, quivering tension he had last heard eight years ago. Never would he forget her words or her voice on the October dawn she had called him out of a waking dream. To say she was not marrying him that day at high noon. She was marrying Terry McPhail!

And second, because since his return to Clayton five months ago to recuperate from his years abroad as foreign correspondent he had seen Lisa but twice and then at a distance. Never, as the wife of the increasingly honorable gentleman now known as Professor Terence Girard McPhail had she invited him to her home.

He closed the door firmly, walked over to his father's swivel chair. Before dropping into it he swung it round to face the window. Then, feet propped on the window, ledge, eyes fixed on low gray clouds bringing snow from the west, he settled back to do some Tina-Johnsoning of his own.

In the two months he had been pinch-hitting as day editor he had learned considerably more about his old home town and its citizens than had appeared in the columns of the *News*. Nothing he had learned, publishable or otherwise, could have affected Lisa adversely.

On the contrary. The name of Mrs. Terence Girard McPhail appeared frequently on the society and women's pages and also, since Lisa was one of the local headliners in swimming and tennis, in the sports news. As for her husband, no week passed, sometimes no day, without more or less important mention of his activities.

As head of the chemistry department of Clayton College, Professor McPhail made news. As director of the chemical laboratory, serving both college and Wayne River Valley, Professor McPhail frequently made news. Sometimes sensational news, at court sessions and coroners' cases, with his testimony and his services in analyzing poisons and other materials. As one of the most popular public speakers in the Midwest, Professor McPhail was constantly being reported on his way somewhere to present his well-chosen words.

And though it had been very hush-hush for years, any day now Professor McPhail might make national news when the story of some chemical concoction of his which the Army had used in the defeat of Japan was released. The whole town knew it was a valuable invention. Anyone who looked at the McPhail residence on Skyview Parkway could see it was a profitable one. No previous head of a Clayton College department had been able to buy a home on the city's most exclusive and beautiful street, live in the style to which the professor and Lisa had so quickly accustomed themselves.

Neither a social, financial, nor professional crisis then could be harrying Lisa. No physical disaster from illness or injury either. The skinny instructor in chemistry who some eleven years ago had arrived from the East to join the college faculty had developed into a substantially fleshed and impressive figure. As of three or four days ago, when Dan had glimpsed him moving with conscious reserve and dignity through the post office lobby, the professor was the picture of health. And Lisa—as long as Dan could remember, he'd never known her to be ill. Certainly her voice had not suggested a sick woman's.

Only some acute personal problem remained to account for that telephone call. But what, he asked himself, had Dan Cumberland to do with her personal problems? Those were McPhail's responsibility now. Unless—the current crisis concerned the professor.

He rejected the obvious suggestion. McPhail, according to the all-seeing eye of Clayton's gossipers, not only adored but was tremendously proud of his young—almost fifteen years younger—and gay little wife. Besides, he was a man of invincible rectitude and convention. Too much so for Dan's own taste. How the recklessly impulsive and only lightly inhibited Lisa had survived eight years of wedlock with such a spouse was as much of a mystery to him as why she had married the professor in the first place.

Abruptly Dan removed his feet from the window sill, sat very still. How objectively he had been considering Lisa and her life! He wasn't quite sure he liked or wanted to find himself in this frame of mind.

He owed a lot to Lisa. To the back of her hand, of course, but no less truly. She had freed him forever from proving susceptible to another woman. And more. The bomb her telephone call at dawn had placed under his dreams and plans, his faith in people and himself, had blown him out of Clayton, sent him wandering over Europe, to find haven at last in the Balkans. The knowledge he had acquired there had made him the New York *Globe's* logical choice when World War II crashed over Europe.

To Lisa he owed his physically ruinous and tragically wonderful years as Balkans correspondent. And to Lisa, when his six months' leave was ended, he would owe still more. Only three weeks to go and then—save for an occasional visit to Marcus P. and Dora—it would be the back of *his* hand to Lisa and Clayton forever.

Luxuriously he stretched his arms above his head, clasped his hands, and pushed upward, to feel his renewed body respond. Three more weeks! Then back to Europe for him, to observe and record the rebuilding of a continent.

He dropped his arms on a gusty breath, swung round to the desk to reach for the telephone. Lisa was out of his system at last! Her emotional crises were all her own—and her husband's.

In spite of himself his fingers curled away from the receiver. An odd sort of pride restrained them. Lisa had failed him, but he had never failed Lisa. And this was the last time she could ever turn to him.

As he reached for a cigarette instead, knuckles struck the door a resounding blow. Impatiently he swung round when it opened a few inches to reveal a copy boy's red head. "Gentleman named Blythe to see you, Mr. Cumberland. Says it's important."

"Mr. Cumberland's not here, Toby, and his son went home an hour ago. Wish the gentleman named Blythe a merry Christmas—"

"And a right merry one to you, sir," a briskly assured voice said.

The door swung wide as a tall, lean young man, almost a counterpart of Dan himself except that the newcomer was fair of hair and blue and brash of eye, marched in. Neatly he slipped something into Toby's receptive hand, closed the door after him, opened it to make sure he had disposed of Toby, shut it again.

Resigned, Dan rose to switch on the ceiling light in the darkening office, accept the card offered him.

"You're already home for Christmas, Mr. Cumberland, but I can't be unless you're a man of good will. Either

here, or over a drink where walls don't have eyes and ears,
I must have words with you."

Dan looked up from the card it had taken more than
one glance to read. "And what would Mr. James M. Blythe, representing the American Protective Association of
Insurance Companies, require of me? Oh, I see." He paused
to decipher a penciled scrawl. "Concerning the Claytonian
and Wayne River hotels."

With mock regret he looked again into the shrewdly
knowing blue eyes. "The Claytonian and Wayne River are
no longer with us, stranger. The first departed in flames
a year ago, but if you hurry you can still observe smoke
rising from the second—"

"Brother, you never uttered a truer word. Stranger!"
Mr. Blythe's solemn wonder was too much to support.
Uninvited, he drew a chair to face Dan across the desk.
"What's stranger than one comparatively young, modern
hotel departing in flames?"

He leaned forward to hold up one finger, then erect
another beside it. "Give up? The answer is two."

WEDNESDAY AFTERNOON, DECEMBER 24

Dan leaned down to open the deep drawer of his father's desk, produce a tantalus and glasses. "You mentioned a drink, I believe. You shall have it, Mr. Blythe. In you I recognize a kindred and skeptical spirit. The first, I might add, I've encountered in Clayton—on the subject of those fires."

While he secured ice cubes from a wall refrigerator, mixed two highballs, and locked the door before passing one across the desk, lifting the other himself, Mr. Blythe maintained a beneficent silence.

"Here's to crime," Dan said with a gusto that later was to haunt him. "Lord knows we can use some in the *News*. But be reasonable, Mr. Blythe. Let the morning gang rustle up their own stuff's my motto. Don't tell me anything that'll break before Friday. No evening paper tomorrow."

His guest made sure of a long swallow before he confessed, "Don't get me wrong. I'm not here to tell you anything. I can't. But"—Mr. Blythe paused to extract clippings from the Monday and Tuesday *Evening News* from a pocket—"I've read these accounts of the Wayne River fire, of course, and just a moment ago in the newsroom I saw a copy of tonight's paper. You don't say nothing mister, but you must mean somethin', the way you keep linking up the *two* fires." At the outrage in Dan's face he hastily drained his glass.

Dan set his own aside. "If it weren't Christmas Eve I'd have your heart."

"Let me explain." Blythe rose to hurl coat and hat into a corner, seat himself more comfortably. "Because I can't find a thing doesn't mean there's nothing to find. Let's look at the record, as someone has advised. A year ago December fifteenth, between seven and eight in the evening, smoke was observed floating about the storeroom of the Claytonian Hotel. The same phenomenon had been noticed on several evenings earlier last winter when the thermometers hovered around zero. Apparently as a result of guests and staff turning on heat all over the place. Local talent on the staff never had found anything wrong before. They didn't then. . . .

"That is, the smoke vanished from the storeroom. They could find no trace of fire. And that was that—until ten-fifteen, when someone in the Harrison Hotel across the street spied smoke hovering over the Claytonian's roof, got excited, called the fire department. By that time smoke was sifting through the corridors and more timorous guests in all stages of dress and undress were beginning to descend to the lobby. . . .

"The fire chief ordered everyone downstairs while he investigated. What he found resulted in his ordering everyone out of the building. Flames running between floors, behind walls, all over the place. Just as they got the last guest out, the whole thing went up like a torch—"

"Visible for thirty miles," Dan contributed, to cut the narrative short. He had heard all this a dozen times before. "I didn't see that blaze, but I did sit in on the Wayne River conflagration the other night. They were much alike, people tell me. Flames leaping to fifty feet above the roof or where the roof had been. Pouring out of every window—"

"So I've heard." Firmly Blythe took over again. "I was on another assignment—down South—last December, but the man who came out for the Association did a thorough job. Found nothing out of line but a set of local conditions, due to twenty-below weather and the war. Water pressure low. Old fire equipment—though new had been ordered. New and inexperienced men on the fire wagons. Plus the delay in turning in an alarm. Everything added up to a bona fide fire. And a cool three hundred thousand in insurance. Which our various companies duly paid the Midwest Hotel Syndicate, owners of the Claytonian."

"Whereupon the Midwest Syndicate bought the Wayne River Hotel and business proceeded as usual," Dan inserted in the pause.

"And on December twenty-first of this year, again in twenty-belowish weather, the same thing happened. In the meantime the new fire equipment had not arrived, the old was older still. Water pressure again was low. More new and inexperienced men on the force. And similar, though not identical, delays occurred. This time the night manager thought the desk had notified the fire department, the desk thought the switchboard operator had called, and so on and on. Understandable, of course. They were all doing their best, remembering the Claytonian, to get the guests down to the lobby."

"That's the bright feature of both fires," Dan commented. "The guests each time lost everything. The management all but a few records. But every life was saved. Clayton's pretty proud of that."

"Noted. The point is—I've spent the past two days here in undiluted labor, trying to find a catch in the coincidence. But again it all adds up to another bona fide fire. And this time to more than half a million in insurance."

Surreptitiously while he listened Dan had glanced at his watch. Almost five. And he had things to do. Find

roses, deep red roses—Lisa's favorite flower—if any were
to be had at this late hour. Arrive home early enough to
dress and mix the cocktails for the buffet supper Marcus
P. and Dora always provided on Christmas Eve for their
old, old friends.

Above all, to break the news to his mother that he was
walking out on the family party at nine or so for a tête-à-
tête with Lisa. For that he needed time and tact. So far as
Marcus P. and Dora—most of their friends, for that matter—were concerned, Lisa had not married Terry McPhail
at high noon that October tenth. She had died a sudden
and very timely death.

Beneath the surface of his mind where such thoughts
insinuated themselves into the conversation, others were
busy, considering and discarding one supposition after
another as to the crisis Lisa faced.

The direst catastrophe he could conjure was that Professor McPhail had been offered a more important post,
East, West, or South. Lisa was definitely a small-town
woman. The height of her ambition was to become one day
the Mrs. Marcus P. Cumberland of her generation. And
she would, Dan knew. Already she had a home on Skyview
Parkway, and a car that duplicated the Cumberland Cadillac even in color. To be forced to leave Clayton would be
the end of the world for Lisa!

The idea amused and charmed Dan. One of Lisa's most
winning ways had been her talent for inspiring in him the
sensation of possessing all wisdom, all power. He felt himself expanding now. If Lisa wanted to remain in Clayton
and it was within his range to help her, Lisa would remain.

He was beginning to look forward to the evening ahead.
Though how on Christmas Eve Lisa expected to be alone
he couldn't begin to explain. But she would! Probably by
one of the harebrained inspirations on which she acted
first, thought afterward.

Of the importunate Mr. Blythe Dan took an increasingly atrophied view. The fellow had told him nothing he, and all the readers of the *News,* didn't know. Dan looked up to meet a question in the hard blue eyes, hastily recalled the last words he had heard.

"Then why are we bothering our pretty heads?" he asked.

"This. Were these fires really necessary? One I can accept. Two—question mark. But there's one more commercial hotel in this town and, as luck would have it, a neighbor of the two departed."

"I don't think you need to worry about a third fire," Dan assured him. "In the first place the Midwest Syndicate doesn't own the Harrison Hotel. In the second, it's an old hotel—fifty, sixty years, perhaps more.'

Blythe's fox-terrier alertness toward those words moved Dan to add quickly, "I'm simply repeating some of Bud Harrison's wisecracks. He's our local cynic. He meant something about depreciation. I'm not sure what."

"I am. Under the new tax laws, owners of a hotel as old as the Harrison by this time have practically written off, through depreciation, their original investment. If the Harrison were a total loss from fire they couldn't benefit from its insurance unless they reinvested it as soon as possible in a new hotel. Otherwise the money would be considered as income and subject to the income tax."

"Aha!" Dan looked wise. "But the Claytonian was only nine years' old. The Wayne River little more than twelve. Depreciation would be negligible in—"

"Look here, Cumberland," Blythe broke in urgently. "I've noted that angle, of course, but that's the sort of information I'm after. The, hell of it is, it's Christmas Eve. And I've got a wife and three small boys in Milwaukee weeping their eyes out right now because I can't be home tonight. But if I take the late train I'll be there by morn-ing—"

"And by leaving there tomorrow night you can be back here Friday—"

Blythe shook his head. "Better if I don't return—im-mediately. Let these birds—this bird Elway anyway—think I'm through."

"Elway? You mean the chap who manages the Midwest interests here? What've you got against him?"

"Nothing—except it's kosher for me to stay here stew-ing over these lousy fires and ruin my family's Christmas. But he's in charge—or was—of both the Claytonian and Wayne River. Does he stay? No! He and his wife left yes-terday to spend the holidays somewhere with friends! Sim-ply got in their car and drove away."

"Maybe his departure's an angle."

"You mean he may have skipped out? Unfortunately, no. At least we can't assume that—yet. Carston, the Wayne River manager, assures me they'll return Friday morning. Know either of them? Carston or Elway?"

"Jack Carston, of course. He's a home-town product. I haven't seen much of him the last ten years, but he and I went through school and Clayton College together. He's no dynamo but honest as sunlight and a hard worker. Elway I don't know, except through the *News*. We're always running briefs about his comings and goings."

"Ever seen Mrs. Elway?"

Dan shook his head.

Blythe whistled appreciatively. "Your loss. But enough of idle chatter. What sort of deal can I make with you to use your eyes and ears for me?"

"Why mine? Bud Harrison's the man for you."

"No good. He's a hotel man himself. And you know this town, most of the people in it. You've got the experience, technique, everything it takes, and, in addition, incentive."

"Incentive? Oh—to break the story in the *News?*" Dan shrugged that off.

Blythe's eyes narrowed, his straight lips smiled. "You're a hard man, Brother Cumberland. But my train doesn't leave till ten-thirty. In five hours I can wear any man down—!"

Dan didn't doubt that statement, and he was impatient to get away. After a moment's thought he conceded, "Oh well, if opportunity ripens I'll ask a question here and there. More than that I can't promise. After all, this is my home. And I'm abandoning it, God willing, January fifteenth. Don't want to leave a bitter taste in people's mouths."

"That's enough. That's all I want." Blythe jumped up to recover his hat and coat, return to the desk to scribble an address on the back of his card. "Just look and listen, and if you turn up anything let me know. No one else."

He wrung Dan's hand, but when Dan unlocked and opened the door he lingered to underline his warning. "If you do find anything, don't—play with fire, Mr. Cumberland. Wire me. Remember that—if you want to make your train January fifteenth."

Wednesday Night, December 24

Lisa opened the door to Dan's ring. "I thought you'd never come," her soft voice confided as he stepped into a wide reception hall. "Do you know it's after ten?"

Dan grinned down on the familiar swirl of unruly short black curls, almost a foot below his eyes. "Sorry, Duchess. The family's entertaining tonight. I've been everything from gentleman's gentleman to ice boy."

He stopped. The better to see him, Lisa had stepped back to the towering Christmas tree glistening with silver and bright with lights. It rose from mounds of gaily tied gifts within the curve of the broad, winding stairs. Now he understood why he had called her Duchess.

In her dinner gown of deep rose red she suggested in miniature a painting he had seen somewhere of a patrician lady of Louis, XIV's court. The tight, low-cut bodice flowered into a bouffant skirt of outrageous proportions. Such flamboyancy of dress and her autocratic manner of holding her small, narrow head were new to Dan.

Beneath his gaze, however, her thick black lashes rose and fell as incredibly as he remembered, yielding only glimpses of lustrous black eyes. Except for tiny lines of strain under those eyes, a firmer, less translucent quality in the smooth olive of her skin, she didn't appear on first glance a day older than on the midnight he had left her so

23

reluctantly to endure the thirteen hours that had to elapse before their marriage.

But when she made no move to offer her hand, speak further, he looked again. As far as he could see, which, considering that skirt, wasn't far, her slender, boyish figure had not changed. Yet that impression of youth was contrived—the sum of massage, expert make-up, and Lisa's own will to charm.

He knew her too well to be deceived, even now. Beneath the surface this poised young matron was taut with pent-up emotion.

Smiling, he presented the long, narrow glazed box under his arm with a bow that brought his eyes on a level with hers. To his dismay, he saw they were wet with tears.

She turned from him swiftly, to place the box on a table, rip it open. When he had disposed of coat and hat she held red roses in her arms, was sparkling up at him over them.

"You remembered," she said in the throaty half whisper that always had revealed her pleasure. "I knew you would."

At a murmur of swishing draperies she pivoted round. The dull, bronze curtains sealing a broad archway on the right had parted to reveal Professor McPhail, impeccable in dinner clothes. Somewhere Dan heard, too, then, the hum of many voices.

Suspicion reared its ugly head. Grimly he cursed his stupidity. When Lisa had said party on the telephone he had assumed the word to be merely a detail of the camouflage she was creating for Tina Johnson's benefit, that when he arrived he would find her alone.

Could it be her intention—hers and the professor's—to display him to their guests in a form of Capulet-Montague reconciliation tableau? Both of them, he knew, were fascinated by footlights.

In fact the footlights of Clayton's Little Theatre had brought them together, illuminated them in many a final-curtain embrace, lighted the way, Dan had often thought in those first lonely years in Europe, to their own highly dramatic romance. Now in his mind's eye he saw the professor throwing open the bronze draperies, stepping back for him to enter, Lisa at his side, his roses in her arms.

Unless he deliberately bolted there was no escape. Professor McPhail was advancing, both hands extended. "This is a very real pleasure and honor, my boy. One we have been looking forward to, my wife and I, for a long, long time."

"Thank you, sir." Dan's resources ended there. Partly in surprise. That salutation had been extracted from him by the almost audible demand of the professor's dignity and air of position.

The thin, somewhat high voice that had accompanied the one-time chemistry instructor to Clayton, he noted, had deepened now, slowed to a sonorous pace. Although McPhail did not betray half his fourteen-year advantage of his wife, Dan noted also, not without satisfaction, that he was fighting a losing battle to retain the semblance of a once full quota of chestnut hair. Now brushed straight back from the heightening forehead, it also heightened the calm of the chestnut-brown eyes, the strength of the somewhat heavy nose and broad cheekbones, the firmness with which the straight upper lip and full lower one closed together.

"Isn't it wonderful of Dan to drop in like this to say merry Christmas so beautifully?" Lisa held up the roses for her husband's appreciation. "Terence, must we waste him on everyone? When there's so much we want to hear. And he can stay only a few minutes."

Dan had said nothing of the sort. He listened with interest for the answer.

The calm brown eyes took on a conspiratorial gleam. With a hand outstretched to each, the professor drew them close. "Our guests are unaware of Dan's arrival, dear. Why not take him up to my study? I'll see that everyone's happy—or presenting a reasonable facsimile of that condition—then join you."

Considerately he removed the roses from his wife's embrace, took them with him as he turned away. Dan looked after him with exaggerated admiration.

"You've always said you were born lucky, Lisa. Now I believe. These old eyes and ears—"

Her hand, small, strong, and, despite the warmth of the house, cold, caught his urgently. "Come along quickly. He'll be back before we can say two words. I thought I had him safely—"

She turned and, almost running, led him up the stairway to a door standing open on the first landing. "In here."

Dan stopped short on the threshold, then entered slowly to move down the long, beautifully proportioned, and luxurious room.

From floor to ceiling, save for tall, deeply indented windows of golden-tinted glass, the walls were lined with books, books chosen solely for their decorative value. Their time-mellowed and faded calfskin bindings, the faded gilt of their titles—all in Italian, apparently formed a rich and subdued background for the long baroque table of hand-carved rosewood in the center of the intricately laid mosaic floor of light and dark woods; for the deep-toned Persian rugs; brocaded chairs, each with reading lamp and rack; for two apparently ancestral portraits hung against the books on the right wall.

Above all, for the magnificent round table, baroque also, that at the far end of the room provided an appropriate desk for a scholar and gentleman of authentic culture. On both tables scientific and other magazines, each in its own hand-tooled leather cover, mammoth Chinese porcelain bowls filled with poinsettias, strengthened this impression.

"Congratulations, Lisa." Dan turned, to find her still standing near the open door. She closed it when he approached.

"Look at me, Dan," she commanded. "Have I changed?"

She was serious, deeply serious, but he was not willing to be—yet.

"I can't remember the French professor's daughter ever running to such yardage," he smiled. "Otherwise she and the professor of chemistry's wife appear very much the same."

"Don't!" she protested. "Unless you're deliberately trying to—to hurt me. Are you?"

"Not at all. I—admired the daughter. Clumsily, I'm afraid, I was attempting to convey the same feeling for the wife."

She studied him a moment, then with a flinging gesture appeared to toss overboard whatever else she had planned to say. Slowly she raised shining eyes, drew a step closer.

"Forget the wife. You loved the daughter—"

"My dear Mrs. McPhail—"

"Stop that!" Lisa whirled round to stand with her back pressed against the closed door. "There isn't time. Terence will be here any moment. Dan, I mean every word I say. You must too. And you've said—a thousand times you've said it—you'd never change—toward me. And you haven't. I know you haven't."

She flung back her head, revealing the soft, lovely line of her throat. Her gaze clinging to his, she moved her short, full red lips inward, moistening them. "Tell me again."

Behind Dan's eyes as he looked at her rose indelible memories of women he'd seen in Bulgaria, Czechoslovakia, elsewhere in Europe; of their mute, unexpectant faces after they had watched their homes turned to rubble, their families dismembered, husbands, sons, brothers die— sometimes horribly—before their eyes. And his gaze on Lisa darkened with sick wonder and pity for the youth they had shared.

How they had suffered—and reveled in suffering— through high school years and college, in scenes like this. How they had burned up emotion over a misunderstood word, a forgotten anniversary, a missed date. All for the pure joy of emoting, of parting and coming together again.

Suddenly Dan understood Lisa now. She wanted to turn back the years, recapture with him the innocent raptures they had generated in the throes of first love.

But he, at thirty-four, felt old, venerable with age and experience. Those years with Lisa seemed millenniums away. And Lisa herself, though outlined against that door almost within reach of his hand, appeared like a tiny, distant figure seen through the wrong end of a telescope. Thinking, he unconsciously, turned his head, and his eyes began to follow with faint interest the pattern of the leading in a golden window.

A smothered sound recalled him. Lisa was waiting, smiling at him through quivering lashes.

To bring himself physically to a level more nearly approximating hers he half seated himself, on the end of the long central table. Then, out of the depths of his wisdom, suggested, "Why not tell me what you want me to do for you, Lisa? I might do it, you know, without this full-orchestration build-up."

Her glance wavered, then she smiled, reassured. "I know you will. Dan darling, take me away from Clayton! Anywhere. Wherever you are."

"But I'm right here," he protested, amused. "In any event you don't need my assistance to leave town. I'm sure you'll find the ticket agents at Union Station reliable . . ."

He stopped. Lisa had shrunk back against the door, was grasping at its smooth surfaces with her small hands. Inwardly he flinched. He knew what it was to see a woman beaten. And he had thought merely to bring her down to earth. Fumbling for words, he rose.

But Lisa was self-restoring. She straightened too, her face tender with pity. "I hurt you so much. You can't forgive me."

"Forgiving can have nothing to do—"

"You love me," she cried. "You know you do. Only you've sealed it over—in eight years. But I can bring it back, darling. I can! Listen. I realize you can't leave Clayton now. Tonight. Or won't. But I can go alone. Friday. Tell me where to go, help me to go there. Then join me—"

"Why?" he asked reasonably.

"Because I love you too. I always have. I always will."

He laughed. "Your true love is Clayton, Lisa. Or am I wrong in assuming it was my opportunity to work on a Chicago paper that caused your overnight switch of bridegrooms?"

Dan sank down on the table edge again, folded his arms, urged paternally, "Come on. Out with it. What is it you really want me to do?"

"I've told you. Oh, I was such a fool, Dan. But I've paid for it. More than paid for it. Now all I want is to be with you, make up for all we've missed."

"Let's do it in Clayton!"

She was too taken aback to guard her words. "Oh no! No, you can't stay here—"

"Why not? Dad wants me to."

"But your work, everything you've done. You can't throw all that away, begin again—here."

Again he laughed at her. "What you really want—or think you do at the moment—is a romantic adventure, isn't it? Safely beyond the eyes and tongues of the college faculty and Skyview Parkway. Don't you know that within twenty-four hours you'd be just as hell-bent to come back?"

"Never!" The intensity of her vehemence surprised him. "Never! I promise you."

Dan became as serious as she. "Lisa dear, it's no good. For either of us. You're no longer the French professor's daughter. I'm not the Dan you knew. Much more than eight years lie between us. You must accept that."

As she listened the glow left her face. She veiled her eyes but not before he had seen their luster dulled too. By anger? Despair? Fear? He could be neither sure nor credulous.

Her dry whisper barely reached him. "You don't want me! Won't take me, help me."

"You haven't asked for the sort of help I can give."

Her lips parted, closed as she turned her head to press an ear against the door. "It's too late. Terence is coming. I won't try to see you again. But one day you'll know what you've done. On that day I'll be dead."

"Lisa! You're talking nonsense—"

As he moved toward her she swooped round him, her skirt flying to right and left like the wings of a bird, to perch herself on the table. By some physical alchemy her eyes were shining again, her face alive and gay.

"Open the door, Dan," she cried. "I hear Terence. I'm sure he's bringing drinks."

Dan opened the door. Terence was.

As he entered Lisa slipped from the table to move magazines aside for his tray. "You're just in time," she chattered. "Dan was afraid he couldn't wait for you. His family's entertaining, too, you know."

"I delayed to prepare a more suitable drink to toast our guest of honor. For Dan, my dear, your wine and punch . . ."

The professor dismissed them with a gesture, lifted a tinkling highball to present it ceremoniously to his wife, another to Dan.

Vexation or alarm flickered across Lisa's face. It vanished as her husband gracefully touched his glass to hers, to Dan's, but her smile was a footlight smile.

"To our meeting on this Christmas Eve," McPhail was intoning. "May it be the first of others, many others, in years to come."

While they placed their lips to their glasses he took a substantial swallow, then added, "Now shall we sit down? Surely you have time to tell us something of your achievements and future plans, Dan. We've heard great things of you, we who, to paraphrase the poet Robertson, I think, must sit and sing though we long to fly."

Lisa and Dan firmly retained their feet.

"Not a quotation applicable to you, sir," Dan protested. "Clayton's very proud and all agog to know more of your invention."

"Ah yes." Professor McPhail drank again, lowered his glass to swirl the ice gently. "How gratifying it has been to an unknown Midwest chemist like myself, working alone, far from the centers of scientific activity, to know I had a small part in bringing victory across two oceans to our brave boys. And to our great nation. I, also, long for the day when the truth may be told. This unprecedented silence, I fear, is creating for me a greater reputation than I deserve."

Dan thanked God for the blessing of an inscrutable countenance. As he listened he tested in his mind a few of the phrases his ears reported. But he wasn't being taken for a verbal ride. Professor McPhail meant exactly what he had said. More; he was pausing now for Dan to reply in kind.

Feebly Dan tried; "Surely not, sir. You're overmodest—"

Lisa, unregarded for the moment between them, looked from one to the other, moved away, turned back. "Stop calling him sir," she interrupted sharply.

The calm brown eyes turned on her. "Dan uses that form of address out of respect for rank, not age, my dear. To be sure, he flatters me—"

Lisa looked up saucily, her resentment only thinly disguised. "I'm disappointed in you both, sirs—and *I* mean *age*. My best friend comes to see me—us, and here you stand exchanging compliments like two old—old Roman senators."

Dan smiled to himself. If Lisa wanted to leave Clayton he knew why now. She was jealous of her husband's work, wanted to win his attention from it, back to her.

McPhail's glance for his wife was fond and gallant. "You begrudge us our exchange of one compliment apiece, you who receive so many?"

With regret Dan looked up from his wrist watch, placed his hardly tasted highball on the tray. "You must forgive me. I promised to turn chauffeur at eleven for some of the parental guests. It's already past—"

With alacrity Lisa placed her untouched drink beside his. Reluctantly the professor, after a hasty swallow, added his glass to theirs.

"I regret this must be good-by as well as good night for me, my boy," he said as he walked between Dan and Lisa to the door. "On Friday I fly East for a meeting of the North American Chemical Society and other conferences. When I return both college and January court sessions will be under way. I have been summoned to testify in one or two interesting cases for which I've made analyses of various kinds."

At the landing he took Dan's hand in a long, warm clasp. "We both labor in the same vineyard, Dan. You up where the fruits ripen in the light and warmth of the sun. I among the roots in the dark but fertile earth. One day the sun may reach me also. Then I hope you will say, 'Well done,' to me, as I say it from a full heart to you tonight."

The sonorously paced words were so clearly enunciated that Dan was taken by surprise when the hand, intended to fall on his shoulder like an accolade, missed its mark. And when Professor McPhail stepped back for his wife and guest to precede him Dan was surprised again to find the brown eyes watching him from behind a glassy sheen.

Halfway down the stairs Lisa stopped, looked back. Dan, two or three steps behind her, stopped too, startled. In that moment her face had grown pinched and white.

He looked round. No one was behind h_m.

Then, great fluffs of skirt caught up tightly in her hands for greater freedom of action, Lisa raced past him. Her eyes, bleak with fear and anger, flashed over him.

While he stood transfixed she reached the partly closed study door, thrust it open, disappeared in a swirl of silk. The next moment the door closed in his face.

Slowly he descended the stairs, her farewell words still echoing in his ears.

"Damn him!" she had said through tight teeth. "He mustn't finish those drinks!"

WEDNESDAY NIGHT, DECEMBER 24

"Is history repeating, or isn't it?" a deep male voice drawled. "From here, I can't tell who's walking out on who."

Dan paused on the bottom step, looked down into the square, browned face and cool, hooded eyes of Thode Brierson, district attorney for Clayton County.

"Hi, Big," he said levelly, and went on to collect his hat and coat.

Thode Brierson was big. More than six feet tall, broad-shouldered, well beefed, he still resembled the full-back Dan had delighted to needle in college days, still retained, even in dinner clothes, something of the collegiate.

"Where ya goin'? Whatcha doin'?" he asked now.

"What're you doing here?" Dan countered. And where had Dan Cumberland been, he challenged himself, not to have spotted so large a mass in the hall below as he and Lisa descended the stairs?

Brierson laughed briefly. "On Skyview? Or in this baronial hall at this particular moment? Don't you read the Clayton *News?* Or know your Parkway? I live on it, play on it."

He extended a small cup of lividly colored punch on the palm of a large, well-cared-for hand. "That's what I'm doin' now. Playin' hide-and-seek. Know a good place to ditch this?"

Dan was not diverted. "That answer cover the baronial-hall angle too?"

Big Thode's lips compressed, then widened in a forced smile. "Partly. Thought I smelled good liquor goin' by. Goin' by is right. Right by the recreation-room doors. Man, that's a room you should see: the entire back of this house! I did exactly what you'd have done—followed it. No luck. The prof marched his tray straight up those stairs, into his private sanctum, and closed the door. But you know Big Thode. Always gets his man. I stuck around."

Again he emitted that short barklike laugh. "Correction—in this case. Always gets a man. Who'd ever have thought to find Professor Terence Girard McPhail serving as busboy to Lisa and her—"

As Brierson talked Dan had buttoned his coat, pulled the collar more snugly about his crossed muffler, jerked his hat down securely over his forehead, produced heavy gloves from a pocket, and drawn them on. The equivalent, for him, of counting ten.

"So that's the secret of your success with witnesses," he said now, and started for the door.

"Sure," Brierson agreed amiably. "Come up and see me in action sometime. I wear 'em down with words until they say what I want 'em to say—to escape me."

"Thanks, but I prefer a door." Dan opened wide the heavy front door, stepped outside, swung it shut, but not latched. For a moment he waited, then opened it an inch.

Thode Brierson—still light on his feet as a cat—was taking the stairs to the landing, three steps at a time.

When Dan closed that door behind him again he knew an actual physical sensation of a door closing within him on a cycle of his life. He stood motionless, curiously quiet, drained of thought and emotion.

Then with a shrug he crossed the porch, descended the steps into thick, soft snow, now falling steadily from an invisible sky.

Again on the bottom step he paused. To either side of the entrance walk a low embankment of cleared snow shut off the sweep of unbroken white that covered the lawns. Just beyond the bank on his right the porch light picked up small stains.

They appeared black, but with a quick contraction of his lungs, he knew they were not black. They were red. As red as blood.

Stooping, he peered over the bank, then with a swift hand scooped at the snow. For an instant he remained bent over, his hand crushing the dark red head of a rose until the long stem that had emerged from the snow with it dropped away. Straightening, he tossed the petals over it, dusted his hands together.

If Lisa's purpose in asking him to her home had been to rouse her husband's jealousy she had succeeded!

At the sidewalk Dan halted again. The big white house he called home was still brightly lighted on its corner, only two blocks away. But here, with the snow falling softly about him, he was moved for the first time with a sense that this was Christmas Eve.

Skyview Parkway parallels a curve of Wayne River to form the northern boundary of the city. Beyond the river low hills, invisible now save for lights in farmhouse windows here and there, roll toward the higher summits of the Agassiz Range.

Whichever way he looked expansive homes, all in their third and fourth rejuvenation since the days of cupolas and towers, wooden lace and other architectural furbelows, presented him with a continuing series of old-fashioned Christmas-card scenes. Set far back from the Parkway in wide lawns, framed in firs, pines, and deciduous trees whose naked limbs were now clothed with snow, they observed a tradition all their own. Across each window a double line of white candles burned.

Sight of the small, unwavering flames winking through the snow tightened Dan's throat. His Christmas Eves to come might be very different; it would be pleasant then to recall this familiar old street in its most characteristic and festive mood.

Turning right instead of left, he walked along with easy strides, the better to see through lighted windows the laden Christmas trees, family groups, and parties. Three weeks from now he would say good-by to Clayton, he thought sadly, but this was his real farewell. Farewell to his childhood, his young manhood. . . .

God in heaven! Am I maudlin? On one cocktail at home and that foul drink of the professor's I merely tasted?

Sternly he abandoned the pleasure he had been taking in his sensations of advanced age, sorrow, and finality. Pulling his hat still lower, he buried his cupped hands in his overcoat pockets and quickened his steps.

But he couldn't outdistance the thoughts now free to claim his attention. Or dismiss his pity and concern for Lisa.

Poor little Peter Pan! Motherless since infancy, petted and indulged by a footless father, by everyone with whom she came in contact—including himself!—for her tininess, prettiness, charming and impulsive ways. Lisa had grown up, or at least acquired more years, accustomed always to the center of the stage.

Now in her own husband she had met her first rival. Not a rival: a usurper. And Lisa couldn't take it.

She'd have to take it, Dan thought ruefully. That and more, if it were true, as it appeared, that Professor McPhail had found in hard liquor another means of fortifying his demanding ego.

She'd have to take it alone, find her own solution. Neither he nor anyone else could do that for her. Lisa could never escape her husband or Clayton—except through divorce. And that she'd never face—unless a satisfactory protector stood ready.

That had been her idea tonight! He—Dan Cumberland—had been the chosen one. And he, poor fool, had not even grasped her intention. He'd been as self-absorbed as she, smugly measuring the degree of his own growth since the days when all his world centered in Lisa.

At that moment words reached his ears. Out of the ether apparently. Only when he stopped, turned round, did he see the young woman who had stepped out of the path to let him pass. She stood now, a few feet away, looking after him. Oddly, he thought. And no wonder. If she hadn't moved aside he'd have walked right over her.

In comparison with his own height she was not tall. And in spite of the great dark cape held together tightly by hands hidden in fuzzy, whitish mittens, the clumsy galoshes on her feet, and peasant's scarf knotted under her chin to cover all but a small oval of her face, not large or fat, either. Those basic specifications established to his satisfaction, Dan took a step toward her.

She stamped her galoshes free of snow, moved back into the path. "Listen!" she said without preamble. And her voice was low, unusually deep and clear-cut for a woman's. "Do you hear a dog barking?" Head bent as if listening herself, she did not lift her eyes.

A smile tilted Dan's lips. As far as young women in their twenties were concerned, Clayton was an almost manless town. And he was an eligible male! In his five months at home daughters of family friends, friends of the daughters, friends of friends of friends, and others without even so nebulous a claim, had impressed that on him. But this young creature's idea of waylaying him at midnight on a snowy Christmas Eve to ask about a dog reached a new high—or low.

Glancing about to discover where he was, to identify her in terms of nearby homes, he saw he had left the Parkway. Somehow he had strayed into one of the narrower cross streets that led eventually to the business district. Which one, because of the heavily falling snow, he didn't know. Here homes were smaller, modern in design, and much more closely spaced than on the Parkway.

When he turned back to his questioner she had lifted her head, was leaning forward as if hanging on his decision. Though he could not see her too clearly, he knew now her eyes were blue or gray. And that was satisfactory too.

"Do you?" he asked, amused. "And if so, where?"

Impatiently she waved a fuzzy blob to indicate the house beside them. A trig white house with attached garage, some twenty feet back from the sidewalk. Because it was dark, completely without lights, Dan had not noticed it. Now, so far as he could see from the unmarred snow before it, no one had left or entered it that evening by way of entrance walk or garage. And save for the soft swish of falling snow, the hum of an approaching motorcar, he could hear no sound anywhere.

He shook his head. "Looks as though whoever lives here has gone visiting for Christmas."

"The sounds I heard came from that garage. Perhaps they left their dog locked in there. And now he's hungry, freezing."

Again Dan glanced up and down the street. Almost every house in the block on both sides showed lights. Cars before several suggested more parties in progress. Again he shook his head.

"Almost every family in this town owns a dog. With all this festivity going on, probably several dogs are locked out of the way in garages tonight. In snow like this it's hard to tell where sound comes from."

"But shouldn't we make sure? Go in?"

At any time Dan's responsiveness to young women was like a paper match. Once lighted, it burned brightly if briefly, but a breath could blow it out. Now this creature's persistence, plus his own awareness that a hypothetical dog was her sole concern, smothered what small interest he'd felt in this encounter.

"You must be a stranger here," he said.

"No. No, I live here."

"Then you know this is the most conservative, conventional, and law-abiding community on earth. Every man's home is his castle, and damned be he who thinks it isn't. Every man's privacy, also, even when he isn't within his own walls. If I had a cute little straight-nose I'd—"

He never completed that sentence. The young woman's lashes, starred with snow, parted to permit the full force of her gaze to concentrate on him. For a breath he figuratively, almost literally, rocked under the impact. In the next she was marching away from him with a swing of her cape that warned him not to follow, even to apologize.

Dan had no desire to follow. All he wanted now was to reach the warmth, serenity, and quiet of his own home. As he turned to retrace his steps he felt he'd had all he could take of tense, emotional young women and their trivial problems.

Sunday Night, January 4

Full length on a couch before the open coal fire in the living room, Dan Cumberland gazed in dreamy comfort at the small running flames. Just back from Union Station, where he'd seen Marcus P. off for a few days' rest in Chicago, he relaxed as warmth expelled the congealing cold of a bitter night from his bones.

The holidays were over. Tomorrow with the reopening of Clayton College, the city schools, all the myriad educational institutions of which Claytonians were so proud, the winter season would officially begin. Life in his old home town was proceeding according to schedule while he had nothing to do and almost two weeks left in which to do it.

The new day editor had arrived January second. Except to look in daily on the News Building, Dan had no further responsibilities there. Last night in a telegram to James M. Blythe he had signed off from any further concern in the Claytonian and Wayne River fires.

He had kept his promise. More than kept it, thanks to various holiday celebrations at which housing and other problems resulting from the second blaze were still being discussed. He had talked with the fire chief, with Jack Carston, with a number of permanent guests of both the destroyed hotels distributed in homes and apartments about the city. The only one he'd missed was Elway himself. And Elway, according to Carston, was still away, in the East, deep in plans for a new hotel, in placing orders for materials.

Everything he'd learned had added up, as Blythe himself had found, to another bona fide fire.

Dan shook his head at himself. Marcus P. was right in frequently accusing him of foreign-correspond-itis. During his remaining days at home he'd remember that chronic skepticism, suspicion, distrust were out. Clayton, Minnesota, and Prague, Czechoslovakia, functioned on two entirely different psychological wave lengths.

Now here he was—on a night when the thermometer threatened to hit fifteen below. With an oil burner purring in the basement, this open fire before him. In the kitchen old Tilda, the cook who had served his family for twenty years or more, was setting raisin bread for his special benefit. Cigarettes, new books, and magazines lay on a low table within reach of his hand. How he'd learned to appreciate warmth, shelter, food, comfort!

His gaze warmed, too, as he looked about the big, familiar room with its comfortable, hospitably worn furnishings. During his years abroad the *News,* in a new and modernly equipped building, had developed into a moneymaker of astonishing proportions. But Dora and Marcus had remained as content with their old house, old friends and interests as in the days when they all survived precariously on the income from a small newspaper, turned out on temperamental presses that shook the walls of its aged brick home.

As the thought penetrated that in another month he might be appreciating the lack of comforts still more, he wriggled his long length into an even more relaxed position. His eyes were closing when the telephone rang. And continued to ring at briefer and briefer intervals.

Dora—bless her!—was playing bridge at the Brownells'. Tilda—bless her!—was slightly deaf. There was no one he wanted or needed to talk with, nothing he wanted to do he wasn't doing right there. He could listen with drowsy pleasure.

The shrill rings lengthened. Assumed a peremptory quality that finally rolled him off the couch, across the room, into the hall. Curse Dale! With only an eight-page edition to get out on Monday mornings, the fellow had to call for advice or something.

As Dan lifted the receiver a harsh, abrupt voice demanded, "That you, Cumberland?"

Dan grunted.

"A car's on the way to pick you up. Make it snappy, will you? You'll want to be here. And how!"

The receiver on the other end of the wire banged into place. Dan stood a moment looking at the instrument in his own hand, then cut the connection. No one on the *News* would speak to Marcus P. in that fashion. No one he could think of would.

He glanced at the grandfather clock ticking mellowly beside him. Almost eleven. "The current Mr. Cumberland will not make it snappy," he assured it.

Outside an insistently penetrating motor siren challenged that statement. The next moment an insistent finger set the doorbell chiming.

Outraged, Dan jerked open the door. A freezing blast struck him in the face. And a large, chilled young policeman looked as if he'd like to.

Dan knew then who had called. Pete Wilson, the police chief. When something with civic angles broke at police headquarters Marcus P. was always notified. As owner of Clayton's only newspaper, he took his responsibilities with tremendous consideration for the good of the town and everyone in it. Now he was on his way to Chicago. And the mail edition of the *Morning News* closed at 12:30 A.M.

"Be right out," Dan said hastily.

In thirty seconds he was inserting himself into the empty half of the seat of a small closed car with a white top. "What's up?"

The young policeman looked a little green. "Plenty."

He sent the car leaping ahead and that was that. As they raced down the icy Parkway, slithered on two wheels round a corner, slewed to a stop two or three blocks beyond, Dan fixed a prayerful eye on the high frozen night sky, glittering with frozen stars.

When he was sure they had stopped he lowered his gaze, looked out, whistled soundlessly, looked again. The house before him was white and trig, with an attached garage on the east side. Lighted now from cellar to roof, it looked familiar but he could not be sure . . .

As his companion leaped out one door he spilled out the other. Before they reached the two low steps to the porch the door opened and a deferential voice said, "Upstairs, Mr. Cumberland."

But as he entered the house Dan's nose stopped him. Faint but unmistakable on the air hung a disagreeable cloying odor. Gas!

He ran up the stairs to the landing, slowed when through the upper balustrade he glimpsed a group of men, silent about an open door. While his lungs protested against receiving that sickening air, heavier here, he went on to stand a moment at the top of the stairs. On his left an open door revealed a bedroom. On his right another open door led to a shining bathroom. Turning right, he passed that door to reach the motionless men.

At his approach the smallest and oldest of the group, a ruddy-cheeked, wiry man with iron-gray hair and startlingly long and bushy black brows over small bright black eyes whirled round. "Who're you?" he shouted. "How'd you get up here?" Then modulated his tones, to add, "Oh, it's you, Dan. Where's your father?"

"On his way to Chicago. Back the end of the week. I'll have to do. What's up?"

At a word from Chief Wilson the men about the door moved aside. Dan stepped forward to look into another and larger bedroom. After one swift glance he centered his eyes for a moment on the room itself.

A room comfortably, almost luxuriously, furnished. Ivoried twin beds faced him, their silken puffs carefully folded back. On one, soft white blankets were open, tossed aside as if their occupant had risen quietly for the day. On the other, their tumbled condition suggested the sleeper had spent a tumultuous night.

Beside each bed lay a small, warm-napped rug. Between them a bedside table was equipped with reading lamp, small radio, an empty onyx ash tray, and an electric clock whose minute hand, as Dan looked at it, moved to mark seven minutes past eleven.

Under the glare of every light in the room a dressing table against the left wall glittered with crystal bottles, jars, mirrors. Against the opposite wall stood a man's chest of drawers, its top spread with a fresh collar and tie, shirt, handkerchiefs. Two still lifes hung on the wall above the beds, but Dan passed them by to observe there were no photographs anywhere.

When he had seen enough of normal things he looked again at what on first sight his eyes had rejected.

In a deep, padded chair to the right of the door sat a woman. Once a strikingly beautiful woman, to judge by ash-blond hair folded about the head lying back against the blue brocade, by the good bones of her face, the slender curve of her throaty and the long, apparently fragile body.

She was not beautiful now. Her open eyes were so
deeply sunken that their color was indistinguishable. Her
parched and drained skin, except above her left temple
where a bruise lay like a purplish shadow, showed unnatural color, a faint lavender rose. Her arms, lying along the
arms of the chair, ended in long, slender hands whose finger tips were dry and shriveled. Skirts of a turquoise satin
nightdress and peach-colored silk robe covered but did not
conceal grotesquely swollen legs and feet. On her upper
body gown and robe were ripped and torn, revealing her
slenderness, almost emaciation, and again that unpleas-
ant, unnatural hue.

On the floor beside the swollen feet a long, compactly
built man with sunken heavy features and thick, close-cut
black hair lay on his back, his sunken eyes, parched, dis-
colored skin duplicating those of the woman's. Black silk
pajamas covered his body except for the upper shoulder of
his left arm where the sleeve had been pulled away.

Dan's gray eyes darkened. He had witnessed too many
scenes where death was present not to know that these two
had been sitting and lying in those positions for days.

"Had enough?" Chief Wilson asked. When Dan nodded he waved a hand. "All right, boys. Finish up. We'll be
downstairs."

The chief himself looked sick, Dan thought, both from
what he had seen and with worry. As the older man led the
way he said wearily, "Except that the man was face down,
that's just the way we found 'em. The way Olaf Thorwaldson found 'em, about ten o'clock."

At the foot of the stairs he turned to Dan to ask, "How
much you going to want on this tonight?"

"Let me check with the desk," Dan told him. "Then
give me all you can. I'll tailor to fit."

A few minutes later he found the chief, not in the living room which stood open to the hall but in the dining

room where doors could be closed and were, by Wilson, as soon as Dan entered. Here the gas no longer was discernible.

On the small, polished dining table a dozen or more sodden copies of the *Evening News,* still folded in the tight squares newsboys tossed in the general direction of subscribers' doors, were scattered. Otherwise, to Dan, the room was merely a dining room, equipped with the usual assortment of furnishings.

The chief pulled forward one of the straight-backed chairs aligned along the walls, dropped heavily into it. Elbow on the table, fingers twitching one of his bushy brows, he said apologetically, "I don't mean anything against you, Dan, when I say I wish your father was here. This case's going to give the station a black eye. That's about the only thing I'm sure of, right now."

Dan swung another straight chair to the table, dug out pencil and paper. "First tell me who these people are, and what's this address??

"Anthony R. Elway and his wife. 355 Penndale Avenue."

Dan's pencil poised in mid-air. "Not the manager for the Midwest Hotel Syndicate?"

"Yep."

"They lived—here?"

"Rented this house a year ago when the Claytonian burned down. Mrs. Elway refused to move into the Wayne River, to live in any hotel again. Wasn't a strong woman—"

"Better give me the facts about tonight," Dan suggested. "I must phone in as soon as I can."

The chief nodded. "Truth is," he began reluctantly, "this thing don't begin with tonight. Maybe goes back ten, twelve days." He poked a finger at the newspapers. "These were on the porch. Date back to December twenty-third. Looks like the Elways came home the night before, never went out again."

Dan's eyes sharpened as he remembered Blythe's comments on the Elways. He started to speak, thought better of it, asked instead, "How'd you discover them tonight?"

"Old story. Barking dog. George Matteson—lives across the street—called the station about nine thirty-five. Gave the desk sergeant hell about a dog barking in the garage here every night, probably cold and hungry, and nothing being done about it. So Foster—the sergeant—sent Olaf Thorwaldson down here to get the dog. He couldn't hear or see anything in the garage, but as this was the second time—" Wilson stopped abruptly.

"Second time for what?"

The narrow blue shoulders heaved, squared. "Might as well out with it, I guess. Christmas Eve late some woman called. Said a dog was barking in this garage, that the house was dark and the dog might be freezing or hungry—What's the matter?"

"Nothing. Just broke my pencil, that's all. Go on. I've got another."

"Well, it was Christmas Eve and we was having a little celebration at headquarters. Seemed kind of rough to send a fellow out to investigate a barking dog. That complaint's so common it's almost a gag. Foster didn't send anyone right away, just told one of the boys to drive round by Penndale on his way home. Couldn't have been much more than an hour later, at that, when Ben Schurz drove by. He couldn't hear or see a thing out of the way anywhere around here."

"What time did that Christmas Eve call come in? Remember?"

"About eleven. Why?"

"Just wondered."

"So—we forgot it," the chief went on. "Didn't hear any more about the dog till George Matteson called tonight.

He wouldn't complain unless there's something to complain about. So Foster hustled Olaf right out. He couldn't see into the garage or raise anyone in the house. Lost a little time—didn't matter, as we know now—when he had to locate the owner of this house, dig him up, and get him out here with keys. Couldn't have entered without him standing by, you know that."

The chief paused conscientiously. "Name's Elmer Ramsey Judson, 520 Third Avenue, West."

Dan smiled to himself. Marcus P. certainly had the chief well trained.

"Well, sir, Judson tried the back door first. There's a door in the kitchen that opens into the garage and all they wanted to do was get the dog out. But the house key had been left in the lock inside and Judson couldn't open it. So they came round to the front door. Judson's key worked there and Olaf started in. Right off he smelled gas and yelled to Judson to leave the door open, get some windows up, and follow him. He reasoned that since the house was dark, if anyone was home, they must be in bed, so he took the stairs." Wilson shrugged. "You saw what they saw."

"What's your theory?"

"Wish I knew. Could be accident. The pilot light on the hot-water heater in the basement was out. Gas pouring out of its valve and the main burner. I turned it off myself. Could be double suicide. With two hotels burning down on 'em, and Mrs. Elway's health none too good, they might've felt they couldn't face another Christmas. Or could be," Wilson concluded heavily, "that one of 'em helped the other to go first, then put out that pilot light."

Dan waited, finally asked, "You haven't considered murder?"

The sagging shoulders stiffened. The black brow beetled with alarm. "For God's sake, *whisper murder!* No, I haven't considered it and won't—unless the autopsies show up something. And I don't see how they can. This house was locked up tighter'n a drum when Thorwaldson and Judson got here. You can see for yourself everything's neat as a pin, nothing's been disturbed."

Clayton isn't Prague! Dan reminded himself, then quickly reassured the chief. "I won't even whisper it." He rose. "I'll just phone in a straight story—no time or space for detail."

But at the door he stopped, turned. "Hi, Chief! What about the dog?"

For a moment the older man looked blank. "Why—no one's seen hide or hair of a dog—so far."

Monday Night, January 5

Word of the Elway tragedy broke slowly over an incredulous city. Claytonians, waking from a prolonged holiday to face the three most arduous winter months and specifically a temperature still hovering around zero, had little time or inclination to read the *Morning News*. Or listen to its brief page 1 story repeated on the early news broadcasts of local station KLRO:

> At a late hour last night Mr. and Mrs. Anthony R. Elway, 355 Penndale Avenue, were found dead in their home by Olaf Thorwaldson, local patrolman, and Mr. Elmer R. Judson, 520 Third Avenue, West, owner of the property.
>
> Attention was drawn to the Elway residence when Mr. George Matteson, owner of the Matteson Bootery, whose home faces the Elways', telephoned police headquarters at 9:35 that a dog in the Elway garage was disturbing the neighborhood. Patrolman Thorwaldson, failing to rouse any response to his rings and knocks, secured the co-operation of Mr. Judson. When they opened the front door a strong odor of gas met them.

On investigation, they found Mr. and Mrs.
Elway dead in an upstairs bedroom, apparently the victims of asphyxiation, and in the
basement a defective water heater from which
gas was escaping. A pile of *Evening News,* half
buried in snow on the porch, offers evidence,
the police believe, that death may have occurred ten or twelve days ago. The newspapers date back to December 23.

But by five o'clock in the afternoon, when newsboys
were making the business streets of Clayton ring with *Evening News* headlines and in the residence districts others
were hurtling folded squares doorward, incredulity was
breaking. Claytonians demanded details.

And the *Evening News* supplied them. Anthony R. Elway
was forty-four; his wife, Dolores Evelyn, thirty-six. The
thermostat at 355 Penndale apparently had maintained an
even temperature of seventy throughout the thirteen days.
In the garage a, small Christmas tree stood ready to be
erected on Christmas Eve. In the dining-room buffet were
wrapped packages which Mrs. Elway obviously had intended for her husband. In Mr. Elway's chest of drawers in the
tragic bedroom were others, still unwrapped, which he had
intended for her. Locked doors, front and rear, and garage,
the undisturbed house—all testified against foul play.

Such homely, intimate details convinced Claytonians
this was no news story reported by A.P. or U.P. from some
other corner of the world where such events were always
happening. This was a local tragedy! A disaster that not
only affected personally friends, neighbors, and business
associates of the Elways but was the concern of every citizen. The entire city reeled under shock and horror.

Its watchword, "You're Among Friends in Clayton,"
appeared to be forever tarnished. That a man and his wife,

residents of the city for three years, professionally, if not socially, prominent for their connection with two of the leading hotels, could have died alone in their home in a crowded residence district and remained undiscovered for thirteen days was unthinkable. That they had done so during the season when Claytonians were at their gayest and friendliest, even more incredible.

Everywhere citizens, feeling their own guilt, sought a scapegoat. They found it in Penndale Avenue.

Penndale Avenue is the first and leading offshoot of Skyview Parkway. In fact it could be considered a part of the river drive, for it parallels an adjoining stretch of Wayne River. Its residences, though less impressive than those on the Parkway, are all occupied by well-to-do, highly respected professional and business men and their families. Members of Clayton College's faculty. Managers of chain stores. Owners of leading shops and services. Lawyers, doctors, two ministers.

How was it possible, with homes set as closely as those on Penndale, with a dog barking day and night, that the neighborhood hadn't been roused within hours? What kind of people lived on Penndale? Why, on Christmas Eve or Christmas, even on New Year's Eve or New Year's Day, had no one had the good will to telephone the Elways, if not to call personally?

Penndale Avenue, particularly the 300 block, of which, the Elway home formed a unit, was in disgrace and deeply felt it. Many of its women were in tears. Mrs. George Matteson took to her bed. Its men were stunned. Even the youngsters, though excited by the coming and going of police cars and others, didn't venture off their home street.

And Penndaleites, in turn looking for a whipping boy, turned on Mr. George Matteson. If, as it appeared, he was the only neighbor with ears and a sense of responsibility, why hadn't he employed them earlier? Much earlier!

By ten o'clock Monday night Mr. Matteson could endure no more. Never a man to suffer injustice meekly, he descended with all guns firing on police headquarters. Finding Chief Wilson absent and no one else there able or willing to give him satisfaction, he plunged across the street to the News Building.

Tina Johnson, on duty for some inscrutable reason of her own, personally escorted him to the private office of Marcus P., closed the door on him, and scurried for the newsroom. Thankfully she spied Dan smoking a final cigarette with Dale and sped him in to soothe the raging subscriber and advertiser.

By this time Mr. Matteson was more than enraged; he was outraged. At the irresponsibility and inefficiency of the police department and the *News*. At having his good name involved without his knowledge or consent in such a civic disgrace.

He had made no complaint to the police Sunday night or any other night, he wanted Dan, all Clayton, to know. He had been at home all evening, reading and listening to the radio, while his wife and daughters attended church. When they returned the whole family had gone to bed. The Elways might have had a dog. His daughter Eleanor claimed to have seen it. But he had never seen or heard it. He wanted that stated plainly on his personal authority in the Tuesday *Morning News*—or else.

Dan listened attentively, remembering that he himself had heard no dog on Christmas Eve, wondering if there had been a dog to hear. When Mr. Matteson's anger, or at least his angry words, ran out he produced Marcus P.'s trusty tantalus. The irate advertiser accepted a chair and a glass.

"I'm sorry Dad isn't here, Mr. Matteson," Dan said then. "But if he were, I know he'd say what I'm going to say now.

Mr. and Mrs. Elway are dead. Unless the autopsies, or other evidence yet to be discovered, prove differently, they died accidentally of asphyxiation. If the autopsies confirm the accident theory, it would be most unfortunate for you and for the relatives and friends of the Elways to have your denial of that telephone call made public."

"I don't see why. I didn't make it. I don't want to be connected with their deaths in any shape or form."

"Why?" Dan asked reasonably. "Because the desk sergeant believed that call Sunday night came from you, knew you wouldn't lodge a complaint without reason—Chief Wilson told me that—Olaf Thorwaldson was sent down to Penndale immediately. Your name, sir, was the means of discovering the tragedy last night. Instead of today, to-morrow, a week from now. Who knows when? You should take credit for that."

Mr. Matteson finished his drink thoughtfully, rose. "Oh well, let it go. Maybe I was hasty. But my wife's sick in bed over this thing, and my girls might as well be. I guess I had to work off steam somehow. Everyone on Penndale feels pretty low about this."

When his pacified footsteps echoed only faintly from the stair well, Dan took an envelope from a pocket, made two characteristically cryptic notes on its back:

? E dg
? tel. PH ¼

After a moment he added a third:

? yg worn in nav cape

He was drawing a heavy line under that third note when he remembered—Clayton isn't Prague! Impatiently he tore the envelope to shreds, tossed them into a wastebasket.

A deprecatory cough from the doorway swung him round. Chief Wilson stood there, watching him. "Tina told me you was up here. Matteson been to see you?" He came in like an old man, sank down on the chair beside the desk.

"Come and gone. He's all right, Chief. Don't worry."

"That's something. Lord, I'm tired. The D.A.'s office—" The chief shook his head at the scotch bottle Dan tilted invitingly. "Look here, Dan, I've been on the police force in this town for forty years, the last eighteen as chief. We've had suicides and crimes, but open-and-shut cases mostly. Clayton's a good town. Folks here don't lose their heads much. If anyone gets too rich he moves away. Too poor, ditto. And we keep those with rough and tough ideas pretty close to Water Street. My aim's been to see that Clayton's a peaceful and decent place for decent folks to live."

"You've done a mighty handsome job of it, Mr. Wilson. Back files of the *News* make dull reading." Dan studied the old man curiously. It wasn't like the chief to fish for compliments.

The bushy brows relaxed to permit the bright black eyes beneath them to smile appreciation. "Oh, there's been some stealing and petty pilfering. Even an occasional shooting or knifing down along Water Street. But my boys can find thieves and bad men as quick as anyone."

Wilson stopped, embarrassed. "But none of us are detectives. I mean, we haven't had much experience in digging out information about people like the Elways. We might miss a trick. That's why I came over tonight. You're not a detective either. But you're used to sizing up all kinds of people, thinking ahead of them, digging out facts. I—if you have time, I'd like to talk things out with you. In case the D.A. decides on an inquest."

"Of course, Chief. But if the D.A.'s interested, why not let his office do the work?"

Chief Wilson's jaw set hard. Then an abashed twinkle sparkled for a moment in his eyes.

"That's what I mean, doggone it. You put your finger on the sore spot right away. Truth is, Brierson and I don't always see eye to eye. Not that I'm saying a word against him. He's a good lawyer. None smarter. But he'd like to see a younger man in my job. At least that's the reason I've heard he's given."

"You should worry—with your record."

"I do. Because since I was twenty-three I've been on the force, everything from rookie to chief. Two more years and I'll be sixty-five. I want to step out with flags flying. If I botch this case—and I made a good start Christmas Eve doing just that—all the good I've done, tried to do, will be forgotten. Brierson'll see to that, and I'll be out on my ear. No, I want to know the answer to every question he can think up. Before he asks it."

"What have you got so far?" Dan asked. "Just in case he decides on an inquest."

"Well, Dr. Forester—the pathology prof at the college—is performing the autopsies. And Professor McPhail—he's doing the analyses of blood and other samples. Then Olaf Thorwaldson, of course, discovered the bodies and the gas escaping. Judson too. Dr. Mollner made the preliminary examination of the bodies. And Ted Bailey, your own *News* photographer, took the pictures. I know, or will know, everything they can say. Oh yes, and Jack Carston—he's the logical man for identification purposes."

"What about that defective heater? Done anything about that?"

"Thorwaldson had one of the gas company men down at the house first thing this morning. Bob Brownell—the

manager; oh, you know him, of course—went down himself this afternoon. Checked every gas appliance in the
place. Only thing out of kilter was that heater. Its safety
valve wasn't operating. He's having the whole thing taken
apart to find out why."

"Would that mean someone else'd have to take the
whole thing apart to tamper with it?"

The chief looked at him sharply. "I'll check on that."

"O.K. What about meter readings? Doesn't a man come
round every month to read the boxes?"

"Yep. Sometime during the second or third week. Bills
have to be made up to go out the first of each month."

"Fine. If you check the meter reading as it stands now
against the December reading and the December reading
against November's, won't that give you something? Frankly, I'm not sure what But it would do no harm to have that
information."

Unexpectedly the chief chuckled. "Police headquarters
ain't the only place in town to pull boners. The gas company's none too happy over this case either. In October they
had to put a new meter reader on the Skyview-Penndale
route. He made the October and November readings on the
Elway meter all right. But apparently he had something
more important to do in December. So he simply made a
'curbstone' reading on his December report. They didn't
spot that till they were making up the bills last week. Sent
a man down to the Elway house then, but it was locked, he
reported, no one at home! They fired the new fellow, but
a lot of good that does them—or us—now."

"Where is this new meter reader? And what's his name?"

"Everson. And heaven only knows where he is. Left
town, probably for California, his supervisor says. Unsta-
ble fellow, crazy about the movies and music, dancing—all
that sort of thing."

"How about getting him back? Or locating him, at least?"

"We-ll, if the last time he was in the Elway house was November—O.K., we'll find him."

"What about the neighbors? Some of them must have known the Elways pretty well. Whether any secret sorrows seemed to be riding them. How they got along together. And so on."

"Would you believe it? I took it on myself to visit Penndale today. Talked with women all round the Elway house. They said they'd hardly exchanged a word with Mrs. Elway, though their husbands, of course, knew him. He wasn't a talkative, friendly man at all, though always polite enough. And Mrs. Elway couldn't or didn't go out like other women do. That place of theirs runs back quite a ways—a hundred and fifty feet or two hundred feet—to the ridge, then drops down to the river. She spent much of her time down there, they say, wandering around in the woods. Then too, Elway was in and out of town a lot. Sometimes his wife went with him. The neighbors seldom knew whether they were home or not. Got out of the habit of paying attention."

"What about Mrs. Matteson? Her husband says she's sick in bed from shock. Why should she take it so hard?"

"Oh, she's one of these high-strung women. Daughters are just like her. Fine family, all of them. Mrs. Matteson was overtired just before Christmas, sewing late, making Christmas presents. Several nights she saw lights burning late in the Elway home, thought perhaps Mrs. Elway was doing the same thing. It just got her down, I guess, because they were all so busy and happy during the holidays, they didn't think about the house across the street being dark."

"Mrs. Matteson saw lights late? When?"

"She isn't sure. She remembers seeing them after midnight December twenty-first because that was the night the Wayne River burned. And the next night too, because she'd finished making something or other and noticed lights when she went to bed. That's all she's sure of. You know how it is. How many houses around your home were lighted or not lighted two weeks ago? Can you remember?"

"Lord, no." Dan shook his head. "Well, what about Judson? Didn't he know the Elways?"

"No. Elway always paid his rent by mail. But, boy, will Judson testify? He's burned up over this. Says whenever the Elways reported anything out of order he attended to it immediately. I'll bet he's licking a pencil right now, preparing a statement for the *News.*"

"Did he ever have a complaint about that heater?"

"Just once. Last March. And the gas company had two— one in June, the other in September. They took care of all three right away. Nothing really wrong with the heater."

"Where did it come from in the first place?"

"From an old firm, Olson and Olson; about eight years ago. Olaf had one of their men down at the house this afternoon. He said the same thing as Brownell. The heater might be defective or merely need adjustment. He couldn't tell without taking it apart." The chief sighed. "That's about all we've done on the Elways today."

Dan leaned back in his chair to gaze thoughtfully at the ceiling.

"I can't suggest anything you haven't thought of yourself, Chief. The only additional source of information I'd want to hear from would be people who knew the Elways well. If they lived in Clayton three years someone must know them. And if they came here three years ago they came from somewhere. Shouldn't be difficult to find out where, check with the police there—"

"So help me, Dan, we've been over every inch of that house. There ain't a scrap of paper, letters, address books, anything personal that mentions the name of a living soul anywhere. For all we know, Mrs. Elway never wrote a letter or received one. The Penndale mailman says he never delivered mail there, supposed they got it through a post office box or the Wayne River Hotel. If Elway wrote any he did it from his office, I imagine. Of course his personal files could have been burned, both in the Claytonian and Wayne River fires. In the records and correspondence Carston has there ain't a personal line of any kind. Just business letters and contracts, and most of 'em were written and received by Carston, acting for Elway."

Dan's tilted chair swung to a level with a bang. "You've wired the Midwest Hotel Syndicate, of course. They must have a complete file on Elway."

At the expression settling over the chief's ruddy face he demanded incredulously, "Do you mean to say they haven't? That they'd trust a man with the management of hotels valued at three hundred thousand to half a million and more dollars without—"

"Oh, the Midwest Syndicate did know all about Elway and his wife," the chief assured him.

"Did! Have they been burned out and asphyxiated, too?"

"They have, Dan. *Mr. and Mrs. Elway were the Midwest Hotel Syndicate, Incorporated.* A Martin White is listed as owning two shares but there is nothing to indicate who he is or where he is. I doubt if he exists at all."

TUESDAY AFTERNOON, JANUARY 6

Tuesday morning as Dan eased himself about the business streets of Clayton, in brilliant sunshine that belied the low temperature, he wondered wryly if he and Marcus P. weren't wasting their time. As publisher and correspondent, their serious concern was to present the news accurately, clearly, and uncolored. Yet everywhere he went—corner cigar store for cigarettes, Clayton Barbershop, Three Brothers Haberdashery, Tollefson's, the tailor—and from everyone he met he heard distorted and rich-hued explanations as to how the Elways died.

By the time he reached the News Building, shortly before two, he had listened to a dozen versions of the composite theory sweeping like a high spring wind over the town. Each differed from the others in certain details, but in the main they were remarkably similar.

The Elways, according to the main outline, had come to the parting of the ways by Monday night, December twenty-second. Mrs. Elway, her health wrecked by the shock of the Claytonian fire, had gone to pieces when the Wayne River burned. Never a lover of Clayton, she had insisted on returning East immediately. Mr. Elway had not only refused but declared his intention of building a new hotel as soon as he could secure materials.

As Monday evening progressed their argument had grown more and more bitter, continued after they were in bed; at length had become so violent that they both had risen. Became so violent then, apparently, that Elway, beside himself with anger, struck his wife, knocked her down.

Failing to revive her, he thought he had killed her. Overcome by remorse, he had lifted her into a chair, thrown himself on the floor at her feet. As luck would have it, that December twenty-second midnight had to be the hour when the pilot light on their defective heater went out again. In the throes of their anger or physical struggle they wouldn't notice the odor of escaping gas. Perhaps when he did, or she did, if she roused, it was too late.

Such a theory, Dan had to admit, neatly dovetailed all that was known of the scene Thorwaldson and Judson had walked in on Sunday night. It accounted for the bruise on Mrs. Elway's forehead, her shredded nightdress and robe, her husband's ripped pajama, sleeve, their sitting and lying positions, for the fact that neither was in bed when the gas began to ascend to the upper floor.

The sameness of the versions indicated a common source. Whose was the master mind, Dari wondered, behind the story? He didn't have long to wait for the answer.

As he crossed the foyer of the News Building to the stairway Tina Johnson popped up from behind her switchboard to summon him with a hiss. But when he leaned over her barricade her pert little face was solemn.

"Miss Tennant's gone home. Had another phone call just a few minutes ago," she informed him. "She hasn't been worth a dime since yesterday morning."

Dan didn't consider the temperamental society and women's page editor worth much more at any time but, knowing Tina, he dutifully asked, "Why?"

"Because her sister's husband just sits and sits in that Harrison Hotel bar, drinking himself stupid. And he's never taken a drink before—"

"Such is life," Dan commented tritely. "But that's his problem, Tina. And you'd have fewer if you paid less attention to Eva Tennant's wire."

Tina froze him with a look. "I just thought I'd remind you her brother-in-law's an old friend of yours. Jack Carston."

He sighed, straightened. "O.K., Miss Fixit. I'll see what I can do to relieve Eva's mind. And yours."

In the Harrison bar he found Jack Carston slumped on a stool at the far end of the semicircular bar that ran the length of the room. At the other end the barman was absorbed in a sporting magazine. Otherwise the gaily decorated place was empty.

For a moment Dan found difficulty in recognizing the man he had talked with only a few days before about the Claytonian and Wayne River fires. Then, though Carston had looked tired and nervous, harassed alike by claims of every description and the makeshift office Bud Harrison had supplied in the rear of the Harrison Barbershop, he had been his dapper, rotund, genial self.

Now the jolly, round face was gray and grooved, the hail-fellow-well-met manner a thing of the past. Head propped on his hands over an untouched whisky glass, he didn't look up when Dan greeted him.

"If you're worrying about that story going the rounds, Jack, forget it," Dan said immediately. "You know Clayton's hunger for gossip. Have a drink with me, then let's both get back to our offices."

Carston thrust his glass away violently. "I'd take that asinine little cluck apart—if I could get my hands on her. The whole rotten tale grew out of something she heard Elway say to me—"

"I can be silent or articulate in the *News,* whatever seems best," Dan suggested.

"You're the only one in town who's said a decent word to me since—since—" Carston turned a ravaged face on him. "You know Bud Harrison gave me—gave Mr. Elway, rather—the back quarter of his barbershop for a temporary office the morning after the Wayne River fire. We had a door of our own, part of that long window that opens on the lobby, and a high screen as a wall between us and the shop. It'd have been fine if this dame—"

"What dame?"

"That barbershop cashier and manicurist. Had her table and cash register on the other side of the screen from my desk. And her ears pinned back permanently. She didn't even go out to lunch those first days after the fire—afraid she'd miss a word, I guess. It didn't matter what she heard that first day—the twenty-second—until Elway came in about half past five."

Carston stopped to rub a hand across his forehead as if he felt perspiration rising there again. "God! I'll never forget that day. Fire still smoldering in the Wayne River, seemed as if they'd never get it out. A high-pressure lad named Blythe had arrived by plane for the insurance companies Burned-out guests—some of them had been with us in the Claytonian too—were weeping and wailing on my shoulder, in person or by phone. I thought I'd had it hard until Mr. Elway came in. People'd been after him, too, even on the street. Even camping on the doorstep of his home."

He pulled his glass toward him, pushed it away again. "Did I say it was five-thirty or so when he came in? Everything was quiet in the barbershop; it closes at five on weekdays. Mr. Elway looked like a man who'd been struck with a cleaver—gashed white—and thrown out in the snow. Dazed, completely sunk. So I tried to cheer him up. Said I'd had definite assurance we could get materials

immediately, begin to build. He never said a word—just
sat there, looking like—"

"A man who'd been hit by a cleaver," Dan completed
for him.

"That's right. That's exactly the way he looked. Gashed
white. Finally I said—though I didn't think it possible
anything more could hit us—finally I said, 'Something
new come up, Mr. Elway?'"

Carston gripped Dan's arm, tried to give an impression
of a blank dazed face, glazed eyes. "Lord love me, he just
sat there, staring at me like that for a minute, maybe two.
I knew he had something to say, though, so I waited. Then
he sort of groaned or laughed, I couldn't tell which. 'Yes,'
he said, 'something new has come up. Someone I've trust-
ed, someone on whose word and loyalty I'd have bet my
life—has come up.'"

Mrs. Elway was the someone, Dan deduced, and marveled anew at the perspicacity of the town gossips. Before
he could speak Carston went on.

"Talking out loud like that seemed to wake him up,
give him a grip on himself. He wouldn't say another word.
Just sat there, tearing one of his big cigars to bits, dropping little squeezed pieces, one at a time, on the floor. I
don't mind saying it wasn't a pretty sight. I had a feeling
he was doing in his mind to—this someone he mentioned
what he was doing right then to that cigar. . . .

"I wanted to get his mind off quick from what he was
doing so I began talking about an idea I had for the new
hotel. To begin on the site of the Claytonian, run her up
four, five stories, say, then build up the Wayne River to
the same level, join both hotels across our private entrance
road, and continue to six, eight, however many stories we
wanted. At the rate Clayton's growing—"

"It is, isn't it?" Dan inserted neatly. "What did Elway
say to that?"

"Nothing. He just went on wrecking that cigar. After a while he got up, looked around that cluttered little office, and said as if he wasn't speaking to me, 'Maybe I'm not meant for this hotel racket. My wife says I'm not. She wants me to get out of it.' He sort of rocked on his heels a minute, then he said, and if you knew him, you'd know nothing could change his mind, 'But I'll be damned if I will.'"

"So that's where the yarn started!" Dan commented. "Little Sugar Bowl Ears heard him say his wife wanted him to give up the hotel business, that he wouldn't—"

"I'll bet everything I own that's how it started. Until Mr. Elway left there hadn't been a sound in the barbershop. But when he'd gone I heard something—like someone walking easy. I slipped out our door, looked in their window, and there she was tiptoeing to the street door. She and I were the only ones who heard what Mr. Elway said. And I never breathed a word, even to my wife."

"Perhaps Elway—"

"No. He never spoke of his wife, his personal affairs, to anyone. Wouldn't have said anything to me if he hadn't been so down. And when he left me he got right into his car and drove home. I watched him start from the lobby entrance. That was the last I—or anyone else except Mrs. Elway, I guess—saw of him. Alive."

Dan's eyes sharpened on the despair in Carston's face. Something deeper than resentment against the barbershop hussy and Clayton's wagging tongues was eating like acid into the ex-manager's mind.

"I'd like to ask a few questions, Jack. Of course if the answers are none of my business—"

"Why not? I'm the boy that knows all the answers!" Carston's cynical anger blazed so hot that for a moment his gray face burned with color.

"What was the status quo between Elway and his wife?" Dan asked.

"You too!" This time Carston pushed away his drink in such disgust it spilled and rolled to crash inside the horse-shoe. The barman went on reading as if that crashing glass were an old story to him.

Carston ignored it too. "I'll tell you what I've told everyone else who's asked me that. Clayton'd be heaven if every husband and wife was as courteous and considerate to one another as those two. Of course I never saw Mrs. Elway after the Claytonian burned. Didn't see much of her during the two years she lived there. But the few times she did come into the lobby—when Mr. Elway was there—they were exemplary. That's just the word for them. Exemplary. Never raised their voices, never argued. They were the most scrupulously—that's another good word for 'em—polite pair I ever knew."

"What was Mrs. Elway like—I mean her interests, her dress, her way with people, especially friends?"

"I don't know, and that's the truth. She stayed in their suite most of the time, had all her meals there, read a lot, played the piano, the maids said. She made most of her own clothes, too, and were they something! Why, just to see 'em, women guests of the hotel used to come down to the lobby when Mrs. Elway went out at four for the long walk she took every day—for her figure, I guess. If it was a figure. I never saw a woman so thin. Except to speak to Mr. Elway or me, she never looked at anyone—and there was plenty who tried to catch her eye. Tall and thin like that, and with that shining, awfully blond hair and white skin that seems to go with it, she was a knockout. Not beautiful, maybe, I don't know, but the first woman you'd look at in a room of beautiful women."

"Not a woman to make or want friends?"

"No, too iced. I don't remember ever seeing her smile or laugh. Nothing here interested her. And no one. Mr. Elway was like that too. Reserved, unsmiling, quiet. But, boy, did he know how to run a hotel! Do you know the first thing he did when he bought the Claytonian? It had been redecorated the year before, but he went over the whole place again. When it was finished it was worth seeing. So was the Wayne River; you saw it. He made it all over, too, and you couldn't find a finer hotel for its size west of Chicago. He did that for every hotel he handled, I guess. Started fresh, everything new. And he bought everything himself—mostly in the East. And he made sure that every nail, every can of paint, every yard of drapery went just where and how he wanted it to be."

For, the first time Carston's face showed interest, his voice quickened. Obviously he could talk about his employer as a hotel man for hours. Dan didn't have hours to spend.

"Not an easy man to work with or for, I'd say," he hazarded.

"No sirree. Hard as nails in some ways. But if you gave him what he wanted, when and how he wanted it, and asked no questions, he was all right. I learned to do that quick, I can tell you. And we got along fine. Why, he brought men here who'd worked for him for years in other places. And you know Chinese Charlie and his gang. They been with Elway almost ten years, made his restaurants something to remember. Men don't follow another man around the country unless they like to work for him."

"I suppose not," Dan agreed. "What about this Midwest Hotel Syndicate? It's new to me."

"Incorporated in Delaware, maybe ten years ago, not more. I don't know much about them except that they're a fine crowd to work for. Gave Mr. Elway complete authority, then let him alone. I managed the hotels locally; he

handled all correspondence and dealings with the Wilmington office."

After three, Dan noted by the clock over the bar. He'd
spent more than an hour with Carston, seemed to have
lured him out of the doldrums. He ought to get Jack out of
here, take him home. But his curious mind had one more
question. Reluctantly he said so.

Instantly all his good work vanished. Carston plunged
right back to the depths where Dan had found him.

"I'll tell you the answer before you ask it," he said
darkly. "No, I'll ask it. I've asked myself a thousand times.
Why do you think I sit alone in this empty bar all afternoon? Asking and asking and asking myself that question!
Why didn't I suspect something was wrong when I didn't
hear from Mr. Elway for thirteen days? Why didn't I investigate, go to his home, do something, anything?"

The eyes he turned to Dan were dredged by grief and
remorse. "The answer makes no sense now. But it did between December twenty-third and January fourth. It was
Christmastime, wasn't it, and Mr. Elway and his wife had
just been through all the shock and trouble and loss of a
second hotel under his management going up in smoke
overnight. . . .

"When he didn't show up or telephone on the twenty-
third, I thought he'd done just what I'd have done in his
place—taken his wife to spend Christmas where they could
have peace and quiet. That's what I told Blythe, only I
made it official. Said I'd had a phone call from Elway.
When they didn't get back the day after Christmas I had
an explanation for that, too, for whom it might concern.
The day after Christmas was Friday. Why should they
come back to Clayton for Saturday and Sunday when they
could be in the Twin Cities or Chicago, having themselves
a little fun?"

"You made that—official, too, Jack, didn't you?"

"Sure. Said I'd had a wire. And when they didn't come back on Monday I made it official again. I'd cooked up two good reasons, fresh and hot. One was Mrs. Elway's health. The other was still better. While Mr. Elway stayed with her he was studying plans for a new hotel, ordering materials. To cover however long he might be away, I said he'd probably have to go on to New York."

Carston's face was twitching. He paused to smooth it with his hands. "He'd been away plenty of times before— for Midwest meetings in Delaware and buying trips— without sending me any word. I took that as a compliment. So I didn't worry about his absence, in spite of a flea Blythe tried to put in my ear that he'd skipped out."

"But you did worry," Dan deduced.

"Sure I worried. Because for myself I had a third and still better reason for his absence and silence. I, Jack Carston, the lad that knows all the answers! I thought he'd been called East, was having trouble explaining those fires to the Midwest crowd in Wilmington. And I wasn't too sure I wouldn't wake up one morning to find a new managing director had arrived. . . .

"But I was all for Mr. Elway. He was a true hotel man if ever there was one. So I kept my fingers crossed and acted as if I knew where he was and that everything was hunky-dory. Those fires weren't his fault. He wasn't even in town when the Claytonian burned. And he was at home on Penndale when the Wayne River blaze was discovered. I was the one in charge, both times. If anyone is to blame I am. And I'm not. Those fires were acts of God—or the devil. Plus twenty-below weather, frozen hydrants, and a fire department that had lost its most experienced men to the war."

Dan placed a quieting hand on the quivering shoulder beside him. "Elway couldn't have asked for a better and more loyal friend than you, Jack. And he knew it or he wouldn't have taken you with him from the Claytonian to the Wayne River. The point isn't that you made a mistake. The point is that you did what you thought was right for the Midwest people and for Elway and his wife."

"The point is," Carston repeated with deadly self-condemnation, "that if I hadn't been so damned smart, trying to play God, I might have saved both their lives! But no, I thought to spare Mr. Elway more bad news until after Christmas. That fellow Blythe was trying to put something over. He didn't get any change out of me when he arrived the afternoon of the twenty-second, so I'd tried again that night. It was almost midnight when I finally got rid of him."

"You mean you didn't tell Elway?"

"That's what's eating me!" Carston pumped his doubled fists soundlessly up and down on the bar. "If I'd done the right thing I'd have gone down to 355 Penndale that night, late as it was. Knocked or broken down the door if I had to. But I saw myself as Santa Claus! And now they're saying those two fine people fought like alley cats! Tore each other's clothes to ribbons! This damned town and its damned gossipers. I'd like to give 'em a theory. I'll bet I know the answer—"

Carston stopped, silenced perhaps by that word "answer." Then suddenly, ignoring Dan's restraining hand, he raised his voice. Raised it deliberately, Dan thought as he listened.

"I'll bet Mr. and Mrs. Elway had gone to bed, were asleep. That one of them woke up, smelled gas. Mrs. Elway probably. He slept like a log. Switchboard operators had to ring and ring to wake him. I'll bet she tried to rouse him, save him. Or he her. And failing, they died together."

Though still ostensibly absorbed in his magazine, the barman's head had raised slightly. He was listening, Dan observed, with both ears almost visibly distended.

WEDNESDAY AFTERNOON, JANUARY 7

By Wednesday noon Carston's object—if he had had one in raising his voice so shrilly—was achieved. And confounded. Claytonians, according to Mrs. Bob Brownell, who dropped in to find Dan and his mother having luncheon before the fire, were on the verge of civil war over a new crop of theories as to how and why the Elways died. Neither of them doubted her. Brownie was the town's champion ear-to-the-ground-er.

Now while the short, prematurely white hair that gave her head the effect of a dandelion top in seed fairly quivered with excitement she pouted out, with all the conviction of an eyewitness, the explanation she herself supported.

"The Elways had gone to bed that Monday evening and were sound asleep. Sometime after midnight Mrs. Elway woke up, feeling dizzy and sick. Then she smelled, gas and got up, naturally, to investigate. But she only reached the top of the stairs. The gas got her there, and she fell or rolled down the few steps to the landing. That was when she bruised her forehead."

"Could be," Dan agreed. "And then?"

"She must have lain there unconscious for a time. When she came to she knew there was no time to investigate, only time to get out of that house. Somehow she managed to go back to the bedroom to rouse her husband. Probably pulling at him, she ripped loose that pajama sleeve. And he must have been drugged with sleep or gas. Her torn nightclothes prove he tried to push her away and, when she wouldn't leave him alone, tore—"

"But Mr. Elway was found on the floor," Dora protested.

"Of course, dear. Because somehow she got him out of bed onto his feet, started to lead him to the door. But he fell and she couldn't lift him or persuade him to move. And she wouldn't leave him to escape herself. So she sat down in that chair beside him," Brownie concluded, pulling the tremolo stop in her voice all the way out, "and died with him."

"Could be," Dan repeated, remembering the words Carston had almost shouted into the barman's distended ears. Reluctant to hear that theory and all the others dissected, he invented an urgent appointment at the News Building, hurried away.

Even in the newsroom, however, he couldn't escape the Elway mystery. Dale was there, arguing his favorite explanation with the new day editor. Seated on a corner of the copy desk, Bailey studied a handful of prints while he waited to present his views. Near by, Tom Jefferson, police court reporter, lounged cynically, but alertly watching for an opening.

At sight of Dan, Dale shouted, "He's mine. I'll bet he's just out of bed, hasn't heard anything yet."

"About what?" Dan asked innocently.

"About what, he asks!" Bailey rose in amazement. "Who talks of anything these days but what happened at 355 Penndale?"

"Keep your seat," Dan advised him. "I've heard all about how they died together—"

"That sob sister's tale! Heard the one about how Elway waited till his wife was asleep, then, slipped down and

turned on the gas himself? With two total fires behind him
and a wife, on the point of leaving him, he didn't want
any Christmas, anything, more at all. But Mrs. E. woke
up, smelled the gas, tried to persuade him to get out. He
refused and when she tried to leave herself he struck her.
Either knocked her into that chair or put her there, then
either threw himself on the floor or fell, overcome—"

Dale snapped scornful fingers. "The real McCoy, Dan,
comes straight from the source. Carston himself told Nick
Bates—you know him, barman at the Harrison—yesterday
that Elway was in a murderous mood the afternoon of the
twenty-second. Tore a cigar to pieces and stamped it under
his feet to show what he'd do to someone who'd let him
down. Mrs. Elway, probably, with her decision to leave
him in Clayton if he wouldn't leave Clayton with her."

"It could've been someone else," Jefferson broke in.
"For all his spit-and-polish manners, Elway was a tough
guy. The kind that makes and keeps enemies. The story is,
Dan, that one or more, of them showed up in Clayton the
night of the twenty-second, had it out with Elway in his
home, and either doped or poisoned him. His wife, too,
of course, to make sure she couldn't talk later. Then they
turned on the gas and—"

"Could be," Dan commented maddeningly. "Any mail
from Marcus P., Dale?" When the night editor shook his
head Dan turned for the door. "Sorry to walk out on your
story hour, fellows. I'm a busy man."

But outside the News Building he had to stop and light
a cigarette while he decided where to go and what to do
for the rest of the afternoon. Thought of hearing more
theories or the same ones over and over wherever he went
was too much. The autopsies hadn't been completed, the
reports mightn't be available until the first of next week.
By that time only a day or two of his leave would remain.

Strange as the Elway deaths were, they could be of only academic interest to him.

Why not walk home? The cold was modifying, the air invigorating. Dazzling sunshine made even the snow-packed sidewalks and streets gleam like mirrors. As he strode along he decided to do more than walk home. He'd follow Fulton Street, on which the News Building faced, straight to its junction with Penndale, then follow Penndale round to Skyview. A brisk two- or three-mile hike on a day like this should clear his wits, assuming he had any left to clear after absorbing all this chatter.

At Penndale sight of. naked treetops rising above the ridge behind the homes along the river's curve touched off a new idea. Below that ridge, between shallow banks, lay Wayne River, where in winters long ago he and his gang had skated and tramped, cunningly tracking rabbits and fox they never found. He could cut back to the ridge between any of these houses, descend to the old river road, and follow it round the bend and on, to ascend again behind his own home.

As he walked along, looking for a familiar house, across whose lawns he could trespass without question, he spied the Elway home a few doors ahead. It must be empty and locked now. He wouldn't disturb anyone going through there.

Turning in at its short entrance walk, he saw from the well-trodden snow that many people had entered there since Sunday night. The beaten path led him round the west side to the back door.

There he understood more clearly why the neighbors knew so little about the Elways. On either side of the long, narrow lawn a lilac hedge, easily eight or ten feet high and three or four thick, extended from house to ridge. Even now, when leafless, it appeared impenetrable. Of the bungalow-type homes to either side, little could be seen but the snow-covered roofs.

He had taken but a few steps down that narrow lawn when a familiar voice hailed him. Reluctantly he faced about. Thode Brierson, almost filling the open back door, beckoned him in.

"Hi, Big!" Dan answered, stood still.

"Where ya goin'? Whatcha' doin'? Come in and see a feller, why don'tcha?"

"Didn't know you lived here," Dan retorted. He turned back slowly. "I'm on my way to the river. Hadn't thought to look at the old stamping ground before."

Brierson stepped down to grasp his arm, draw him into the house. "Take first things first, boy. Keep me company for a while. Isn't as if you were a stranger. You were among those present Sunday night, I've heard tell."

Stamping the snow from his feet, Dan stepped into a warm, immaculate white kitchen. Evidently the faithful thermostat was still maintaining the house at an even seventy. But he felt uncomfortable there, noticing everything. For some reason he'd never thought of Mrs. Elway in terms of pots and pans and linoleum.

As Brierson dug into a broom closet for something Dan raised his head sharply. "Thought you said you were alone."

"Alone? I am." Big Thode turned round a yardstick in his hand.

"Someone just went out the front door.'

"Spooks!" Brierson laughed. "That's the effect this house has on you. One reason I dragged you in. Come on."

He led the way through a swinging door into the dining room. "You're almost right, at that, in thinking I live here. Among the thousand and one angles on this case, of course, is the chance of foul play. But the house was locked fore and aft when Thorwaldson and Judson, got here Sunday night. There isn't a sign anywhere of forced entry. Or of anything being disturbed or taken away.

Except for that one bruise on Mrs. Elway, there wasn't a mark of any importance on either body. And her bruise might have been caused by the well-known open door."

As he talked Brierson pointed the yardstick to right and left as if he were showing the house to a prospective tenant. "You notice anything while you were here?"

"Not a thing," Dan started to say. But automatically his eyes were everywhere. Not looking for signs of entry, robbery, or petty thieving. But for a hair, any kind of hair so long as it came from any kind of a dog.

The spotless rugs and upholstered chairs and divans betrayed no sign that a dog had ever lain upon them, rubbed against them.

"But I was here only a few minutes," he added deliberately. "All I saw really was that upstairs bedroom and the dining room."

"Take a look around then, why don't you? I'll be glad to have your ideas. No matter what the autopsies show, we've got to hold, an inquest. Only way to quiet the rumormongers. They're really going to town on this case."

"I know," Dan said feelingly. "I'm a refugee from rumors myself."

Brierson headed for the stairs. "I'm making a few measurements. Be through in a sec."

Dan followed him. "Anything been rearranged or taken away since Sunday night?"

"Nothing but the bodies. Why?"

"Anyone been sent in here to clean, put things in order?"

"No. Why?"

"Just wondered."

"Because the whole house is so shipshape? Why not? This Mrs. Elway didn't have anything else to do but take care of it and herself. Elway spent most of his time uptown or out of town."

Brierson went on to disappear in the Elways' bedroom. Dan turned to look into the small room to the left of the stair well. It looked like a bedroom, was a bedroom, though obviously unused.

Thoughtfully he returned to the stairs, retraced his steps to the kitchen. The first low door of the kitchen unit revealed two small pans, one white, one cream, suspended on hooks. They could have been used for dog food and water. But were they?

Turning, he found the door at one side that opened into the garage. It was as immaculate as the house. Almost filling it was a dark red sedan, its nose level with the door. On the far wall garden implements and snow shovels were racked. In one corner were oilcans and an automobile kit. In the other the little drying Christmas tree. Nowhere any sign that a dog had been fed or bedded there.

Idly he walked round the car, opened its door, and looked in. No dog hairs on its upholstering either. Nor, he noted with interest, any reason to believe the Elways had intended to leave Clayton. The gas gauge showed the tank was empty.

Yet that young woman in the dark cape and the angry man who had lodged the complaint at police headquarters had both heard a dog in here. On Christmas Eve. And again last Sunday night. Both had said from the sounds they heard the dog might be freezing or hungry. Freezing was impossible; the garage was heated. But hungry . . .

He stopped, struck again by that similarity of phrasing.

Had there been two people? That young woman had an exceptionally deep voice, plus a shattering capacity for anger. What if she had called the station Sunday night, deliberately deepened her voice, deliberately used George Matteson's name? Or what if her own name were something like that—Georgia Mathews, for example, or Masterson?

When Brierson descended the stairs he found Dan in the lower hall, absorbed in the telephone book.

WEDNESDAY AFTERNOON, JANUARY 7

"Renewing your youth—with telephone numbers?" Derisively Big Thode flipped the book closed under Dan's nose, went on into the living room to throw himself down on a divan. "Come on, have a cigarette and chin awhile. And take off that overcoat."

Dan perched on the arm of a chair, kept his coat on. "What's on your mind?"

"At the moment nothing but interest in my fellow man. Specifically, you. Of course we've bumped into each other occasionally: can't miss in a town this size. But I've never had a chance to catch up on your adventures."

"Adventures are for the inefficient, I've heard."

"Experiences, then, in your case, of course. I'll bet you've had plenty, boy!" A shutter closed in Dan's eyes before the gleam in the pair focused on him. To Brierson, adventures, experiences meant only one thing. "Come on, Dan. Give."

"All right. You asked for it." Deliberately Dan settled himself in the chair. Deliberately and clearly began to analyze the position of the Balkan States, the relation of each country in the group to the others, their relations with Russia, with western Europe, with the United States.

Once started, he almost forgot his listener in the pleasure of discovering the clarity and perspective his six months' rest had given him. And Brierson, strangely, was the perfect audience. He smoked and listened without interruption.

As Dan talked sunlight withdrew from the room, the short winter afternoon slipped away. When he came to a final period he got up, shrugged his overcoat into position, stooped for his hat on the floor beside his chair.

A reading lamp flashed on. He turned to find Brierson watching him with an expression suggestive of the alleged cat after swallowing the alleged canary.

"Hell's bells!" Dan groaned. "I must be slipping. Why aren't you asleep?"

"Not me! That was damned interesting, fella. First time anyone ever gave me an earful on the Balkans that made sense. Why stop?"

"I've kept you too long as it is." Dan turned for the dining room.

"Hi! Where ya goin'?"

"Out the back door."

"Are you kidding?" Brierson lumbered to his feet to scoff. "Think you can promenade along the river, let alone get there, in that outfit you're wearing? And at this hour? It'll soon be dark, man."

"Nonsense. It's only four o'clock. And I know every foot of that river. I'll be home in fifteen minutes."

"In five. I'm driving you."

Dan stepped back, grasped him by the shoulders, lifted his hundred and ninety pounds clear of the floor.

"O.K., wise guy," Brierson agreed when he was once more on his feet. "But if you aren't found till the snow melts in the spring, I'll be damned if I'll waste an inquest on you." His face lighted. "Hey, wait a minute. What about this case?"

"Well, what about it?"

"Nothing, as far as I know now. Looks like a clear case of accidental death to me. Nevertheless, as I told you, we'll have to blow some of the taxpayers' money on a hearing."

"That's your pidgin."

"Yours too. If you observed anything Sunday night, that should come out in the evidence."

"Me?" Dan shrugged. "All I know is what I read in the papers."

"But you were here—"

"And what I learned Sunday night you read in the Monday *Morning News*."

Brierson sighed with exaggerated relief "If you mean that, I can cut down the witnesses by one. But you've always been such a devious guy, fella." His voice remained level, but his eyes hardened. "A man never knows you're carrying a grenade until it hits him."

"Meaning?"

"Nothing—unless you've cooked up some subtle theory on this case."

"Before the report on the autopsies is ready?"

Big Thode faced him a moment before dull color began to creep up his throat into his heavy cheeks. "I should have broken you in two when you were a freshman," he said with forced jocularity. "You were a skinny little wise guy then, and I guess except for pounds and reputation you aren't much different now."

"Forget it," Dan told him. "I was just playing dead. I'm leaving Clayton in another week."

"That right?" Brierson's heartiness returned. "Well, well! Back to the bigger and blacker headlines and a book one day, I suppose." He turned toward the dining room, turned back. "Come on. Use your head. Let me drive you home."

When Dan refused, Big Thode went on through the dining room to the kitchen, unlocked the door. "So long then, and thanks for the lecture, Mr. Cumberland. I'll be proud to tell my grandchildren—"

Dan stepped outside, stopped to adjust his muffler, turn up his collar. With the sun the sparkling air had gone. The variety he encountered now had a penetrating chill. What an idiot he'd been to sit so long in that warm room in a topcoat!

He might have turned left, followed the path round to Penndale and so home if he had not heard then the click of a lock turning. Brierson was still in the kitchen; waiting to see what he'd do.

Though he knew himself for a stubborn fool, Dan struck off across the snow for the ridge. Before he reached it, snow was packing itself inside his broad-beamed oxfords, clinging to his trousers, but without pausing he started down.

Deep snow banked the slope, embedded bushes and trees, smoothed treacherously over hollows and hummocks and over all but the largest fallen trees and branches. Slipping and sliding, guiding himself by a grasp on this branch or that bush, he plunged along.

Halfway down he noticed the going had eased. Remained easier as long as he kept within a winding course outlined by shrubs. Gratefully he realized he had stumbled on a path of sorts.

Warm and breathless, he reached the comparatively level area along the river. There the prospect brightened. Wayne River, frozen deeply and drifted with show, lay eight feet below. Along the bank, years before, an optimistic park board had cleared a road that Clayton might boast a marine drive. But floods every few years when the Wayne rose to fill the channel between the ridges on either side had put an end to that ambition. The trees were gone there, however, and much of the snow had blown down on the ice. What remained was hard-packed. If he stayed close to the edge he could push along steadily if slowly.

As he pushed he knew pleasure in the wild bleakness and isolation of the scene. The lonely river curved eastward to a bend that marked the end of Penndale, the beginning of Skyview. Across the river, as here, naked trees laid ebony patterns against the white ridge slopes, the higher trees, against the darkening sky. He even enjoyed the cold, still, biting air.

In ten minutes or so he had rounded the bend, glimpsed dimly ahead the long curve Skyview followed. Just before the river turned again he could climb the ridge to his own back door.

Shortly he spied through the trees ahead a large black mass. As he drew nearer he saw it was a structure of some kind, round in shape, ten or twelve feet high, made of corrugated iron, apparently roofless.

It lay snugly in the lee of the ridge, perhaps forty feet away across deep ripples of snow. Curious, he stopped. No windows offered interior views and the broad double doors facing the river were not only barred but secured by a heavy padlock.

As he stood, wondering, the skin on the back of his neck tightened. A shiver ran over him. He moved on, impatient with his incessant curiosity about whatever came under his attention. The thing couldn't be anything more important than an indestructible playground for small boys or an enclosure in which some of the estimable ladies on Skyview could sun-bathe in summer.

Suddenly he stopped again. Cold hadn't caused that shiver. He was warm! Had he heard some sound, caught some movement? He listened, turning his eyes slowly over the slope, over the level stretch as far as he could see behind him.

Not even the upper branches of the trees were in motion. The stillness was absolute.

He faced round to look up and down the river. Nothing there but ice and snow, the snow directly below the bank webbed with ski tracks. Nothing moved across the river, either, though now its bank and ridge were barely visible and on the hill slopes beyond farmhouse windows were showing lights.

Pleased, if anything, to have recognized that feeling of warning, he started forward again. In Clayton he hadn't talked or thought much about his years overseas, but the dissertation he'd given Brierson had brought them all back to consciousness. And with them, apparently, had come that prized sixth sense. Or perhaps its reappearance was a sign he was now rested, relaxed, fit and ready to go back.

So thinking, he was only for an instant aware of the ground beneath his feet taking sudden wing. The next, unaware of anything, he lay face down across the ski tracks on the river below.

When he opened his eyes his mother, sitting quietly beside him, smiled.

"Don't move, dear. You're home, in your own room, and all right."

Except for a blinding headache, Dan saw nothing extraordinary in that.

"You fell," Dora explained. "Coming home last night in the dark along the river. You'll remember in a day or two. By the grace of God a young woman found you. She was skiing along alone, came on you almost at once. She wrapped you in a long cape she had with her, went for help. A farmer named Jansson and his son from across the river brought you home."

Of all her words, only one had any significance for Dan—why he didn't know. "Cape?" he repeated, stopped. Even that effort cracked his head open.

"You would ask about that! She wasn't wearing it, dear. She was carrying it. She'd taken it along to use when she stopped somewhere to build a fire for a picnic. Lucky for you." Dora's gray eyes, so like Dan's own, dimmed a little. "Lucky for Marc—and me."

MONDAY AFTERNOON, JANUARY 12

Full length on the couch before the open fire, Dan fixed his eyes on one blue flame licking the coals. Unostentatiously anxious near by, his mother knitted, unaware that each faint click of her needles echoed like crackling thunder in her long son's head.

And Dan would not tell her. He'd raised enough hell since yesterday, achieving this couch. And his clothes. If Dora ever imagined a little thing like needle clicks bothered him, he'd have small chance of leaving Clayton, as per schedule, Thursday evening for New York.

Until yesterday he hadn't really got it clear in his mind that he was Dan Cumberland, foreign correspondent, on six months' leave. Now that he had, he wasn't going to forget again. Funny about a crack on the back of the head! A man forgot everything, including how he got it. Even now he didn't remember exactly.

He could recall the river bank, that he was walking along the edge. But even though it was almost dark there had still been light enough to distinguish nearby trees, the sullen gray of the frozen river. Of course the snow itself had given some light.

Yet he was so accustomed to getting around in darkness, sometimes in complete and hazardous darkness, in streets and on country roads strange to him, that he had

developed a form of cat's eyes. How then could he have
tumbled off a river bank, once as familiar to him as the
palm of his hand?

Wryly he grinned at himself. He knew what he was up
to, what he was going to say in a moment. How he got that
crack on the back of his head was an important item of
information. But more important—compellingly important to him for some reason—was the item about the young
woman with the cape. How had she happened on him so
quickly and opportunely? How could she have saved the
life of Daniel Forsythe Cumberland, yet vanish into darkness again without anyone—even Marcus P.—being able
to find out who she was, where she came from, where she
went?

People could disappear in Europe, voluntarily or otherwise. Could disappear in cities like New York and Chicago.
But this was Clayton! And between them, Marcus P. and
Dora had infinite resources for learning anything they
wanted to know. The impression gained on him that they
did know, for their own purposes wouldn't reveal the gal's
identity.

He turned his head—God, how good it was to be able
to turn without splitting it in two!—to look at his mother.

Serene and ample and kind, her face, with the cute little second chin she tried so hard to hide, appeared intent
on her needles. But her eyes met his.

"Tell me again." He smiled.

She didn't need to ask what. She smiled, too, and for
the twentieth time told him again.

"You left the News Building a little after two last
Wednesday afternoon, Tina told us. Evidently to walk
home—the long way. On Penndale, if you hadn't intended
to before, you decided to go down to the river, come home
by the old river road. Thode Brierson told us that. He

tried to delay you until it was too late and dark to go, then
to dissuade you."

Dan understood now that cat-canary look.

"Poor Thode! He's awfully upset. But of course he's
never learned that for him to try to stop you from doing
anything is the surest way to make you do it. Why you've
never been friendly with him, dear, I can't understand.
It isn't like you to hold that little difficulty in college
against him. He's lived it down, done very well for himself
and his family. Everyone likes him, trusts him now. Marc
says there's talk of running him for the state legislature."

Dan cocked an eyebrow at her. "That's a new paragraph. What's happened since last you told me this yarn?
Big Thode been here in person?"

"Not since he came last Thursday, as soon as he heard.
But he's telephoned every day. No, both Marc and I have
noticed how you close up every time his name is mentioned. I just thought I'd—"

"Say a kind word for him? Well, you have, darling. Now
go on."

"Where was I? Oh you went down to the river behind
the Elway house, followed it around the Skyview bend.
Not far beyond it there's a little break in the bank, Marc
says, but it was filled with snow. Evidently in the dark it
looked like solid ground to you. You stepped onto it—and
down you went."

"But the crack's on the back of my head—"

"Fortunately. Dr. Mollner thinks—everyone does—that
when you felt yourself going you twisted round, tried to
save yourself, fell backward."

"I remember everything in general up to there," Dan
told her, then, assured that his voice was level, natural,
asked, "And the young lifesaver who found me—what did
she say?"

"We only know what she told Mr. Jansson. She said she was skiing upriver on her way home from a picnic, saw you fall. She reached you in a minute or two, wrapped her cape around you, and went for help. Jansson's was nearest and she got him, and his son to go for you with blankets and a car. She returned to the river with them, of course, but when you were safely in their charge she put on her skis, took her cape, and went on—to wherever she was going. We don't know another thing about her, dear." Dora cocked a knowing eyebrow of her own. "Really we don't."

"Don't be silly, my good woman!" Dan advised. "I outgrew Clayton's romantic conventions long ago. My object in asking is not matrimony."

Under her smile his irritation grew. "It's ridiculous, impossible, for anyone to vanish into thin air in a town this size. Someone must know who she is. There can't be a dozen young women here who are expert skiers. She must be one, to ski on that river alone. And there can be only one who skis with a big blue cape over her arm."

His mother dropped her knitting to look at him oddly. "How do you know her cape was blue? I didn't say so. I don't know what color it was."

Figuratively Dan bit his lip. "I don't know. I suppose I assumed blue because the only capes I've seen lately are Navy capes and they're dark blue."

Unexpectedly Dora laughed. "Marc had that idea too. About Navy capes, I mean. And there's one in Clayton. You must remember it—"

Dan looked blank, then laughed too. "Captain Billy's! Lord, I haven't seen or heard of him for a thousand years. Don't tell me he's still here."

"He is. Cape and all. Marc even went down to the old steamboat—"

"You're making this up—"

"I'm not, Dan. Captain Billy still lives on his old boat, down below the foot of Radisson somewhere. Near the railway bridge, I think. He's almost eighty-five now, and lives pretty much on his memories of the days when he was a captain on the river. But he's strong and well and perfectly happy now."

"Now?"

"His grandson, Neil Crane—he's done awfully well in Minneapolis—came back to Clayton four, perhaps five, years ago and took Captain Billy home with him. But the old man was so miserable without his boat that Mr. Crane had it hauled up on shore and remodeled so the captain can live on it the year round comfortably and safely. That's where he is now, and happy as a lark, Marc says. Sleeps all day, paces his bridge all night, no matter what the weather. Mr. Crane keeps a man there to look after him, of course."

"And he still has his cape?"

"Not only has it but still wears it. I'm not clear as to the arrangement of the boat, but I believe part of it's a little two-storied apartment for Captain Billy, sleeping quarters below and his old bridge above. Because a mutiny on that boat fifty years or more ago is one of his most vivid memories, he remains locked in there, won't let a soul on the bridge. Marc couldn't talk with him, of course, but he drove down one night with Pete Wilson and there the old man was, wrapped in his cape, pacing back and forth on his bridge—"

"No chance of anyone getting that cape then, that I'd bet on." Dan laughed again. "Remember the day Jack Carston and I climbed aboard the old hulk and Captain Billy peppered us with bird shot? Lord, that was twenty years ago! I'm growing old, darling." He grinned at his mother. "Not trying to change the subject, ate you? You're sure Jansson didn't learn the girl's name?"

Dora sighed but took up the tale. "In the rush of getting you home neither Mr. Jansson nor his son thought to ask her. Marc's been over all that with them. They said they assumed from the way the young woman spoke you and she knew one another. She told them who you were, where to take you."

"What about that chap from the *News*—who skis? He hasn't traced her?"

"Darling, Marc told you. The river is crisscrossed with ski tracks on both sides. Until Tom Jefferson went down there no one had any idea to what an extent the Scandinavian farmers are using the river this winter. He got a good story out of what he discovered. It's in the feature section of yesterday's paper."

"With pictures? I'd like to see it."

Dari moved to sit up. Dora gently pushed him back, departed to find the *Sunday News*. When she returned the telephone was ringing. She gave him the entire paper, went on to the hall.

Dan listened for a moment to her exclamations and questions. Evidently Brownie had struck a new mine of gossip somewhere. Then he opened the paper to find the ski story for himself, study the photographs, perhaps pick up a lead on his mysterious rescuer.

Sports, advertising, and feature sections fell away as a headline on the back page of the news section caught his eye: Elway Death Jury Views the Bodies.

Beneath the headline was a small cut of three men: Lars Larson, feed-store owner, unmistakably of Norwegian extraction; Vilhjalmar Jorgenson, bookkeeper, as unmistakably of Danish; and the narrow, simon-pure American face of Harry Williams, clerk in the Clayton grocery.

All six eyes looked straight back at Dan, set, a bit grim. Evidently Bailey had snapped his camera on them after they viewed the bodies. In the Evergreen Mortuary, the story said.

His eyes skimmed the paragraphs, stopped on the final lines:

> Due to a burst pipe in police headquarters, the inquest will not be held in the assembly room there at ten o'clock Monday morning, as previously announced. The hearing has been transferred to the county courthouse and postponed until two o'clock in the afternoon.

Dan's interest in the Elway case didn't brighten. But his interest in that courtroom soared. He was fed to the eyes, he told himself, with staying in the house. He felt fine, his mind was as clear as a bell. More, he'd never witnessed an inquest. Why not see and hear this one, learn the finale to the Elway case, and prove to his family he was as good as new, perfectly able to hop aboard his train on the fifteenth?

Even to himself he wouldn't admit his basic reason for attending the hearing.

He listened. Dora was assuring Brownie she had a very sick boy in the living room, couldn't possibly get away for the afternoon.

Dan's feet hit the floor. For a moment he swayed, then, erect and balanced, marched to the telephone, took the receiver from his mother's hand.

"This is the sick boy, Brownie. Just let me know where you want Dora when. She'll be there."

A protesting Dora was there at two o'clock. At two-twenty Dan, a free man, entered the main courtroom of the Clayton County Courthouse.

MONDAY AFTERNOON, JANUARY 12

He entered at a dull moment on a dull scene. The spacious oak-paneled room, with its lofty oak-beamed ceiling and once handsome parquet floor, the pride of Clayton thirty years before, now was dingy and dust-filmed. Gray light of a sunless winter afternoon, filtering through long-uncleaned panes of five tall windows, made it appear dingier still.

Across the front of the room, flanked on either side by doors, ran the judge's high bench. Above it a stereotyped mural, portraying a blinded Justice in the act of passing judgment, gave the court its only color.

Neither the judge's bench nor that of the clerk of court just below it was occupied, but in a square indentation in the bench wall at the right of the judge, had there been one, sat a small, haggardly gray man. In a disheveled gray suit several sizes too large for him he held himself erect by elbows braced on the chair arms and chewed furiously on his own lips.

At a table on the nervous little man's left a pretty white hand was turning this way and that to permit the light of a desk lamp to reveal almond-shaped nails, recently lacquered a screaming scarlet. Attached to the hand was a slender young creature, perched on the edge of a straight chair. Pad and pencils identified her as the court stenographer.

In the jury box, set against the left wall of the room, the three jurors crowded together at one end of the first of the four banks of seats. They appeared lost and obviously felt that way. Motionless, impassive, they sat with folded arms, eyes fixed on space. Piled on the broad railing before them were their hats and coats, those of many other men.

What action there was centered about a long table running parallel with the jury box. There Dan recognized Thode Brierson's heavy shoulders hunched about his ears as he leaned across the table to talk with a gray-haired man whose patient, tenacious face revealed that he was accustomed to spend many hours in drab, overheated, airless rooms such as this. Between the two, papers and photographs were spread. At their elbows a bundle of newspapers was tied up with string.

But Dan was only momentarily interested in the courtroom as a whole. His eyes were for the audience. To his surprise, only the first of the two sections of long, broad, pewlike oak benches was filled. He had expected to find the room crowded to the doors. And to recognize among the crowd a young woman in a heavy blue cape.

Only three women were in attendance. They sat together in the last row: two large, middle-aged women in black and an earnest young thing in brown whose face was almost hidden under a cartwheel of a hat and behind enormous horn-rimmed spectacles. One of Clayton College's potential journalists, Dan deduced from her notebook and busy pencil. Disappointed, he moved down the narrow aisle to a front seat he had spotted.

He had tossed his coat over the back of the bench, brushed aside a small white pamphlet, and settled down for a long afternoon before he recognized his neighbor.

"Glad to see you up and about again, Dan. You took quite a tumble, I hear," Professor McPhail's sonorous voice murmured in his ear.

"Good Lord, am I in the wrong pew? Is this seat reserved for witnesses?" Dan looked beyond the professor to the row of men in business suits, devoid of encumbering coats and other winter paraphernalia.

"Not at all. I'm a witness, of course, and so are my neighbors, but others are behind us. I'm delighted to have you as a seat mate—if you should be here at all."

"Oh, I just fell on my head. Solid bone. I'm fit as a fiddle. What's up? And what's happened?"

"You've merely missed the opening preliminaries and the first routine questions to the first witness." McPhail's calm eyes directed Dan's attention ahead. "You know him, I think. Jack Carston. . . ."

Incredulously Dan looked at the little gray man still chewing his lips in the witness box. That man—Carston! Since he had last seen him the ex-hotel manager must have lost twenty pounds. And aged a year for each pound lost.

"You know Thode Brierson, of course,' the professor was saying. "That's the coroner he's talking with—Dr. Stephen Moorehead. He should or could occupy the judge's bench, but they're trying to keep this inquiry as simple and informal as possible. To spare the Elway families and other relatives—when they're found—as much distress as they can. They're agreeing now, I think, to use the photographs instead of questions to verify gruesome details."

As McPhail spoke the D.A. and coroner sat back. Brierson assembled a half-dozen large photographs fanwise in one hand, rose, and approached the witness.

Nothing about him now suggested the collegiate. Dan envied him his tailor, his posture, and, when he spoke, his deep, clear, incisive voice. Dora was right. Big Thode had done very well for himself.

"You have testified, Mr. Carston, that you were associated for almost three years with Mr. Anthony R. Elway. That during the first two years, when you were manager of the Claytonian Hotel, you also knew Mrs. Elway. On the night of last January fourth you were called to 355 Penndale by Police Chief Wilson to view the bodies of a man and a woman. Will you look at these photographs, please, and identify the two people shown in them as dead?" to glance at the uppermost photograph, then he shrank back. "Mr. and Mrs. Anthony Elway."

"Will you speak louder, please?" The D.A. gestured toward the little table not three feet away. "The court stenographer can only record what she hears."

The witness moistened his lips. "Mr. Anthony Elway—and his wife."

"Thank you. That is all."

Brierson turned back to the long table. Carston stumbled to his feet, stood a moment with one hand braced against the wall of the judge's bench, then slowly moved across the floor to the first row of seats.

As he went the coroner intoned from a slip of paper, "Patrolman Olaf Thorwaldson."

The tall, broad-shouldered young Norwegian policeman bounced up from the second row, walked straight to the table, to stand, right hand raised, while Dr. Moorehead repeated rapidly:

"You do solemnly swear that the testimony which you shall give at this inquest concerning the deaths of Anthony R. Elway and Dolores Evelyn Elway shall be the truth, the whole truth, and nothing but the truth, so help you God?"

"I do." The patrolman was in motion as he spoke. A moment later he dropped solidly into the witness chair.

Brierson began at once. "You are Olaf Thorwaldson, of 940 West Seventh Street, and for the past three years have been engaged as a police officer of Clayton, Minnesota?"

"Yes sir."

"On Sunday evening, last January fourth, the desk sergeant at police headquarters sent you to 355 Penndale, to release a dog from the locked garage there?"

"He did."

"Tell us what you did and saw."

"Well, as soon as I got there I tried to get into the garage because I couldn't hear any dog barking or whining. But its car doors, both front and back, were locked down. I mean they latch automatically on the inside into floor catches. There was no way I could use my skeleton key. So then I went to the neighbors to ask what they knew about the dog and where the Elways were. The family on the right didn't know anything at all about them. Neither did the neighbors on the other side, but they told me Mr. Elmer Judson owned the property. I called him up and he came right out in his car. We tried the back door first, but it was locked and the key in the lock inside. Then we went round to the front porch to try—"

"Did you notice anything on the porch?"

"Yes sir. Folded newspapers all over, sticking out of the snow." The patrolman's alert blue eyes turned on the table. "Those in that package there. I opened them out like that, tied them up—about midnight, January fourth."

"Good. Did Mr. Judson open the front door?"

"He unlocked it. I opened it."

"Describe what you did then."

A smile flickered across the policeman's lips. "Well, sir, as soon as I opened that door I smelled gas, and Mr. Judson, right there beside me, had a lighted cigarette in his mouth. I spun around, jerked it out, and threw it down the steps into the snow. Then because it was ten o'clock or later and the house dark, I headed straight for the stairs, yelling for him to leave the door open and get some windows up too."

"You didn't turn on any lights?"

"Yes sir. Every one I could find as I went along. But I didn't see anything until I came to the front bedroom. Then I stopped in the door and shouted for Mr. Judson to come up. He was with me when I went into the room. He told me the—the people we found there was Mr. and Mrs. Elway."

Again Brierson produced the photographs. "Are these correct representations of what you saw when you entered the bedroom?"

Thorwaldson's gaze was steady. "Just like they was. We took one look and knew they was dead. Then Mr. Judson—he ran downstairs and outside. I called the station to report. Then I took a look around the downstairs to find out where that gas was coming from and finally I went down to the basement. I traced it to a water heater there."

"You turned it off?"

"No sir. I left everything just as it was for Chief Wilson to see. He turned the gas off."

"The whole house had a strong odor of gas?"

"In the basement, no, sir. Couldn't hardly smell it there at all. But I noticed it all through the downstairs, and upstairs it was strong."

"Did you do anything else, notice anything else?"

"Just that the house and everything in it looked like a house would. Nothing disturbed, I mean, no sign of entry or struggle. And it was warm and comfortable. The thermostat was set at seventy. But by the time I'd finished looking around Chief Wilson was there. He brought two more patrolmen and Bailey, the *News* photographer, with him. Soon after Dr. Mollner arrived. And the chief sent me out to get Mr. Carston—"

"Thank you. That is all."

"Dr. Henry T. Mollner," Dr. Moorehead read from his list.

Hat in hand, wearing his coat, Dr. Mollner came and went in less than a minute. He had been called to the Elway home about ten-thirty, had arrived to see exactly what the photographs presented—impatiently he waved the prints away. The odor of gas was still noticeable when he arrived. And his very superficial examination of the bodies suggested that death had resulted from asphyxiation. But in all he had not remained in the house ten minutes.

Brierson excused him. He rushed away.

Ted Bailey followed, equaled the doctor in speed of testimony. He had been at police headquarters January fourth when Thorwaldson's call came in; had accompanied the chief to the house, taken the photographs, and made the six prints Brierson placed in his hand.

"Thank you. That is all."

Four witnesses in ten minutes, Dan marveled. Where had he ever acquired the impression that legal procedure proceeded by oxcart?

The speed and complete detachment of the inquiry roused his ire. Brierson, the coroner, and jury might be investigating light rays, lizards, or lovebirds for all the sign they gave that the strange and tragic death of two human beings was their concern. A man and a woman, moreover, who for three years had lived and breathed and had their being in this very city.

In many parts of Europe Dan had seen men, women, many children die, had seen many more dead, but never before had he been placed in the position of thinking of human lives as disembodied integers in some sort of arithmetical game.

How many points made game, he wondered cynically, in a case like this? Apparently you started with two points—the two bodies. Then, as each witness testified, added others . . .

Automatically his hand sought his pockets for pencil and paper, found a pencil. He remembered the white pamphlet he had thrust aside, secured it. On the front cover black running script declared, "It's a wise young man who knows his own strength!" The back cover was virgin white.

There he began to keep score: two points for the bodies, one for Carston's identification. Two—no, three; no, four—for Thorwaldson. One each for the locked house, the undisturbed house, the gas-filled house, the discovery of the bodies. One for Dr. Mollner; no, a goose egg for Mollner. He had contributed nothing but a supposition. One for Ted Bailey and his camera . . .

Oh hell! Irritably Dan thrust pencil and pamphlet into a side pocket. There was more to this than he had thought and he had missed hearing the name of the elderly man with gooseberry eyes crowding a large soft body into the witness chair.

MONDAY AFTERNOON, JANUARY 12

He looked up just in time. "You are Dr. Clifford Forester, professor of pathology at Clayton College?" Brierson was asking.

"Yes—I am." Dr. Forester's cold, clipped words revealed that his rosy, fine-textured skin was the only colorful thing about him. He took a spectacle case from a pocket, snapped it open to pinch a pair of glasses on his shining nose and peer at the district attorney as if he, too, were a specimen.

"During your six years at Clayton College you have performed autopsies—"

"During the past eighteen years, here and elsewhere, I have performed more than one thousand autopsies."

"On January fifth of this year you were asked to make autopsies on two bodies, identified to you as those of Mr. and Mrs. Anthony Elway."

"I performed the autopsies Tuesday afternoon, January sixth, at Evergreen Mortuary."

"Please tell us in your own words what you found."

"First of all, that both bodies were unusually well preserved. Considering the history of the case, they may have been dead ten or twelve days. I can only say, however, they had been without the breath of life three days or four."

Once started on his own work, Dr. Forester forgot his audience. His chilled voice went on as if he were lecturing a class.

"The pinkish tone of their skin, the characteristic pink color of every organ in both bodies, and the bright, almost cherry-red color of their blood, plus their well-preserved condition, all indicated to me that carbon monoxide gas poisoning had caused the deaths."

Dan stiffened alertly. That was the most important statement made so far, the most important, in his judgment, that could be made. Yet neither spectators nor jury showed interest. The coroner continued to draw doodles around the edge of his list of witnesses.

Even Brierson's attitude showed no change. "Did you find any injuries, any signs of struggle?" he asked immediately.

"The body of the man bore no evidences of injuries, though here I must qualify. About his upper arms and on his legs below the knees were faint bluish discolorations. If they were the result of bruises, such bruises were of a most superficial nature. On the woman's body I discovered the same faint bands of bluish color on upper arms and lower legs, and in addition a pronounced discoloration of the left temple. This temple bruise could have been caused by a blow, say with the palm of a hand, or as a result of one of the household accidents we all are heir to—running into a door, falling against a step or wall . . .

"Because there had been so much drying of the skin surfaces, due to lost body fluids, it is impossible for me to say whether these bruises or surface frictions were caused before or after death. The skin on both bodies was much parched, particularly on the tips of fingers and toes."

Brierson lifted an arresting hand. "Would this parching, Dr. Forester, indicate that death had occurred more than three or four days before the bodies were discovered?"

"It offers most effective evidence that the couple had been dead some time. So, too, does the condition of the eyes; in both bodies they were much sunken from drying. The swollen legs of the woman's body also indicate she had been sitting in that position some time, permitting the fluids to settle in the lower body."

"Continue then, please."

"The bruise on the woman's forehead was the only true external evidence of struggle or accident. But when her brain was opened I found a hemorrhage surface in the left temporal lobe. Such hemorrhages are seen in cases of concussion. Depending, of course, on when and where she received that blow, it is possible she was temporarily unconscious before her death."

"You do not say the blow caused her death?"

"No. Definitely not. Evidences of carbon monoxide in her lungs demonstrate she was alive and breathing when she died. Both the man and the woman died—as has been the case in every instance of gas poisoning I have seen—an anesthetic sort of death. That is, without struggle."

Brierson dropped his notes on the table, looked questioningly at Dr. Moorehead. The coroner shook his head.

"Thank you, Dr. Forester. That is all."

Dr. Moorehead sat up, cleared his throat, said loudly, "Professor Terence Girard McPhail."

Instantly the lethargic atmosphere cleared. In an expectant rustle, as spectators shifted for a clearer view, the professor rose, walked with slow dignity round the long table to pause before the coroner, lift his right hand. As if hearing the oath for the first time, he listened carefully, bowed his head to respond, "I do." Then like an actor walking out in a long-familiar stellar role he advanced on the witness chair.

"During the past week, Professor McPhail, you performed the chemical analyses on the blood and other samples taken from the bodies of Mr. and Mrs. Elway. Will you state in your own words, please, what you found?" Brierson's formality reflected his respect.

"Samples of the blood and other materials from each body were turned over to me on January seventh by my colleague, Dr. Forester. I tested the blood samples first. And I at once observed the characteristic cherry red, or pink, he mentioned in the blood of both. I also noted the fact that it had not completely coagulated. As those appearances are characteristic of carbon monoxide gas poisoning, I then submitted both samples to the spectroscope. To determine, of course, whether any definite and positive evidence of this gas were present in any quantity in the blood. The spectroscope observed clear evidence that carbon monoxide was present."

Ripples of movement and excited murmurs drew Dan's head round. Although McPhail's finding had merely corroborated Dr. Forester's, the audience had received it as an original and highly important statement. Quiet returned quickly as the professor went on.

"Next, though some time later, I performed the stomach analyses. On the membranes of both I observed marks such as would be produced by an irritating poison. And the bright cherry-red color of the blood vessels in both was clearly visible."

"Your conclusion is then . . . ?" Brierson's question fell into complete silence.

"That carbon monoxide was present in both bodies. Not only present but present in sufficient quantities to saturate the blood of both bodies. To cause death."

A sigh ran over the room. Professor McPhail paused. So did the district attorney. One by one the frozen jury thawed and settled back in their seats as if that were all they needed to know.

When Brierson spoke again his voice was solemn. "Professor McPhail, ordinarily such testimony as you have given would be sufficient. But in consideration of the history of this case, of the wide interest and other features"—he didn't say rumors, but his emphasis on the last word said it for him—"above all, out of concern for the families that one day must learn of this tragedy, you were asked to make other analyses."

"I was." The professor was equally grave in voice and manner. "It appeared imperative to anticipate and lay forever any suspicion that may have arisen or might arise in future concerning any other poison that could have contributed to these tragic deaths."

Again he paused for the whispers and rustlings to quiet.

"I made a very systematic and elaborate analysis to detect the presence of the ordinary classes of poisons. First I tested for those that would be vaporized—chloroform, ether, carbolic acid, many more. I found none of these present in either body. Next I tested for the very poisonous materials—arsenic, lead, bichloride, also many others. I found nothing. Thirdly, I tested for another group known as alkaloids. Again nothing."

The slow, measured tones became slower still, weighted with authority. "Finally I turned to the powerful drugs, poisons such as digitalis, various forms of sleeping pills, and many other drugs that if taken in sufficient quantities can prove fatal. Again—nothing. . . .

"My conclusion is, therefore, that *carbon monoxide gas was the one and only poison to be found in either body*. That carbon monoxide poisoning was the one and only cause of death."

With a gesture of finality Professor McPhail sat back in his chair.

"See what I mean?" a voice behind Dan said. "Never misses a trick, and you can understand every word he says. Believe it, too."

Brierson apparently agreed. He relaxed his formality during his next questions. "Have you any conclusions as to the time of death?"

"I can go no further than my colleague, Dr. Forester. And for the same reasons. However, I can venture an opinion." The professor paused as if to think back. "In my opinion Mr. and Mrs. Elway could have died any time between December twenty-third and January first."

Dr. Moorehead cleared his throat loudly to still the rising chatter. "Did you find any evidence, Professor, to suggest whether one body might have been dead longer than the other?"

"Nothing. That is not to say, however, one did not outlive the other. I can only repeat: both had been dead more than three days."

The coroner grunted, sat back. Brierson resumed.

"Is the carbon monoxide gas you found in the blood and other samples of both bodies present in the gas furnished this city by the Wayne River Valley Gas Company?"

"It is."

"Is the gas supplied by the gas company—the gas supplied 355 Penndale Avenue—heavier or lighter than air?"

"Lighter. It could be used to lift balloons."

"Then gas escaping from the water heater in the Elway basement—gas containing carbon monoxide—would have taken an upward course?"

"Lighter than air, it would rise. More than that, as it rose, it would penetrate. Penetrate walls, ceilings, floors. And in addition, of course, it would seep under and around closed doors, through every slightest crevice."

"Have you any information as to the amount of gas necessary to cause death? Have you found any indication that the necessary amount was present in the bodies?"

"I have already said yes to your second question. I will add here, however, that no one can live in air that contains

one per cent of carbon monoxide gas. Less than that—a
mere trace—if inhaled over a long period, is sufficient to
cause death. From the carbon monoxide content I found in
the body samples, I should, say the air in the Elway bedroom at the time of death contained more than a trace."

"By January first, say?"

"The gas would not accumulate in the upper story of
the Elway home. In turn as it penetrated the lower walls
of the house it would continue to move and rise, not only
into and out of that tragic bedroom, but throughout the
house. It would penetrate the outer walls, escape into the
open air. That is the reason why this inquest today is concerned with the deaths of only two of its citizens."

His pause was impressive. "If that gas had concentrated
within the walls of the Elway home, by January fourth,
when Olaf Thorwaldson opened the door, Mr. Judson beside him with a lighted cigarette between his lips . . ."
Professor McPhail opened his hands dramatically. "They
would have been merely the first of many unfortunate victims on Penndale at that moment."

Consternation broke out behind Dan. Evidently Penndale was well represented among the audience.

Professor McPhail certainly had a way with him. He
had built his testimony into climaxes like those of a play,
this second one more dramatic than the first. Dan found
himself waiting with impatient interest for the third.

But it was the coroner's dry voice that rose in the pause.
"From the bruise on Mrs. Elway's forehead, Professor, and
the bluish discolorations on arms and legs of both bodies,
isn't there a possibility that some sort of struggle took
place before death?"

The professor smiled. "Some form of struggle," he repeated significantly, "but not necessarily one of violence. I
personally am convinced the Elways were engaged in some
lively activity. Romping about or dancing, perhaps, to the

radio. There was one in the room, as the photographs show, ouch exertion naturally would accelerate their breathing. They would inhale the gas more rapidly."

"What do you mean by romping?" the coroner asked dryly.

McPhail bowed in acknowledgment of the question but turned to the district attorney. "Beyond my own analyses, my knowledge of this case has been derived from the Clayton *News,* not always available to me as I have been out of town a great deal since December first. Yet as we are all curious as to how and why two able-bodied adults were unable to detect and escape the fatal gas, perhaps I may be permitted to offer an opinion—as an answer to the coroner's question."

"Certainly," Brierson assured him.

"Remember then that this tragedy probably occurred before Christmas. As one *News* story reported, Mr. Elway was accumulating in one of the drawers of his chest gifts he intended for his wife. Most of us here are married men. All of us know the nature of women. I suggest that after they were in bed for the night Mr. Elway told his wife, possibly teased her, about what one or all of those gifts might be."

Professor McPhail smiled again, conscious of the responsive interest and nods among his listeners. Almost visibly the scientist gave way to the popular amateur actor and speaker.

"I can see him falling asleep—or pretending to do so. I can see his wife, overwhelmed with curiosity, slipping out of bed to quiet it. I can see him waking to find her opening, even peeking into that forbidden drawer. See him spring out of bed to prevent her. *Voilà!* A tussle, half in fun, half in earnest."

Even Dan, though his teeth were set, could visualize the intimate and vividly personal scene the professor's resonant and dramatic voice, even more than his words, had conjured. The prof was enjoying himself. So were his listeners as their smothered laughter and comments testified. The jurors roused to slide slyly wise glances at one another. They were all married men: sure, something like that could have happened—probably did, Dan gathered from the murmurs behind him.

And although he deplored the professor's idea of entertaining the court he had to admit that McPhail was the first to view the Elways as people, to give to what had happened a homely, human naturalness and logic.

On that note of common understanding Professor McPhail evidently hoped to end his testimony. With a glance at Brierson he moved to rise. Dr. Moorehead's voice stopped him.

"Even if they were dancing or engaged in a friendly tussle, Professor, isn't the odor of gas strong enough and disagreeable enough for them to have become conscious of it?"

McPhail turned courteously. "It would take some time for a concentration of gas to reach that room in sufficient quantity to disturb them if they were thoroughly absorbed. Normal people, under normal conditions, or, I should say, under less active conditions—reading, talking, playing a quiet game of cards—could hardly fail to recognize the odor of gas and attempt to get out of it or find the cause and eliminate it. But if they were in lively motion—"

"Does anything in the testimony given here, including your own, Professor, indicate that Mr. and Mrs. Elway were?"

To the surprise of the entire room Professor McPhail nodded.

"Yes. Three things. Two have not been mentioned in the oral testimony but they are evident in the photographs. One of these is Mr. Elway's ripped pajama sleeve. The other is his wife's torn nightdress and robe. And the third is the bluish bands Dr. Forester observed on the upper arms and below the knees of both bodies. Both Mr. and Mrs. Elway were tall, almost equal in height. The bands on the arms, therefore, suggest to me that, dancing or tussling, they had grasped each other just below the shoulders. And the bands or marks on the lower legs suggest to me that, either dancing or scuffling about the room, they may have knocked into this and that or even"—the chestnut eyes sparkled wisdom at his intent audience—"or even, if and as opportunity offered, exchanged a gentle kick or two—"

Unrestrained laughter swept the room. The prof was quite a guy. And the Elways were real people. Human. Regular. Dan could actually feel that impression spreading on the close air while he conceded that the professor had brought another climax to a quick boil. In fact, to its pleasant bubbling, again was moving to rise.

Once more Dr. Moorehead's tenacious voice defeated him. "Is it your idea, then, Professor, that the gas began to penetrate the room while Mr. and Mrs. Elway were in lively motion? That, exhausted, they flung themselves down, he on the floor, she in a chair, and fell asleep? That the gas overcame them while they slept?"

McPhail sat back, now as completely reserved and cold as Dr. Forester. "My intention was to offer a possible and simple human explanation. In doing so, I realize I have violated the rules of evidence. I have no personal knowledge as to why Mr. Elway died on the floor, his wife in a chair. Let me repeat what I do know. My analyses support Dr. Forester's findings that their deaths resulted from inhaling monoxide gas."

"Thank you very much indeed, Professor McPhail," Brierson said hurriedly. "That is all."

Dr. Moorehead cleared his throat. Meekly, almost surreptitiously, behind a discreet hand.

MONDAY AFTERNOON, JANUARY 12

When Professor McPhail stepped out of the witness box he took the life and color he had injected into the proceedings with him. Spectators and witnesses reacted visibly and audibly. Several who seemed to have attended for the sole purpose of hearing him departed. A few made no effort to conceal their extremely dismal view of the coroner.

Even such evidence of his popularity did not appease the professor. Stonily he resumed his seat, folded his arms. Dan looked at him with concern. On the skin of his face and throat, even his hands, a fine moisture clung.

"Well done, Professor," Dan murmured.

The set face did not turn, but after a moment words came, harsh and dry. "That—yokel! He knows better than anyone else how necessary it is to quiet the infernal chatter about suicide and foul play." McPhail stopped to exchange an expressive glance with Brierson, who was assembling new notes at the table in preparation for the next witness.

When he spoke again his voice was normal. "The D.A. is an understanding man. If Moorehead would let him he'd handle this case with utmost tact."

Again the professor broke off. This time to pin his attention on the solid-looking businessman with a shining bald pate taking the witness chair. Dan needed no identification of this witness. Bob Brownell, manager of the gas company, was Brownie's husband.

"I spent the afternoon of January fifth," Brownell shortly was stating, "at 355 Penndale, personally checking every gas appliance in the house. Except for the water heater, I found everything operating perfectly,"

"Will you explain the nature of this heater and what you found wrong with it?"

"The heater is a standard type of construction, including an ordinary water boiler, heated by an ordinary Bunsen-type burner—"

"That burner"—Brierson moved his hands graphically—"is simply a round piece of tubing with a bunch of holes in it?"

"Yes. Though I would describe it as a casing with arms on it. These drilled arms—or holes—permit the gas to emerge and, when lighted, to heat the water in the tank above."

"Do you light the main burner by turning on the pilot light?"

Mr. Brownell frowned. "You do. But if you will permit me, I'll describe first various devices on the heater that enable it to operate efficiently—and safely."

Brierson permitted him.

"One, a thermostatic valve in the pipe which, plus the temperature of the water in the boiler, operates a thermostat. This thermostat is set at the point desired by the consumer. When the water is heated to the desired degree a thermostatic valve turns off the gas."

Brownell extended a plump left hand, turned back the little finger, then the next. "Two, a safety valve. Three, a pilot light. Finally there is—or should be—a flue pipe to carry off any fumes." With four fingers folded into his hand, he opened them one at a time as he concluded, "The Elway meter was equipped with devices one, two, three. It lacked number four. Is that clear?"

"Completely," Brierson assured him.

"Very well. Now—the safety valve operates thermostatically, according to the degree of heat it derives from the pilot flame. When the pilot flame is burning the expanding tube forces open a valve that permits gas to enter the main burner. When the pilot light is low or turned out the tube contracts and shuts off the gas to the main burner."

Dan listened with wondering ears to Mr. Brownell's loquacity. Ordinarily the gas company manager was a man of few words, perhaps because his wife was a woman of so many. Even Brierson was impatient. Now he interrupted determinedly.

"In other words, Mr. Brownell, the Elway heater was automatically controlled. Yet on January fourth the pilot light was out and gas pouring freely from both valve and main burner."

"Permit me. The Elway heater was equipped to operate as I have described. But if the safety valve failed to function the consumer would then have to operate it by hand control. That is, the consumer would need to light the pilot himself, with a match. The pilot light would then open the main burner and light it. Now—"

Mr. Brownell settled himself more firmly to pat a forefinger of his right hand into the open palm of his left. "On January fifth I had the heater taken apart, examined carefully. There was nothing wrong with its thermostat. There was nothing wrong with its safety valve. That is, we found no obstruction inside it, no sign of corrosion anywhere. There was nothing wrong with the heater or its controls. No sign of tampering, either, with the heater or the meter box. Yet obviously, if the pilot light were out on January fourth and gas escaping, the safety valve was not functioning. Therefore we must assume that the safety valve was suffering from what we call 'metal fatigue.'"

Spectators were moving restlessly, many whispering and talking. Someone groaned with boredom. The jurors appeared to have lapsed into a coma. Mr. Brownell set his jaw, went on doggedly.

"With the safety valve working properly, there is nothing anyone can do by hand to that water heater the automatic control won't check instantly. But with this safety valve defective, the pilot light could either go out of its own accord or be turned off by hand."

The coroner found his voice; "You mean someone had to go down into the basement, light the pilot light, and then, when the water was hot enough, go down and turn it off again?"

"No, I do not. Someone would have to light the pilot valve, that is true. But even with the safety valve out of order, the thermostat would turn off the gas when the water reached the desired temperature."

"So I thought," Dr. Moorehead commented. "But it would be possible, wouldn't it, with the safety valve not functioning, for the pilot light and burner to be turned on by hand and not lighted?"

Mr. Brownell gave him a prolonged look. "Yes," he said. "In that case, of course, the gas would flow unchecked—"

"The witness has testified, Coroner," Brierson inserted politely, "that he found no signs of tampering." He studied his notes, decided to abandon a couple of sheets, turned with decision to the last page.

"Let me ask you this, Mr. Brownell. What was the rate of normal gas consumption of the water heater at 355 Penndale?"

Mr. Brownell's answer was to shake out a white handkerchief, mop his brow—with relief, Dan thought, to see those pages of questions dropped. Finally he said, "Its rate was twenty-four and a half cubic feet per hour."

"Did you check the meter to see how much above normal it registered?"

"I did. It registered between seven and eight thousand cubic feet above normal."

"That's the amount you believe then flowed from the main burner and pilot valve into the house between, say, the night of December twenty-second—"

Brownell sat forward with a jerk of alarm. "I didn't say that. All I can or will say on that point is that the Elway meter registered seven to eight thousand cubic feet above normal. Whether the entire amount was released by the heater or not, I don't know. Whether it was released during the period of December twenty-second or -third to January fourth, I don't know."

"You don't know?"

Curiouser and curiouser, Dan thought as he watched the phlegmatic Brownell positively squirm with embarrassment.

"I—I don't have that reading. Our last—record for that meter was made in November." The square-jaw set firmly. Mr. Brownell sat back as if to indicate he had already covered the subject more than adequately.

Brierson hesitated, but the spectators agreed with the witness. Their restiveness decided him. "Thank you, Mr. Brownell. That is all."

For a slow and deliberately moving man, Brownell left the witness box behind him in nothing flat. Peering round Professor McPhail, Dan watched the white handkerchief appear again in active mopping-up operations.

Mr. Elmer Judson was the last witness. A tallish, angular accountant, his long, angular face set with determination, he could hardly wait for the formalities of oath and routine questions to end.

When he had established Judson's ownership of the Penndale property Brierson stepped back as if fearing the man would leap at him.

"During the past year did your tenants, Mr. and Mrs. Elway, ever complain to you about their water heater being defective?"

"They did not. This afternoon is the first time I've heard anyone say it was. Mrs. Elway did telephone me last March to say the pilot light had gone out. I called the gas company and within an hour had a report back from their serviceman that the heater was O.K."

"When you were in the Elway home the night of January fourth did you go down to the basement with Patrolman Thorwaldson, examine the heater?"

"No." For the first time Judson's assurance faltered. "I left the house as soon as—just after—as soon as I could. I waited outside until Chief Wilson came. He said I could go home, I—wasn't well."

"You haven't been back?"

"No!"

"Did you have any personal contact with Mr. and Mrs. Elway?"

"Except for the afternoon of December sixteenth, a year ago, when I showed them both around the Penndale house, I've never seen either of them."

"Thank you. That is all."

"No, it isn't—if you'll pardon me. I want to make a definite statement for the record of these proceedings. I buy the very best equipment for my properties from the most reliable firms. I keep it in perfect shape, make repairs as soon as I'm told they're needed. And I want to state here and now that no plumber, city inspector, serviceman, or anyone else has ever told me that heater was defective."

"Thank you."

A much less angular Mr. Judson returned to his seat.

Brierson faced about to the spectators. "Is there anyone in this courtroom who has any further information to

offer, anyone who wishes to make a statement in connection with this case?" His gaze fell on Dan, moved on
to Professor McPhail, then quickly over the rows behind
them.

No one spoke.

Turning also, Dan discovered that most of the audience, including the three women, had already slipped
away. Those who remained were shuffling and stamping
into rubbers and galoshes or standing to flail the air. with
cramped arms as they wriggled into heavy overcoats. His
eyes lifted to the hexagonal clock high on the rear wall,
remained there incredulous while Dr. Moorehead pronounced the final words of the inquest.

"As no one appears to have any further information, we
will conclude this hearing. The jurors will now adjourn to
make their findings."

Just ten minutes past three! Impossible, Dan thought
until he checked with his own watch. It seemed to him
he had been sitting on that hard bench, breathing that
overheated air, for hours. His mind was drugged with the
contradictions of the witnesses, the uncertainty as to time
of death, and general confusion of the testimony, yet not
too drugged to guess what the verdict would be.

He felt himself rising to shake hands with Professor
McPhail, with others whom he knew, to make—he hoped—
appropriate answers and comments. When they had gone
and he turned to pick up his own coat the room had emp-
tied.

Shortly after five o'clock Dora Cumberland returned to
find Dan waking, to all appearances, from the nap he had
embarked on before she left.

"Good boy." She smiled and as a reward presented him
with the cold square of the *Evening News* she had picked
up on the porch. "You've slept more than three hours."

She stood a moment, looking at him expectantly, but when he said nothing she departed to interview Tilda.

Dan opened the paper, turned to the local news page. Yes, there it was—its headline ran across two columns:

CARBON MONOXIDE CAUSE OF ELWAY DEATHS
INQUEST JURY FINDS

He skimmed the first summarizing paragraphs to the final statement.

> Later the jurors returned the following verdict:
>
> "Said jurors upon their oath do say that, according to the testimony given at the inquest, we find that said Anthony R. Elway and Dolores Evelyn Elway died as a result of carbon monoxide poisoning caused by gas escaping from a water heater in the basement of their home at 355 Penndale Avenue, in the city of Clayton, Minnesota.
>
> "We do not find criminal liability upon the part of any person or persons in connection with their death.
>
> "Signed: Lars Larson
> Vilhjalmar Jorgenson
> Harrison F. Williams

For the verdict to have reached the *News* in time for the evening edition, Dan knew, the jurors must only have had to select from a series of prepared legal statements the one that embodied their verdict. Evidently Larson, Jorgenson, and Williams weren't plagued with the kind of minds that had to know the score, play by play.

Reminded of his own unfinished tabulation, he patted his side pockets, sat up to make a more thorough search. He found his pencil. The little white pamphlet was gone.

After a disgusted moment he shrugged. A sign from heaven, perhaps. The Elway case was closed. And three nights from now he would be New York bound. Let it go. Forget it.

Forget it he did in a battle with Marcus P. and Dora, over his intention to leave as planned, that raged throughout dinner and afterward. His parents, defeated but unconquered, hardly had retired from the field to wage their own private war across a cribbage board when a special delivery boy tumbled up the front steps.

Dan returned from answering the bell with a long white envelope in his hands. "For me," he said in answer to his father's inquiring glance.

Under the glow of a reading lamp he studied his name and address printed with a dark blue pencil across the white. Otherwise, except for the stamps, the envelope was blank.

Puzzled, he tore off one end, shook out the contents—a small white pamphlet whose cover declared, "It's a wise young man who knows his own strength!" He turned it over to find his own brief notations on the back.

"Anything important?" Dora asked.

Dan showed the front cover. "Just a little homework someone thinks I should do on my own strength."

"Throw that in the fire," Marcus P. advised testily. "The town's peppered with those booklets. I can't get newsprint, but the Dairymen's Association can buy all the paper it wants to boost milk sales—"

His son didn't hear him. He was reading the small, square paragraph centered on the inside cover.

This is one report that is for you and you alone.
Once every month or six weeks, fill in the
charts and check on your own physical progress.

The same dark blue pencil that had printed his address
on the envelope had underlined heavily the first sentence.

Dan might have followed his father's advice had not
the booklet opened of itself to the center. There, fixed in
place by the staples, was the headline clipped from the
Evening News: Carbon Monoxide Cause of Elway Deaths.

Beneath the clipping, on the small chart for recording
his increasing weight—if he drank sufficient quantities of
Dairymen's Association milk—he found three short lines,
also printed in blue:

Reading Room—Public Library
Nine-thirty—Monday Night
Destroy

MONDAY NIGHT, JANUARY 12

On the dot of nine-thirty Dan entered the public library, walked round a horseshoe desk in the center of the reception room to the wide arch that opened on the reading room.

In the fireplace bisecting the opposite wall a bright fire burned. At a long table to right and left a dozen or more men and two or three women bent over books and magazines. Without exception the sagging forms of the shabby, insufficiently clothed men betrayed the reason for their presence there—warmth. For a moment no one looked up, appeared to be expecting anyone.

Then a small figure, smartly clad in dark red, rose at the end of the table on the right to wave a black-and-white gauntleted glove.

Marcus P. and Dora were right, Dan thought as he looked at her: he certainly wasn't up to any mental work yet. Who else but Lisa would have contrived such a melodramatic device to get him out of the house? Who but Lisa would have designated the public library? Lisa, who never opened a book!

Reluctantly he walked toward her. "Fancy meeting you here," he said tritely as she held out her hand.

"Oh, Terence is making a speech about something in the auditorium downstairs. I couldn't take it so came up here to wait. Aren't you going to sit down?"

"For one minute—"

Her hand closed on his arm. Her shining eyes studied him anxiously. "How are you really, darling? I've worried terribly about you—

"Lisa! Is that what you brought me here to ask?" His anger at his own stupidity turned on her.

She looked first blank, then hurt. "Here? Dan, you can't resent me speaking to you when you practically walk over me."

His suspicion lightened. "Sorry. I'm still irritable over being shut up in the house—"

"You were at the inquest this afternoon, Terence said."

Again suspicion tightened, but he said lightly, "My maiden voyage."

Lisa's gaze cooled, but not for him.

"Mr. Cumberland?" another voice said, a voice unusually deep and clear-cut for a woman's.

Dan turned, sprang up as he saw at his elbow the blond librarian who'd been sorting books behind the desk when he entered. Now she held two or three index cards in her hand.

She lifted clear dark gray eyes to look straight into his. "I'm sorry we don't have the books on Greece you telephoned about, but I've found others. If you wish, I'll show you where they are in the stack room when it's convenient."

"Certainly. Right now." Dan picked up his hat with alacrity, smiled good-by at Lisa.

But she was rising. "I'll come with you. I've never seen—"

"Didn't you read the sign?" Dan looked horrified.

"What sign?"

With a finger he sketched a big square on the air. "'Stop! Man at work!'"

Her small mouth curved, but her eyes lost their smile. She looked from him to the retreating librarian. "You have changed—if blondes interest you."

"Immensely. Who is she?"

"As if you didn't know!" Her black eyes bit at him. "Don't you think I recognize that old book trick? How many times did we pull it when I was a student librarian?"

"Shhhhhh!"

Saved by someone who was actually reading, Dan lifted a hand in salute, hurried away.

The young woman was waiting for him at the desk. Silently she led him into a long, overcrowded stack room where books in narrow aisles almost rose to the ceiling. Her tall, slender figure, demurely clad in blue suit and white blouse, disappeared down the second aisle on the right.

When Dan reached her she said at once, "I'm sorry. We can't talk here—tonight."

"Why not? If you're thinking of Mrs. McPhail—don't."

"Mrs. McPhail? Oh no . . ."

His eyes appreciatively recording the clear, fair skin of her oval face, the shining, soft fair hair rolled about her head, he said with an urgency that surprised himself, "But we must talk tonight. I recognize you now. You're the young woman with the disappearing cape. My family has turned Clayton upside down hunting for you—"

At her troubled look he added, "We don't need to talk here. When are you free? I have a car—"

"I leave at ten, walk down Fulton Street."

"Good. I'll wait for you."

"Around the corner, then. I'll walk by and if no one is following me—"

"Following you!"

"It may mean nothing. He does it so openly—now. But tonight—for the first time—he's come inside."

Dan looked from her to the bookshelves beside him, took down two books. "There's nothing remarkable about a personable young man like me taking his favorite librarian home. I'll look at these till ten, then meet you at the desk. Just leave it to me. Now where is this man?"

"At the table on the left. All in gray."

Dan returned alone to the reading room, saw with relief that Lisa had gone. The other women too. Looked to the left.

Halfway down the table, head propped on his hands, sat Jack Carston.

Dan walked over, drew out a chair. "Hi, Jack!"

Carston jumped, turned on him suspiciously. "What brings you here?"

"Why not these?" Dan tapped his books but his eyes looked through the glass partition to smile at the blond librarian, again sorting books behind the desk.

"Are you kidding?" Carston kept his voice down, but it was strong and angry. "She never goes out with anyone."

"No? Stay right where you are till ten o'clock and see." Dan brought his attention back to Jack, studied the thin, haggard face, the pink-rimmed eyes, dim for lack of sleep. "And what are you doing here?"

Whatever stiffening had held Carston erect appeared to be dissolving. He extended a fumbling hand toward a battered gray hat on the table. "Nothing, I guess," he said uncertainly.

"Then let me take you home. I can do it easily and be back here by ten."

"Home! That's the last place I want to go." Carston crammed his hat on his head, pushed back his chair, then before Dan's concerned gaze, confessed, "Clara's left me. Taken the kids and gone back to Wyoming to her mother."

"Clara! Nonsense, you know better than to believe that. But why didn't you tell me this afternoon? When I looked for you after the inquest you'd gone."

"I'm not telling anyone—anything—yet." Carston looked again at the reception desk, rose. "Well, so long."

Dan walked with him to the door, but Jack stopped him there. "Don't—be kind," he said angrily. "I can take anything but that."

"But you're ill, Jack. Let me take you home to Dora. She'll fix you up, and you'll be doing her a favor. She thrives on nursing people and is furious because I escaped her."

"Yes, I heard you had a fall." Carston stopped, turned the knob of the heavy door, but before opening it asked abruptly, "When you leaving?"

"Thursday night." As disappointment showed in the averted face Dan added, "Why? Something I can do for you? Come on, you can tell me as we go—"

Carston jerked his arm free of Dan's hand. "Let me alone. There's nothing you can do for me, anyone can do. Well, so long. I'll be seeing you again—maybe."

He opened the door, stepped outside, let it close of itself behind him. Dan didn't try to follow. His impression that Carston for some reason of his own was faking this down-and-out condition deepened.

When he turned back to the reception room the desk was cleared of its books, its occupant gone. A trickle of readers emerging from the reading room informed him the library was closing for the night. He stood aside to watch the sorry figures, most of them old and beat, shuffle out of the warmth and light. To the flophouses, probably, or worse, on Water Street.

His eyes lighted as the librarian in her demure blue became a silhouette against the fire. She placed a screen before it, came toward him, turning out table lamps on the way. An amused sparkle moved in Dan's gravely watching gaze. This poised, efficiently confident young woman was anything but demure.

"I'd hoped we could talk here," she said when she reached him. "But—"

"Why can't we? What worries you now?"

"Maybe nothing—again. But Mrs. McPhail—"

"What about Mrs. McPhail?"

"She—I'm afraid she followed us into the stack room."

Inwardly Dan ground his teeth on Lisa though he smiled reassuringly. "I made the mistake of telling her not to come. But I doubt—well, if she did listen, she'd be none the wiser."

"No, perhaps not. However, if she happened to mention your going there with me to her husband—Professor McPhail is a member of the library board, and I'm not really a librarian. I'm only here during reading hours, eight to ten. After eight the stacks aren't open to the public."

"Forget it," Dan advised airily. "I'm a man of parts. Got rid of your follower just like that, didn't I? Knew him, as a matter of fact. He's harmless."

"I know him too. That is, I know who he is. Sometimes I've wondered if he didn't follow me to ask me something or tell me something. Once or twice I've slowed my walk to—to let him catch up with me. But he always slowed up too."

"How long's this been going on—his seeing you home at night?"

She hesitated, perhaps to check back. "I don't know exactly. A week, perhaps more."

"Oh, I imagine he did it merely because right now he's lonely and low in his mind." Dan grinned ruefully. "Unless you've a worse reason than that, let's go before this refined atmosphere undoes my wits altogether."

She left him on that for the small office behind the desk. He expected to see her emerge, wrapped in the heavy dark cape, the kerchief about her smooth hair. He was not disappointed when she reappeared, though she wore neither cape nor kerchief. In a smartly cut karakul coat and

close-fitting black hat with a wisp of veil over her eyes, she
had an exciting chic which Dan much preferred to beauty.

When they were seated in Marcus P.'s powerful closed
car, however, she lost a little of her poise. Dan thought he
knew why. She'd probably read too many books by foreign
correspondents.

"Hungry?" he asked soberly. "Mrs. Tolt's Tea-Room is
still open." If that invitation didn't reassure her, nothing
could.

"No. And I can't ask you to my home—to where I live,
I mean."

"Come to mine then. My family will break out flags to
meet you."

"No, no. Couldn't we just sit in this car somewhere?
Where no one can see or hear us?"

"We'll drive out to the airport. That's the popular thing
to do here. Watch the planes—if any—come in."

She said nothing while he sped the car west beyond
the city limits. To the great level field outlined by lights
where dark hangars and other paraphernalia emphasized
the brilliance of the illuminated airport building. Outside
the line of lights the field was ebony, and the half-dozen
cars parked there were discreetly spaced.

Dan shut off the engine. "If privacy is what you want,
this is it. But I don't need it for what I want to say. That
is, if it were possible to put into words how grateful—"

"Please," her deep voice protested. "Don't talk about
your accident—now."

"Talk about it! The Cumberlands are going to expound
on it, Miss—er—Miss . . . ?"

"Sandys. Barbara Sandys. You can speak of it later or,
if necessary, I will myself. Not yet."

She was silent again, obviously to choose her first
words. As Dan waited, his eyes on her clear-cut profile

silhouetted against the glass of the door, his interest in what she had to say diminished before his deepening curiosity and interest in the young woman herself.

"Mr. Cumberland, I want you to find the man who killed Dolores Elway—and her husband."

MONDAY NIGHT, JANUARY 12

Inured as he was to startling phrases and events, Dan was startled now. After a moment he gained equilibrium enough to say more or less levelly, "My answer to that is, the case is closed. You know that."

"I don't know that."

"No? Then my answer is—three questions. One: if you have reason to believe the Elways didn't die accidentally, why haven't you gone long before this to the district attorney? Two: and I don't mean to be rude—where does Barbara Sandys appear in this picture? And three: and again I ask this politely, why come to me?"

"The inquest is over, but the case is not closed," she told him quietly. "It will never be closed until their murderer is found. I didn't go to the district attorney because at this moment I only know they didn't die accidentally of carbon monoxide poisoning. I have no proof, no way of securing it myself. That's why I sent for you."

Dan gasped mentally. "You want me to find this—proof for you! But I'm not a detective, and I'm leaving Clayton Thursday night."

"I don't need a detective. I need someone like you who can find the truth and analyze facts, not just accept or discard them, as was done at that inquest this afternoon."

"You were there!" Dan laughed suddenly. "You were the young student in brown behind the big spectacles and notebook? Of course you were! Is that where you found the pamphlet you sent me?"

"I waited to speak to you there. But several men were around you and I saw it on the seat. I'd watched you writing on it—"

"Well, since you were there, you know the inquest left many questions unanswered, but on the whole Brierson followed a pretty straight line through the main points. The evidence itself, as well as the jury's verdict, makes a very strong case, Miss Sandys. A very much stronger case than you and I—assuming the proof exists—can break in a few hours."

"The proof exists somewhere," she insisted. "And we have all the time we need to find it—and the man it points to."

"You may have. But I leave Clayton January fifteenth."

He heard her draw in her breath, felt her move as if to brace herself against the back of the seat. When she spoke her deep voice was calm but even more inflexible, if possible.

"Mr. Cumberland, you owe your life to me."

Dan drew in his own breath. "I do—certainly," he admitted, too stunned to find ready words. "And my mother and father also feel forever in your debt. They searched Clayton for you, to tell you that—to do—to offer—" Before her insulated silence words failed him.

"There is nothing your parents can do for me or offer me. It was your life I saved, and you're the only one who can—can pay for what I did."

"If it were possible I'd do—try to do even this, Miss Sandys. But it's out of the question. I've given my word, I'm under contract—"

"If you had frozen to death there on the river, could you fulfill this contract?"

"But—"

"If I had discovered you an hour or hours later, I might still have saved your life. But it might have taken weeks for you to recover. In that case—"

"Wait!" he begged. "The point is you did find me right away. I am well enough to travel and work. I must go back—"

"You can't leave Clayton until you discover who killed my sister—and her husband."

"Your sister!"

"Dolores Sandys was my sister. All the family I had. Do you think I'm going to allow someone to take her life and do nothing about it? I don't care about Anthony. He deserved to die—a dozen deaths."

Dan's thoughts raced as he both heard and felt irrevocable purpose in the young woman beside him. Christmas Eve in the snow she had looked to be no more than twenty. Tonight in the library he had guessed her age at twenty-six or -eight. But now she talked with the control and assurance of a woman twice that.

Aloud he said gently, "Believe me, I understand how you feel. And I want to help you. I can—if you'll accept the kind of help I can offer." He paused, remembering he had used almost those same words before—to Lisa. "I'll wire my newspaper in New York tonight. Now. From the airport office. Ask to have the best detective available take the first possible train or plane."

"No."

"You must let me do this. And you must let me arrange for you to draw on my bank—no, on my father—that will be easier for you."

"No."

"But a trained and experienced detective, Miss Sandys, would, know a thousand times better than I—"

"He wouldn't know Clayton."

"You believe the murderer is here? You're sure of that?"

"I'm sure the information we need to find him is here."

They sat in silence for a minute, two minutes, Barbara Sandys adamant, Dan, for once, helpless before a woman. She hadn't used any of the wiles or influences he knew how to counter. She'd simply told him what she wanted of him, claimed his aid as her right. As it was, he had to admit.

At last he found an idea and his voice. "Perhaps you'll accept a compromise. I have three days left. Let me use one of them, two—to scout the town, see what I can learn. I'm not even sure the case can be reopened."

"I am. The verdict of the jury itself says 'that, according to the testimony given at the inquest, we find . . .' That means, I know it does, that if new evidence is found or old evidence reanalyzed a new hearing can be called or maybe a trial—"

"But why—why," he asked again, "did you wait until tonight, until the inquest was over, to tell me who you are? Don't you know the police and district attorney have searched everywhere to find the families of the Elways? Why didn't you go to them or to a lawyer of your own choice? To someone, anyone. And days ago."

"I've told you one reason. I had no proof. Another is—I wanted to hear the testimony at the inquest. Another is—I don't want to tell anyone but you who I am. Besides, who would believe me—a substitute in the library and a—" She broke off, began again, "Who would believe now, after I've lived in Clayton almost a year, that Dolores Elway was my sister?"

"That you can prove. Must prove."

"Not unless it's necessary—to find her murderer. No, not even then. Dolores suffered enough. And our family. I'm not going to allow her life to be known. Ever."

"That won't make the task you've set yourself any easier."

"The task I've set you. Though I'll help, of course."

"You haven't accepted my offer—"

"No. You'd be wasting time."

Anger began to rise in Dan. "Miss Sandys," he said, as coldly determined as she, "you have a legitimate claim to almost anything you wish to ask of me. But you can't ask the impossible. Nor would I undertake it. I'm afraid we'll have to compromise—"

"I'll do this," she offered unexpectedly. "I won't ask you to say yes until tomorrow night. You haven't had time to think of all that's happened in terms of murder. But when you do—and when you've scouted round, as you said—you're going to change your mind. I know you are. I'm so sure of it I'm willing to wait."

"That's very good of you," he said dryly.

"And I can give you some help now," she continued as if he had not spoken. "I didn't tell you al_ I know about Mr. Carston. My sister was afraid of him—not because he actually threatened her in any way," she corrected hastily as she sensed his rising protest. "She told me he tried to make opportunities to see her—alone. She was afraid he might have learned something about her—wanted to—"

"Blackmail her?" Dan turned to face Miss Sandys squarely. "If that's the kind of thing you base your belief in murder on, you're wrong all the way through. I've known Jack since we were both knee-high. He's no mental giant. A born follower. He could neither cook up an idea like that nor carry it out. That sort of thing takes a devious mind and courage Jack never had."

"I'm sure you should talk to him tomorrow. Make him tell you what he knows—or suspects."

"Perhaps his following you means he suspects who you are."

"No. If he did I'm sure he'd have spoken to me before this. He suspects me, I think, of knowing something just as I suspect him. He—both of us were on Penndale during most of those thirteen nights; I didn't always see him, but somehow now I think he saw me—"

"You don't think he's your man!"

"I—don't know. He could be. Oh"—her voice faded out with weariness—"there's still so much I should tell you, but could we go back now? I'm suddenly very tired. It—it hasn't been easy to send for you, talk to you like this."

Dan started the car gladly. He himself felt as if he were driving a rocking rowboat. His head throbbed and every bone and muscle in his body ached. Nevertheless, though he said nothing, question after question clamored for answers in his mind.

He drove automatically until her hand on his arm recalled him. They were driving down Radisson, Clayton's main business street, passing between the charred walls of the burned hotels on one side, the Harrison Hotel on the other.

"Stop at the next corner, please," she told him. "I'll walk home from there. Don't follow me, will you? Just come to the library tomorrow night, any time after eight."

With misgivings Dan watched her vanish down the now dimly lighted street. As he started the car again he remembered the Harrison bar; Jack Carston might be there. Wearily he parked, climbed out, walked back.

Carston was not there though he had been until a few minutes before. Chatting with Bud Harrison and others, Dan remained until the bar closed at one-thirty.

He reached home to find his parents waiting up for him in what seemed a highly exaggerated state of alarm. When they were assured he was physically intact Marcus P. gave him a clue to their agitation.

"You're to call McPhail at his home. He's kept the telephone hot for you since eleven-thirty. Something extremely urgent, I gather."

"But it's almost two o'clock!"

"Good. Call him."

Dan did. The professor himself answered, sonorous, calm, amused, all at the same time.

"Your father must forgive me, Dan, for disturbing him unnecessarily. All is well now. The missing one has returned and—"

"Lisa?"

"She accompanied me to the public library tonight where I spoke before the local teachers' association. When I finished she was not to be found. Assuming she'd returned home, I felt no concern. But when I reached home myself, no Lisa. I'll spare you the details of my search for her, but at last I found someone who'd seen your car parked in front of the library. Quickly—too quickly—as it turned out, I put one and one together. And remained undisturbed— until almost midnight. Then, remembering your accident, I became alarmed. Several times, I regret to say, I ventured to call your home. However, Lisa returned a half hour ago—alone. She'd had a most amusing adventure."

The chuckle at the end of the line invited a question. Patiently Dan asked it.

"The little cabbage had tired of waiting in the library and gone out—as she thought—to my car, curled up under a rug in the tonneau, and fallen asleep. When she wakened she found herself at the airport, listening in on a most unique *affaire d'amour*. She was too embarrassed to reveal herself, of course, so played mouse while she waited their convenience in returning to town. Luckily, when they returned, she was able to escape her predicament unobserved, secure a taxi, and now is sleeping the sleep of the unrighteous little creature she is."

Dan listened to the end, replaced the receiver, turned for the door at the end of the long central hall that led into the garage.

"You're not going out again!" Dora protested.

"Just to the car. I forgot something."

He found it—as he knew he would. On the floor of the tonneau, beneath the crumpled rugs. A smart black glove whose gauntlet was slashed with white.

TUESDAY MORNING, JANUARY 13

Dora moved aside the coffee percolator the better to command an unobstructed view of her husband.

"Darling, if you don't break up that cold you're going to break up our home. Your disposition is growing progressively worse. Do be reasonable. No one wants to stir up a mess like that Elway case again. Dan merely asked you if it could be reopened and if so, how one went about it. I'd like to know the answer to that myself."

Marcus P. lifted his napkin as if to hurl it to the table but, under her steady gaze, folded it instead. From somewhere he dug up a truly sweet and penitent smile.

"Sorry, Dora. It's that blasted Mollner with his blasted shots and advice that's embittering my life. You'd think a man had never had a cold before—"

"It's more than three weeks, sir, since you acquired it," Dan reminded him.

"You'd never have had to call Dr. Mollner if you'd canceled that Chicago trip," Dora added. "You were almost well—"

"All right, all right." Marcus P. threw up his hands. "Leave me alone and I'll answer Dan's question. Yes, Brierson can reopen the case whenever new and authenticated evidence convinces him it should be reopened."

Dan smiled at Dora, turned again to his father. "With that cold you shouldn't be running around the streets, should you? And that reminds me, since you won't need the car today, I know a fellow who can use it."

Marcus P.'s goatee quivered irately. "If you want it to— oh well, drive me downtown, then take it. But remember this, son. The Elway case, is closed, the bodies cremated."

"When?" Dan asked. "On whose authority?"

"Last night, I suppose. On the D.A.'s order. The urns will remain in the Evergreen Mortuary until—" Marcus P. stopped, his anger kindling again. "What's come over you, Dan? You showed no interest in this case all along.

Now when at last it's over you open up."

"I sat in on the inquest yesterday, thought up a lot of questions I didn't hear answered."

"Name one."

"I'll name two. Where's the Elway dog? Who turned out the lights?"

"Lights?"

"Certainly. The Elways weren't in bed asleep when the gas overcame them. One, or both of them, was up, moving around. Late on December twenty-second Mrs. Matteson saw lights in that front bedroom after midnight. Yet the house was dark until January fourth. Who turned out the lights?"

Mr. Cumberland rose to look at his son closely. "Well I'll be damned," he said with mock amazement. "Hurry back to New York while the *Globe'll* still have you, son. The Clayton *News* requires brains."

He marched out.

"What did become of the dog?" Dora asked. "And who—"

Dan stooped to kiss her. "You figure out the answers, darling. I've a tough job of chauffeuring to do."

It wasn't so tough. Marcus P. didn't open his mouth till they reached the News Building. Then he said quietly as he turned to leave the car, "Sorry I blew up, son. But as a favor to Clayton, if not to me, forget the Elway case."

Dan's first stop was Jack Carston's home on Elk Street. A one-story little gray house, almost hidden behind firs and winter shrubs. Although he received no answer to his rings and knocks, he felt sure Carston must be asleep inside.

Bud Harrison had told him that Jack had left the Harrison bar for home. Bud had also mentioned that Jack spent very little time in his makeshift office; didn't arrive till noon, left it again in an hour or two. And it was not yet half past nine.

Tentatively Dan tried the door, found it locked. He turned to the broad front window on his right, facing south across the porch. Its shade was drawn down to the sill. Below the window lay the *Morning News*.

Dan picked it up and, turning it idly by its corners, stood irresolute a moment. Then, descending the steps, he walked round the south side of the house. The windows there were closed, their shades down too. Dan took hope from that. If Clara still retained interest in preserving her furniture from the winter sun she intended to return.

The back door also was locked. And the windows on either side of it closed and shaded. So were the windows on the north side of the house.

Back at the front steps, Dan paused only a moment, then with long strides returned to the kitchen door. His skeleton key did its duty and he entered the kitchen.

A very untidy kitchen, he saw when he had raised the shades, completely unlike the white and immaculate equivalent he had seen in the Elway home. On the dinette table dishes used and unused were strewn, and among them lay two jagged slices of dry, hard bread. Cupboard doors stood open. On the gas stove a coffeepot tilted at a crazy angle.

As he stood listening to the silent house the drip-drip of a faucet grew louder in his ears, The hot-water tap of the kitchen unit, he noticed then, was its source. Without thinking, he walked over, turned it off.

Then he went through the house. It didn't take long—a dining room and living room on the north side, both in the order Clara had left them. And across a narrow hall two bedrooms, joined by a small bath. The bright little bedroom at the rear of the house, with its two small beds, obviously had been furnished for Jack's two small children. Only the main bedroom and the bath held interest for Dan.

In the bedroom a wide bed, its blankets tossed about, pillows crushed and twisted, indicated that Jack had slept there. But when Dan thrust a hand among them he found no warmth. If Jack had slept there last night he had risen long since.

Dan looked at the clothing strewn about—all Jack's. All ready for laundry basket or dry cleaner. He looked again into the disheveled bathroom where towels lay crumpled in corners, others in the tub. The dapper, meticulous Jack had certainly changed!

Returning to the hall, Dan found the telephone, called Bud Harrison. A sleepy voice answered, none too willingly. But when Bud understood at last who was calling he came alert.

"Jack Carston not home?" he repeated irritably. "Oh, think nothing of it, Dan. He's probably asleep in one of those Water Street joints. They stay open all night. And he has no yen for his home these days. You know that."

"You said last night he'd gone home."

"I'm afraid I did." Bud was silent a moment. "Look here, Dan. I know you like the fellow, feel sorry for him. So do I. But I've got to consider our guests and town trade. And I've put up with Jack a darned sight longer than I would with most men who're trying to drink themselves to death or soak up courage from a bottle or whatever he thinks he's doing. Funny thing is, he seems to go overboard just on the smell of the stuff. Buys plenty but always spills it or forgets it or something. Last night—well, it's true; he did leave the bar shortly before you arrived. I had Nick invite him to go. In other words, put him out."

"Jack! But why? He isn't the type to be noisy or disagreeable,"

"No? Well, he was both last night. And about you, Dan. If I hadn't known you could take care of yourself, I'd have told you."

"He made threats against me?"

"Not threats, no. But he certainly made it clear to anyone who'd listen that there's no love lost between you. Even tried to deny you ever had been friends." Bud yawned. "Oh, forget it and him—and let me. I've still got two good hours of sleep coming."

Dan rang off, more disturbed than he would admit. Thoughtfully he drove back to Radisson, parked the car, and walked down a sloping, unpaved road to Clayton's original main thoroughfare.

Now known as Water Street, it lies along the ridge of the river, a rickety two blocks of small frame buildings, old and unpainted. Most of them house bars, flophouses, cheap eating places. A few display tawdry merchandise in their dusty windows.

One by one Dan entered every door open for business or that would open to his knock. Only in Chinese Charlie's Chop Suey House did he encounter a familiar face, hear a word about Carston.

The Chinese admitted Dan reluctantly, stood with him just inside the closed door, his small black eyes flickering over the boxes of tea and noodles scattered about his small display window.

"When Mistah Cahston come Watah St'eet, he come heah," he told Dan quickly. "I give him one good d'ink, he go sleep. I take cay-ah him. Last night he no come." When Dan continued to tower above him, silent, he added, "He no go his homeside? You think t'ouble happen, maybe?"

"I don't know, Charlie. And I don't know where else to look for him. If he comes down here, call me, will you?"

"I look, ask too. Mistah Cahston good man. I cook fo-ah him in one hotel, then in oth-ah. I quit. Come he-ah."

"Why did you leave the Wayne River Hotel?" Dan asked. "You made the place famous with your steaks and Chinese chow, Charlie."

The black eyes shone opaquely, at him. "Mo-ah bettah have little business Chah-lie's own. Mistah Cahston, he say good luck. He help plenty."

"Little business!" Dan smiled. "Most of the town is down here every night." He turned for the door. "Well, I guess that's all, Charlie."

"Minute," the Chinese said, his eyes again on his window. "Why oth-ah man have int'lust why you come this side?"

"What do you mean? Some other man?"

"Tall, thin man," Charlie said. "I watch you long time befo-ah you come my side. He watch too."

"Where is he now?"

"He go. No see now."

"Do you know him? Ever see him before?"

"Mo-ah bettah you go now, Mistah Cumbahland. One day Chahlie know something maybe. He tell you." He opened the door with finality.

Dan stepped outside. The door closed quickly on his heels and a key turned. He looked up and down the brief street, could see no one. Water Street slept during the day, came to life in the evening. Every window now was either blank or closely curtained.

Wearily he returned to Radisson, picked up the car, and drove round to the News Building to find his father waiting.

"Almost half past twelve," he greeted Dan. "Dora'll have our lives." He shot an all-observing glance at his son. "What's eating you?"

"I can't find Jack Carston—"

"Be thankful for that. Seen him lately?"

"Last night."

"Oh, then you know. Damn fool—with a wife like Clara and two fine youngsters."

"He's had lots of trouble lately, Dad."

"Who hasn't?" Marcus P. retorted.

His morning shot looking for Carston, Dan made two or three telephone calls after he drove his father to the News Building for the afternoon, then returned to his original quest for information on the Elway case.

Police headquarters was just across the street. He sought and found Pete Wilson there. His first question brought the chief's comfortably elevated feet down from his desk.

"What d'ya mean, Dan, do I know anything that didn't come out at the inquest?"

"Well, what about the Elway dog, for example? It was never mentioned."

"Still harping on that dog? Olaf thinks it ran out of the house when Judson opened all the doors. After they smelled gas they had no time to think about a dog. Anyway, it must've been pretty thin and weak—couldn't go far. Remember, the snow was deep and the weather bitter cold. It may be living high on rabbits down behind the

ridge somewhere, or dead and covered by snow by this
time. If so, there'll be no finding it till spring,"

"But there was no sign of a dog having been in that
garage or in the house either."

"Then why're you asking about the Elway dog if there
wasn't one?"

"O.K., forget the dog. But who turned off the lights?"

"What lights?"

Patiently Dan explained.

"Why, I don't know, Dan. I never thought of those
lights—if there was any. No one else did either, I guess.
But we didn't go far wrong at that. Maybe the Elways woke
up in the dark, too dizzy and sick from that gas to think
of lights, stumbled around trying to reach the door, didn't
make it. The case is closed, son," the chief reminded him
comfortably. "Forever, I hope. This is no time to be asking
questions like that."

Suddenly the chief sat up, beetling his heavy brows.
"Just asking questions or've you got something on your
mind?"

"Just asking questions. I attended the inquest yesterday. Thought up several no one asked or answered. Maybe
it's just a sign, Chief, that my wits are aching for action
again. I'm leaving this week, you know."

"Good. Not that you're leaving Clayton, of course. But
because you don't mean anything by such questions. It'll
take this town a long time to forget that Elway business.
The sooner folks stop, talking the better."

"Anything special on your mind—about it?" Dan asked.
The chief sat back, elevated his feet' again. "Nope. That
verdict suited me down to the ground. My motto's always
been—"

"I know. To keep Clayton peaceful and decent. More
power to you, Chief." Dan rose. "By the way, how about
asking your boys to keep an eye out for Jack Carston? He

looked like a sick man when I saw him last night. He isn't
at home. I've been out there. And he isn't around town."

"That—rat. He's a disgrace to the streets. Know where
the boys are always finding him? Reeling around in the ruins of those two hotels, still thinking he's managing them!
Once Ben Schurz even found him asleep in the Claytonian
debris." Wilson pronounced it "debriss." "I'd be doing him
a favor to run him in as a vagrant."

"Don't do that," Dan protested. "Just find him and call
me. I'll take care of him."

"Your father all over again." Wilson smiled and got to
his feet to walk to the door with Dan. "Soft as rice pud-
ding inside. I'll find him for you—be glad to."

But at the door Dan erased the friendly approval in the
older man's face. "You took that request so well, Chief, I'll
make another. Is the Elway home still intact? If so, Mother'd like to see it."

Half an hour later, with that lie on his conscience and
an apprehensive Dora beside him, Dan opened the back
door of the Elway home.

"Just look at everything," he repeated as they stood in
the kitchen. "When you've finished I've only one question
to ask you."

At first reluctantly, then with growing interest, Dora
moved from room to room, floor to floor. Except for the
dining room where two or three chairs still stood about the
table and in the living room where Brierson had crushed
the divan cushions and left cigarette ends in a tray as he
listened to Dan through that wintry Wednesday afternoon,
the house was unchanged. Even in the main bedroom one
bed was still quietly opened, the other tumbled. On the
chest of drawers the fresh linen still awaited a wearer.

Dora's intelligent eyes recorded everything, revealed
nothing of what she was thinking as Dan opened doors,

pulled out drawers, lifted covers of boxes and baskets. She lingered longest in the kitchen before the open door to the refrigerator, then, when they ascended the stairs, stood silent for minutes in the bathroom.

"Take me home now," she urged suddenly.

Dan was disturbed to hear a tremor in her voice, catch the shimmer of tears in her eyes. "Of course, darling. But—"

"*Now,*" she insisted.

Until homeward-bound they did not speak again.

"Do you mean that's exactly the way the house looked when Mr. Judson and that policeman entered it?" Dora asked then.

"Almost exactly. Of course men from police headquarters and the D.A.'s office searched the place for various reasons. But they put everything back as they found it."

"The poor woman . . . Oh, that poor woman . . ."

"Why poor woman?"

"Because no woman would leave her house like that if she went to bed at night intending to get up in the morning—as usual. Mrs. Elway didn't expect to, intend to, Dan. When she went to bed that night she knew she'd never—never—"

"Don't let it get you now, Dora dear. Just tell me what you think."

"I don't know. It's all so confusing. That refrigerator cleared of everything perishable, all the little things one leaves about a house put away. Not in the order one would expect them to be; more as if she just wanted to get them out of sight. And then there's the fresh linen on that chest of drawers in the bedroom, the Christmas tree and gifts. And in the bathroom, the kitchen too, and the laundry in the basement—all fresh towels on the racks in the bathroom, yet not a sign of soap anywhere, not even a little piece. Dan, there wasn't a thing in that house that wasn't clean and fresh. Not a single thing to be—continued!"

"To be continued?"

"Nothing in that kitchen, no fruit, butter, or cream— things like that—to use for breakfast if they planned to leave on December twenty-third. Nothing partially consumed . . . Oh, I don't know," Dora said worriedly. "If we left our house in that condition it would be because we were leaving it. Never coming back. Never wanting to."

Dan said hastily, "Thanks, dearest. You've told me exactly what I want to know. Now forget what you've seen."

"I can't forget it. I'll never forget it, Dan. As long as I live I'll think of that poor woman on that last day going through her own house like a stranger. Like a woman who'd never seen it before—putting it in order— for strangers to see."

A little after four Dan stepped out of an elevator on the fourth floor of the Wayne River Bank Building, crossed the square foyer to open a glazed door on which square black letters announced T. O. Brierson, Attorney at Law.

"I have no appointment," he said to the pretty young thing typing in the outer office—the court stenographer of the inquest. "Just happened to be in the building."

"Dan Cumberland, in person!" a hearty voice said behind him. He turned to see Thode Brierson coming through an open door, hand outstretched. "Come in, come in."

With one hand he drew Dan into his private office, with the other closed the door. "Your honorable presence in my humble office calls for a—what'll you have, boy?"

"Just a cigarette. I'm doing my good-bying early, Big. And my congratulating late. I'd always heard that inquests were dull, dragged-out affairs. Not the way you handle 'em—"

"I value those words, coming from you. But I can't take much of the credit. Except for McPhail, the witnesses were men who don't enjoy the limelight. Wanted to say what they had to say and get away."

"That explanation doesn't cover Bob Brownell."

Big Thode laughed. "Imagine Bob with stage fright! He was positively dripping. I felt sorry for the guy, finally. Let him go."

"The prof's quite a showman."

"I'll say." Brierson sat down before his desk, closed a half-open drawer with a bang. "Am I glad to write R.I.P. over that case!"

"You sound very final."

Brierson didn't feel as hearty as his voice indicated, Dan was sure. The attorney's eyes showed pink veins of strain; he held his great shoulders erect with a visible effort.

"If you know a stronger word than that, use it," Brierson told him curtly.

"That's good enough." Dan shrugged the subject off. "I did have a reason for dropping in on you while I was in your neighborhood. Jack Carston. You and he were pretty good friends at one time."

Thode crushed out his cigarette, lighted another before he answered. "Still would be—if he'd have it that way. You saw him yesterday at the inquest so I don't need to tell you he's falling apart. Sees every man's hand against him, himself a failure—down and out."

"He's got good stuff in him."

"Had, you mean."

"Had! Good Lord, nothing's happened to him—"

"Happened? Oh—no. I mean, he's got plenty of rotten stuff in him now. Swallows anything. Even canned heat, I hear."

"Canned heat? Is that a drink?"

"No, just what it's called. That jellied-up alcohol that comes in cans to cook with. Never heard of it? Well, I hadn't either till Bud Harrison told me about it the other day. Seems it's quite the popular dish down around Water Street somewhere."

"And Jack has a taste for that!"

"He's been seen down there, and something more than liquor's responsible for his cracking up so quickly."

"That doubles my reasons for coming in, Big. I had a talk with the chief a few hours ago. Asked him to find Carston for me when I couldn't locate him myself. I was worried after what I saw of him last night. He looked like a man with one foot edging toward a grave."

"What d'ya think I can do about him?"

"Not you alone. But you, Bud, and I ought to be able to finance treatment or whatever he needs to get him back on his feet."

Brierson riffled his fingers on the desk a moment, looked up. "Sure, if you're in on it too. Personally, I doubt if he's worth it. How much do you want?"

"Thanks, nothing now." Dan stubbed out his cigarette, got to his feet. "I'll have to see Bud, of course, and first of all Carston. Perhaps I can persuade Bud to act for us. I'm leaving Thursday, you know."

"You're kidding! With a crack in your head not a week old?"

"I'd say that's a fine example of a pot calling a kettle black."

"What's that mean?"

"Looked in a mirror recently?"

"Nonsense. Nothing the matter with me. No sleep, that's all. That inquest had to break just as I was up to the ears getting ready for the opening of court next week. But when it's over Beth and I are heading South for a month in the sun."

As Dan descended in the elevator to the street floor he thought he could use a month in the sun himself. And he had two more interviews to go through. Would have had three if Dr. Moorehead had been in town. But the way things were shaping up, by ten o'clock tonight, he promised himself, he'd be free for two long days of rest.

In the gathering. darkness he drove out Radisson to College Boulevard, followed it south to the idyllic spot where Clayton College lay among wooded hills. Before Science Hall he stopped the car, sat a moment watching the lights flash on along the walks, the muffled figures of students here and there wending their weary way dormitory- or busward.

Stiffly he slipped from under the wheel, mounted the steps, and pushed through a revolving door. The same odor of mixed chemicals he'd sniffed a thousand years ago, it seemed to him now, greeted him familiarly. A minute later he entered the open door of a first-floor office, to find Dr. Forester standing behind his desk, packing papers into a brief case.

"Sorry not to have been able to see you earlier, Mr. Cumberland," he said, offering a soft hand. "And now I've only a minute or two, I'm afraid. A committee meeting's been called for five."

"That's all right, sir. I have just one question."

Dr. Forester nodded to a nearby chair, continued to busy himself with the buckles on his brief case. "I looked up your record while you were a student here, just to be prepared. Your science courses didn't include pathology."

Dan smiled. "No. And my question doesn't concern pathology, primarily. The fact is, Dr. Forester, I attended that inquest yesterday, listened to your testimony—yours and Professor McPhail's—with great interest."

At mention of McPhail's name Dr. Forester stiffened. "Indeed? A very routine case. Not worth the detailed discussion my colleague saw fit to give it. Unless you had some personal concern in it, Mr. Cumberland?"

"No. I'd never witnessed an inquest before, took the opportunity when it offered. As I listened a strictly lay question, from your point of view, occurred to me."

"In connection with my analyses?"

"In a way. I wondered, sir, if in your exceptionally wide experience or to your knowledge a situation had ever arisen in which the conclusions of the pathologist and those of the chemist disagreed. That is, revealed different causes of death. Would such a thing be possible?"

Dr. Forester's cool manner turned to ice. "You heard Professor McPhail's testimony supplement mine, did you not?"

"Of course, sir. My question was a general one."

Pale lips pursed with distaste. "You're a newspaperman, I believe. A foreign correspondent?"

Dan suppressed a smile, nodded.

"Then that explains your interest in the melodramatic and sensational, doesn't it?" Dr. Forester tucked his brief case under his arm, looked about his cleared desk. "I'm afraid, young man, a meeting of minds between a—a journalist and a scientist is impossible. I have had neither time nor interest to explore the headline possibilities in my field. Now if you will excuse me . . . ."

He hurried round his desk and without offering Dan another soft clasp went on out the door.

Dan returned to town, stopped the car before Mrs. Tolt's tidy tea-room on Bell Avenue.

A half-dozen women still lingered over teacups at small round tables set closely about the long room. At others waitresses were preparing for the dinner guests. But the booths along the left wall were unoccupied, Dan found, until he reached the last one. There Lisa, all in black, save for an enormous scimitar of seed pearls at her throat, sat alone, impatiently waiting.

"This is the last place I'd have expected you to suggest," he said as he slipped into the seat opposite her. "Have you ordered? . . . Good. Coffee for me. Lots of coffee," he told the little blue-uniformed waitress who appeared at his elbow.

"Must you be so grim?" Lisa asked when the girl had gone. "Or are you trying to intimidate me?"

"You know why I'm grim."

She quivered her lashes at him, smiled through them. "Well, you made me feel pretty grim last night. But not for long, darling. I must thank you for the most fascinating evening of my life."

"What do you intend to do about it?"

"About what I heard? I intend to use it."

"I know that. How?"

"You know how."

Dan shook an aching head. "I'm not the man I was when I telephoned you this noon. You'll have to tell me."

"I told you. Christmas Eve."

He looked blank, then incredulous. "Lisa, you aren't still—"

"I didn't sleep a wink all night, planning. I haven't been still a minute since Terence left to catch his plane this morning. I'm all packed, angel. Just two bags. They're in the checkroom at Union Station right now."

When he continued to look at her unbelievingly her light manner vanished.

"You yourself gave me the opportunity I've been praying for, Dan. And I'm going to take it. I've got to get away from Clayton. And I can't do it alone. I've never been anywhere alone. And I can't stand up to Terence alone—think of everything ahead of him. He'd find me, bring me back."

"I'm not leaving Clayton till Thursday night."

"I don't want you to. If we left the same time Terence would guess immediately what had happened. But you must plan how and where I'm to go, get my tickets. Then tell me what to do until you come."

"I'm leaving New York February first for London."

"What a coincidence!" She smiled brightly. "So am I. But I'll stay there, angel, wait for you. I know I can't follow you around Europe."

"And my alternative?"

"You haven't any, silly. Unless you want all Clayton to know who—"

"Careful!"

"What I heard, then. I've already arranged—"

"Arranged?"

"Arranged. You get me to New York or wherever you can join me Sunday, and nothing will ever be known of the sister or what was said."

"You've even rehearsed the words for this—plot, haven't you?"

"I'm not going to fail. This time."

Perhaps she caught the gleam in Dan's eyes. She leaned forward to say softly but clearly, "I've written down every word I heard, Dan. That's one reason why I couldn't meet you earlier. If you won't help me or don't join me in New York Sunday, I've placed an envelope where a telegram will deliver it—to someone who'd be very glad to know what I heard."

"To Professor McPhail?"

"Why on earth would it interest him?"

"I can't imagine why it would interest anyone—legitimately."

Lisa's small face darkened with quick anger. "What do I care whether it's legitimate or not? I'm going to leave Clayton, thanks to you. Tonight—before Terence returns in the morning."

Dan pulled his wits together, studied her thoughtfully. Lisa was a facile and resourceful little liar, but somewhere in what she said was always a grain of truth. He tried a new approach.

"Tell me why you must go away and I'll consider it."

"I can't."

"Then do what you like with your information."

"You don't mean that!"

"Certainly I mean it. In the first place, how many people in this town will accept your word against mine? In the second, your tale can do no more than cause trouble and—though this, of course, means nothing to you—more suffering for a young woman who's already had more than her share. Well, that's too bad."

Lisa's glance wavered. He followed up his advantage.

"You wouldn't try to use what you heard to hurt anyone needlessly. If you're so desperate to get away you must have a really good reason. I want to know what it is."

"And if I tell you, you'll help me?"

"If I believe you, yes."

She sat back as the waitress arrived with Dan's coffee. When they were alone she compromised.

"I'll tell you what I can. Not all. You'll see why. I've got to get away because I'm afraid, Dan. Terrified to death—of Terence. I've got to get away before he discovers what I've done."

If he hadn't been so tired Dan could at least have smiled. Malice was the worst offense he could imagine among Lisa's sins. "What have you done?" he asked patiently.

Her soft, breathless voice took on a hard edge. "Terence isn't the paragon husband he appears to be, Dan. He's had several—affairs is the Clayton word for it. None very serious, really, until the one that began last spring. And it was dangerous too."

"The heroine, I take it, has a husband."

Lisa nodded. "I've never tried to do anything before, never let him suspect I knew. This time—I did." Her small face grew smaller, her eyes larger, at some memory. "Dan, something dreadful's going to happen any minute. And I mustn't be here when it does. Terence'll know I'm responsible,"

"I hope he beats you!" Dan was openly skeptical. "You read those lines in some pulp magazine."

For a long moment she looked at him. Then, heedless of the filling tables about them, she opened the scimitar pin, tossed it on the table. Before Dan grasped her intention she zippered open her snug-fitting jacket, slipped down the left shoulder.

His startled eyes focused on the smooth olive flesh there, now one dark bruise. Without a word she pulled the jacket into place again, zipped it closed, and replaced the pin.

"Terence did that. Last night," she said to the sick look in his eyes. "He—he thought I'd run away with you. He's been afraid I would ever since you came back. He doesn't care about me—only about his reputation. And he insists on being free himself. All he wants is that I—all his possessions—remain just the same, always. Don't look like that. It's true. I'm just another prop to him. Like that study of his you admired so much. We give him face, make a—an impressive backdrop for him."

"How'd you get that shoulder?" Dan asked grimly.

"He did that and more before I could tell him—convince him—last night that I'd gone to sleep in the wrong car."

"Convince him! Lisa, you can't think ahead of McPhail because you imagine everyone believes exactly what you want them to believe. How many dark green twelve-cylinder Cadillacs are there in Clayton? How many of them were parked in front of the library last night? Of course McPhail knows in whose car you didn't go to sleep! You acquired that bruise when he forced you to tell him every word you heard!"

She shook her head weakly. "I—I didn't tell him," she managed finally.

Again he looked skeptical. "I wish I could believe that."

"I didn't tell him. I swear it, Dan." Lisa thought a moment. "Do you think I'd tell him it was you in that car with another woman when I—I've been trying ever since you came back to—to make him believe you were still—still fond of me?"

Dan centered his mind on her first sentence. He wanted to believe her. But he had been under no illusions last night as he listened to the professor's amused explanation of Lisa's absence. McPhail knew in whose car his wife had spent several hours.

Before Lisa's heedlessness, once so appealing to him, he now was helpless. Yet he still felt the pull of his old responsibility for her. And that bruise on her shoulder was real.

She looked so small, so helpless herself, sitting there in the center of the wide, dark seat, waiting for him to solve her problems as he always had. Again, beneath his anger and concern, he knew that heady sensation she alone could give him.

"You win," he said finally. "I'll help you. But not because or while you hold a gun at my head. Produce that envelope!"

Lisa's worry lines smoothed out magically. She sighed with relief, smiled. "Idiot! There isn't any envelope. I knew you'd help me when you understood."

In answer he reached across the table, picked up her extravagantly sized black purse. She sat rigid until he smiled at the conglomerate trivia its capacious depths revealed.

He was about to close the bag when the small gold triangle of a zipper caught his eye. He drew it back, opening the flat side pocket that lined one side. A moment later he held a long brown envelope in his hand.

When he looked up he half rose in alarm. Lisa's black eyes were wide open, fixed on the envelope as if frozen there. Her face appeared frozen too, with the small, full red lips parted to speak, too stiff to utter a sound.

He tucked the envelope into an inside pocket of his suit coat, rose. "Now let's go."

"Don't— Give that back to me." Her words were ragged, barely audible.

"So—it doesn't contain your memoirs of last night! What is it then? Answer me or I'll find out for myself."

"It—it's something else. For you. To read—if anything happens to me." Tears welled in her eyes, rolled unchecked down her pale cheeks.

"Then it's safe with me for a long time." He felt as drained as she looked. "Let's go. I'm taking you home."

"Home!" The word galvanized her. She sprang up.

"To my home. Where else? Don't you read the papers? Know I've a crack in my head? Do you think I can work out a plan for you on a moment's notice? Or secure tickets and reservations?"

But Lisa shrank away from him. "No, no. I'd sooner face Terence than your mother."

TUESDAY NIGHT, JANUARY 13

An hour later Dan lay on the couch, listening to his mother's stern descent of the stairs. Of all the difficult moments of this long and difficult day none had been harder than the one when Dora looked up from her book to see him enter her living room, Lisa clinging to his arm.

If he had struck Dora in the face, he knew, he couldn't have hurt her more. But she stopped beside him, placed a hand on his forehead, rubbed it gently back and forth.

"It's all right, dear. This is your home. If you want that—woman in it, that's your privilege. But I'm afraid we must talk a little about it—because of Marc."

He drew her hand down against his lips. "You're wonderful, Dora. And believe me, I'm sorry—"

"We'll all be that—later—if Marc discovers she's here. It's the grace of God he's late. I've warned her, Dan, not to make a sound. But there's nothing for her to do in that guest room. She won't read and she isn't the type to lie on that bed long, staring at the ceiling."

Dora drew up a chair beside him. "I locked her in—with some food. I almost wish she'd choke on it—before Marc comes, of course."

"Don't worry. Lisa'll change her mind by morning. If not, I'll find a place for her—somewhere. But she's so helpless and frightened right now, Dora."

His mother bit back the words on her lips, suggested instead, "Lisa's lived in Clayton most of her life, Dan, must have friends who'd—"

"That brute will look for her every place but here. What he needs is a good scare—"

"Darling, must you wear yourself out on other people's troubles your last days at home? You're not well yet, and now you're exhausted. It takes a clear, rested mind to solve one's own problems, let alone other people's."

"Don't rub it in. I've been blundering around all day." Dan raised a smile for her. "Oh well, just one more thing to do tonight and Lisa to arrange for in the morning. Then two whole days right here by the fire with you."

"What about me?" Marcus P. came in from the hall, rubbing chilled hands. "Does my son and heir rate all the attention in this house?"

He was smiling, but his cold obviously was worse. He did not suffer illness gladly and now his eyes were bright with anger as well as inflamed. As he sat down near Dan he placed a hand on his chest to ease his racking cough.

Through dinner he controlled his fretfulness but when they were once more in the living room he turned on Dan. "Let's get this straight, son. Are you or aren't you trying to raise hell in this town?"

"Is there any to raise?"

"Well, you've lined Wilson, Brierson, and me against you if you are. That's a strong combination to break down—in two days."

"What are you talking about, Marc?" Dora asked.

"The Elway case. Again! Dan's been driving up and down the streets all day, putting his nose into other people's business. Lord, Dan, can't you wait till you're back in Europe to go busting around asking impertinent questions? This is no place to do it. And this is no time. The chief and Brierson did their damnedest to collect and present all the evidence they could find at that inquest. And their damnedest is pretty damn good. You couldn't trick or bribe any of those men on the jury if you offered them the mint. Nor any of the witnesses either. Yet you—with your questions about dogs and lights and Lord knows what else—presume—"

"More or less in passing, Marcus P.," Dan assured him. "I really went to see the chief and Thode about Jack Carston."

"If Jack wants to go to hell, let him. It's his own business."

As the telephone shrilled in the hall Dan and Dora exchanged sighs of relief. Even Marcus P. appeared to welcome the interruption. "I'll answer it," he said, and hurried away, coughing as he went.

A moment's silence followed his hoarse hello. Then both his wife and son stiffened to attention as Marcus P.'s voice, deadly quiet with anger, said clearly, "Professor McPhail, this is the second time you've had the effrontery to call my home to ask about your wife. Mrs. McPhail is not under my roof—and never will be."

The receiver smashed into its cradle. Marcus P. came back to the fire, his anger against his cold and Dan submerged in a larger wrath. "I want you to tell me if McPhail calls this number again. There's a law on the statute books—"

He stopped to look up at the ceiling. Something had fallen with a clatter just above his head. "What in God's name is that?"

"Nothing, dear," Dora told him. "Nothing for you to be concerned about, I mean. Tilda—"

"Breaks dishes in the kitchen. That crash came from upstairs. In the guest room." The keen brown gaze left the ceiling to flick from Dora to Dan. "Who's up there?" Without pausing for an answer he started for the hall.

"Marc, wait." Dora rose anxiously. "Don't go up. We'll tell you—"

"I'm not going up. I'm calling McPhail to apologize, tell him his wife is on her way home."

With a stride Dan was in front of him. "Not—for a moment, sir. Lisa is upstairs. I brought her here, that's true. Because she can't go home. She's leaving McPhail—"

"Then let her leave him from her own house. I won't be placed in the position of lying to a man like that!" Marcus P. quieted suddenly to look up in stark dismay at his son. "Dan, after all these years, you aren't—"

"Of course he's not going to marry her!" Dora was beside her husband too. "But the child's in real trouble, dear. Even physically bruised. She turned to Dan for help—to leave Clayton and her husband—"

Marcus P. was looking at his watch. "You two can dupe me just seven minutes longer. At exactly half past eight I'm calling McPhail—either to say his wife's, here or that she's been here and gone."

At half past eight Lisa was gone—as far as the deep, dark tonneau of the Cumberland car. Dan, at the wheel, drove slowly toward the library, forcing his heavy-footed brains to one more effort.

As he passed the high school he saw it was surrounded by cars. Neatly he slid the nose of the Cadillac into the last parking space, got out, and locked the doors. Without a glance for the tonneau he walked on up the street to the library, two blocks away.

He had to wait a moment for Miss Sandys to emerge from the stack room. She joined him quickly at a display shelf of new books, her eyes bright with expectancy.

"You made an extraordinary request of me last night," Dan began at once. "Now I must make one of you. Where do you live? I'm not curious. This is important for a very strange reason."

"I—have a room—"

"Good. Where?"

She hesitated and faint color showed in her face. "On Captain Billy's steamboat. I take care of him."

Dan had no time to be surprised. "Good," he repeated, and meant it. The old steamboat would be just the place. "Would you be willing—just for tonight—to change places with Mrs. McPhail?"

He grinned at the swiftly merging expressions racing across her face. "Correction; would you accept the hospitality of the Cumberland guest room, let Mrs. McPhail occupy your room? There's no time to explain, but she can't go home and she can't stay in mine."

Miss Sandys fingered a book into place, looked up. "It must be urgent, Mr. Cumberland, or you wouldn't make such a request of me. I'd like to say yes, but I . . ." Her candid gray eyes searched his drawn face, softened. "Yes, if Mrs. McPhail . . . Yes, I will. But your family mustn't know who I am."

"We'll talk about that later. Now if you'll let me have your keys I'll take Mrs. McPhail to the boat, come back for you."

Her disappointment in his going was clear, but she turned quickly to get her purse.

"This key is for number one cabin," she told him a moment later. "Mrs. McPhail will find everything she needs there. And tell her not to be nervous. No one comes near the river these cold nights. And Captain Billy never leaves his bridge."

"I'll be back in an hour," Dan said gratefully, turned away, turned back. "Carston here tonight?'

"No. Not yet, anyway."

"If he comes in keep him here, even if I'm a little late, will you?"

Lisa cried out in protest when Dan stopped the car at the foot of Radisson. "Here you are, Lisa. Last stop for tonight."

She looked fearfully from the old houses that marked the end of the street on one side to the dim white glow of snowy woods on the other. "Where are we going?"

"To the last place in the world anyone would think of looking for you. Captain Billy's steamboat."

"I don't believe you!"

"You will when you see your cabin. If Miss Sandys can live in it you can bear it for one night."

Still protesting, she let him lead her down the faintly beaten path among the trees to the river. There the old steamboat, last of the fleet that until a half century ago had given life, supplies, and new citizens to the valley, loomed white in the darkness.

It was merely a memory of a steamboat now. Its hull was firmly founded in the bank. The entire superstructure had been removed and replaced by a low rectangular building amidships and a square two-story tower forward, both painted white.

A small green light shone at the top of the ladder that led to the deck. Others marked the doors of the midship structure. Elsewhere the ship was dark except for the bridge which formed the upper story of the tower. There in the blaze of light pouring from the unshaded windows that lined its upper walls the broad shoulders of Captain Billy, made broader still by a Navy cape, and his leonine head with its nautical cap, moved back and forth.

They found cabin number one to be a large square room with a small adjoining bath. But Lisa was not impressed with its warmth and light and old-fashioned furnishings. She tossed her purse on the high bunk topping a set of wide, deep drawers, moved straight for a window. There, hands cupped about her eyes, she peered out across the open deck to the scattered lights on the hills of the far shore.

Dan felt the hot little radiator, examined the Yale lock and inside bolt on the door, looked half enviously at the deep chair placed between a low table with a good reading lamp and a book-lined wall.

"Very cozy, I'd say, Lisa. Now you're all set. And if you're smart you'll use tonight to catch up on sleep."

She whirled round. "You aren't leaving me here! Alone!"

"With Captain Billy on the bridge, all's well."

"I won't stay. You can't leave me here. It isn't safe."

Dan had reached the end of his rope. "If you can suggest a better place I'll be glad to take you there."

She was silent, but when he turned for the door she sped round to bar his way. "You can't leave me here alone. I'm not safe anywhere without you."

"Nonsense. Miss Sandys lives here summer and winter, comes home at all hours. If she isn't afraid—"

"She is afraid—if what she says and you believe about her sister's death is true!" Lisa's eyes dilated suddenly. She gripped Dan's arm tightly. "Dan, if that's true, can't you see I'm not safe here?"

Dan looked at her levelly. "Why? No one knows Miss Sandys and Mrs. Elway were sisters—except you and me, Lisa."

She bit her lip, turned from him swiftly. As swiftly turned back. Tossing her hat to the bunk beside her purse, she rumpled her hair and smiled up at him gaily. "You don't have to leave immediately, darling. Stay here till I'm used to the place, at least."

He glanced at his watch. "Nine-thirty. And the library closes at ten. I must get back, take Miss Sandys to Dora." As her face clouded again he said quickly. "If I can I'll drive round here later. But I'll hope to find you asleep."

Reluctantly she accepted the key. "Hurry back," she whispered. "I'll wait for you."

Outside the closed door he listened until he heard both lock and bolt fall into place. Captain Billy, he saw as he stood there in the cold silence, was still faithfully pacing his bridge.

"Lisa," he called softly, "if anything disturbs you, go to Captain Billy. Pretend you're a passenger—"

In answer she beat her small fists on the door.

The thin stream of old men was trickling out of the reading room when Dan again entered the library. Miss Sandys, already in hat and coat, was waiting for him, her eyes anxious behind the black wisp of veil.

"Is everything all right?" she asked at once. "Professor McPhail has been here. Looking for his wife—or you, I think."

"He didn't explain why he came?"

"No. No, he only asked a few questions about the evening readers and so on, then went all round the library. As a member of the board, he does that every now and then. But always before he's been so impersonally courteous. To-night he—I can't describe exactly how he looked at me. As if he really saw me for the first time. And knew me—or something about me."

"Does he know where you live?" Dan asked quickly.

"No, I'm sure he wouldn't know that. I'm too unimportant."

Dan smiled to cover his own uneasiness. "Maybe he's just a case of arrested development. Saw tonight for the first time what your mirror sees every day. All set? Let's go."

As Dan drove into the Cumberland garage and killed the engine Dora appeared in the house doorway. Her gray eyes appraised Barbara Sandys briefly before she smiled.

"I shouldn't have rushed Marc off to bed," she told Dan. "He'd have enjoyed meeting you, I know, Miss Sandys. Come in."

But in the hall she left them. "Dan will show you your room when you're ready, my dear. I just came down to heat some milk for my husband." Small worry lines creased between her eyes and she said to Dan, "I hardly know what to do with him. He won't have Dr. Mollner, anyone . . ." Then her face smoothed, and she smiled reassuringly, turned for the kitchen.

Barbara looked after her thoughtfully before accompanying Dan to the living room. In the archway she stopped to gaze about the big, comfortable room.

"Come in," Dan invited, drawing a chair closer to the fire for her. "And don't worry about Dad. He takes illness as a personal insult—"

"I'm not worrying about your father." When Dan didn't notice the slight accent she gave to the last word she added quickly, "I was appreciating this room. It's a long time since I've been in a real home."

Dan waited until she was seated to say gravely, "I've kept my promise, Miss Sandys. And I'm afraid—from your point of view—the result is disappointing. I feel as you do there are many unexplained angles in the deaths of your sister and her husband. But from my experiences today I'm convinced they must remain unexplained. It would be impossible to do anything without the cooperation of the chief of police and/or the district attorney. Both of them—and others I talked with—are firmly opposed even to further mention of the Elway case."

"Your father is a powerful man in Clayton."

"He's adamant too."

"Why?"

"For the same reason they all have. Clayton is a school and college town, Miss Sandys. It turns out students of all kinds as Detroit turns out automobiles. Hundreds of families have moved here to send their children to Clayton schools. Thousands of youngsters come here every year to Clayton College, the Clayton School of Music, private schools, business colleges, and so on and on. Clayton must uphold its reputation as a safe and decent place for decent people. Its economic life depends on that." Dan's voice took on an ironic note. "The larger justice, Miss Sandys, is concerned with the many."

"Then we'll have to do without their help," she told him.

"Without mine too," he started to say.

"Wait. Mr. Cumberland, I know my sister didn't die an accidental death or take her own life. She was murdered! Not for anything she'd done—except to marry Anthony Elway. I know that on December twenty-second, perhaps the last day of her life, she was terrified of some man—"

"Perhaps of her own husband," Dan suggested. "I've been told that after the Wayne River fire she threatened to leave him if he remained in Clayton, and that he—"

"No, no! They were going to leave Clayton together the night of the twenty-second. I saw her for a few minutes late in the—morning. She was so upset she could hardly talk."

"Wasn't it natural for her to be upset—over the Wayne River fire? After the Claytonian—"

"She was shocked, naturally. But it wasn't the fire it-self that frightened her. She was terrified that some man would prevent their leaving."

"And you believe they were stopped? By this man?"

"I don't know what happened. I can't explain why they were found dead in their bedroom—unless, of course, they changed their plan, thought to leave early the morning of the twenty-third. I do know they intended to leave the twenty-second, and that Dolores' mind was entirely on the future. She wasn't thinking of—death. Only of safety."

"When did you last see Anthony Elway?"

"I've never seen him to talk with. He didn't know I was here." She stopped, said firmly, "That's all I can say."

"Why did you come to Clayton? Did your sister send for you?"

"No. I found out where she was, came of my own accord. I wasn't going to let her know I was here if I found her well and happy."

"She wasn't?"

"Dolores loathed Clayton. But she wouldn't leave Anthony. So I found a way to stay here, to help her if she needed me."

Dan made a mental calculation, smiled at the thought of this young sister standing by to help a woman almost twice her age.

That smile stopped Miss Sandys for a moment, then she went on. "Every morning Dolores walked along the river. In summer and fall I did too. When the river froze I skied."

"Always in the morning?" Dan heard himself asking stupidly. He was puzzled by this young woman's frankness on some topics, her complete reticence on others.

To his surprise a crimson flood poured into Miss Sandys's pale face, receded. "That's the way Dolores wanted it."

Hastily Dan turned to a less sensitive subject. "How'd you happen to find your way to Captain Billy's steamboat?"

"Shortly after I arrived last May I saw an advertisement in the *News* for a woman to take care of an old man. I'd managed my father's home since I was sixteen, so I answered it. Mr. Crane—Captain Billy's grandson—was here from Minneapolis to see how his grandfather had weathered the winter. He suspected the man he'd left in charge of the boat had neglected Captain Billy and teased him. The old man was all worked up about mut_ny."

She smiled a little. "Captain Billy's really a darling. All he needs is someone to see he has the proper food and clothing, and he's happy. Perhaps not happy, but alive, interested. He loves that old boat as if it were a person, and the river—"

"No wonder Mr. Crane took you on." Dan smiled.

She looked up impatiently. "That's enough about me, isn't it?"

"Not half enough. What are you going to do now—that there's no reason for you to remain in Clayton?"

"I'm staying until you find the man who killed my sister."

"But—"

She leaned forward, said slowly, "Isn't it time for you to explain, Mr. Cumberland, what connection you have with my sister's death?"

Dan was speechless for a moment. "You aren't serious!"

"Very serious. I found you on the river lying on your face. But according to the *News* your doctor said you were suffering from a blow on the back of the head. Perhaps I'm wrong—trying to tie too many things together. But when I remember meeting you in front of my sister's home on Christmas Eve, then watching you as you listened so closely to what was said at the inquest—well, what happened to you looks to me as though someone tried to kill you too!"

TUESDAY NIGHT, JANUARY 13

Dan hid his admiration, amusement, and interest. This quiet young woman was much more resourceful and alert than he had suspected. Much more tenacious than any woman, young or old, he'd encountered in the valley. But aloud he said coolly, "That's odd, isn't it, when the Janssons found me lying on my back? They told my family that and also said you'd found me that way."

"That's true." If she felt his distrust she gave no sign. "I didn't think it necessary to tell the Janssons anything. All I wanted of them was to take you home. But I found you lying face down. As I didn't want to move you any more than I had to, I spread my cape on the ice beside you, turned you over on it, and folded it around you."

She stopped the words on his lips with a gesture. "You can believe me or not, as you wish. But you should know this. You were just a short distance beyond the bend when you fell. I saw you fall—forward. And I saw something else. Someone else, I mean. Just for an instant. It was quite dark and I couldn't see clearly."

"You mean you couldn't tell whether it was a man or a woman?"

She nodded. "I didn't know, of course, until I turned you over that the man on the ice was you. And I thought the man on the bank—or the woman—was a friend, that

181

he'd come down to help. But he didn't. He looked down, turned away, disappeared."

"Disappeared? Just like that?"

"When you fell I lengthened my strokes to reach you as soon as I could. That brought me directly under the bank. I couldn't see up and over, it as I could at a distance. When no one came down I thought he'd gone for help. After I'd done what I could for you I even waited, expecting to hear voices on the ridge. When I heard nothing I ran across the river and up the hill to the Janssons'."

"Why cross the river—with Skyview Parkway lined with homes?"

"The other bank is lower and has an ice road along it," she said simply. "Ice-cutting crews use it all winter. And a car can come down there easily. I didn't know how badly you were hurt—there wasn't much blood—but I didn't think being carried up that Skyview ridge in a blanket or over someone's shoulder would be very good for you."

"You think quickly, Miss Sandys."

Faint color showed in her cheeks again but she said steadily, "You suspect me of thinking quickly now? I don't need to tell more than the truth. When the Janssons had gone I climbed the bank to see what caused you to fall. I could find no reason for you to trip or stumble. You'd evidently been watching your way, for a few steps behind where you went down there was a break filled with snow—"

"Good Lord, Barbara! If you suspected someone of knocking me over the head, why didn't you drive back with the Janssons? At least skip for home as fast as your skis could carry you!" Dan threw up his hands angrily.

"But I never dreamed of such a thing at the time. I hoped the Janssons would get you home quickly, before your friend started back with help." She stopped, said softly, "Thank you for calling me Barbara. It makes me feel you trust me, even if you can't believe what I tell you right now."

Dan rose to stir up the fire. "You must forgive me if I'm wrong," he said when he straightened. "It's my nature, unfortunately, to test every word I hear, especially every woman's word. It was almost dark as I walked along that river bank. And so still it was uncanny. It even infected me with a feeling that I wasn't alone down there. Isn't it possible you may have imagined you saw a man on the bank above me or have been misled by a tree?"

"No. I've skied up and down the river there almost every day."

Dan shook his head. "I know that river bank too. It would have been impossible for anyone to come up behind me without my knowing it. Even more impossible for anyone to push me."

"I don't believe anyone did. I think you were struck in the back of the head by a chunk of ice."

"That's possible. Those trees were loaded with snow and ice. A piece may have been on the verge of falling, needed only the vibration of my passing—"

She pressed her lips together, said no more. He smiled ruefully. "I'm trying to talk us both out of your idea that someone was responsible for my fall. Because I'm sure it had nothing whatever to do with the death of your sister."

"And you're trying to talk me out of believing her death was no accident, aren't you?"

"Certainly I am. Do you realize, Barbara, this description you've given of my falling on my face is the first concrete statement you've made? You've repeated over and over that your sister was murdered. You've said she was afraid of someone, hoped to leave Clayton with her husband to escape some threat that hung over them. How far would you—we—get using that sort of argument on either Brierson or Chief Wilson?"

"What more do you need to know?"

"What more! Well, I'd say hardheaded men like the D.A. and the chief would appreciate a suggestion about the man you suspect of being guilty."

She pulled herself together for another effort. "I can think of no one—except Mr. Carston. And I have nothing to prove what I suspect about him. I told you Dolores was afraid of him. And you've seen for yourself how he's changed since the Wayne River, Hotel fire. I used to walk past the Wayne River almost every evening on my way to the library. Usually he was in the lobby or behind the desk. A jolly, round little man, always smiling and joking. Now he's a wreck. And he was manager of both hotels when they burned. I've wondered if he were responsible for the fires somehow. If Anthony found out and he—Mr. Carston—had to—"

"Climb into that basement at 355 Penndale, turn on the gas to insure his own safety?"

"He wouldn't have to break in. He could have gone down to Penndale to see Anthony about something—"

Dan left her suddenly, to pace restlessly about the room. He came back to say, "I've a hunch also about Jack. What I've seen of him in the past day or two is one of the reasons why I did what I did for you today. He's a wreck of a man, as you say. Two fires, the deaths of Mr. and Mrs. Elway, whom he admired tremendously, and now his wife and children leaving him, are enough to break a stronger man than he. But once or twice I've thought he isn't as far gone as he pretends to be. He sits for hours in the Harrison bar—over a single drink. He shambles around town, into all sorts of places he's never been before. My guess is he's putting on an act. That he knows more about those fires than he's said. Perhaps more about the deaths of your sister and her husband too."

"That's almost the same thing I said."

"Not at all. But we'll leave Jack Carston till we find him. What else do you know or suspect?"

"I can make a concrete statement about Bruno."

"Bruno? You don't mean the dog?"

"Of course I mean the dog."

Dan whistled. "Well, where is it? What happened to it?"

"I have him. On the steamboat."

"And what is your concrete statement about Bruno?"

"He was fat and shining when he came to me. Doesn't that suggest someone must have fed him every day—of those thirteen days? To keep him quiet. Postpone discovery. A dog locked up for almost two weeks without food or water would be thin and weak."

Dan turned on her suddenly. "You called police headquarters on Christmas Eve!" When she nodded he added, "And you were the George Matteson who called again on January fourth?"

"I called them Christmas Eve about an hour before I met you. I was waiting around there for someone to come. But the police did nothing and you'd do nothing. Every day after that I called Mr. Carston in the Harrison to ask for Anthony, but he was always so sure Anthony was in Chicago or New York and he always had such good explanations that I was fooled. Finally I couldn't stand the suspense any longer. I had to know. And I thought if a neighbor complained to the police they might listen. That's why I said I was Mrs. George Matteson. But by that time I was so angry and worried I was hardly articulate. The policeman who answered the phone didn't hear the 'Mrs.'"

"Now we're getting somewhere. Your sister had told you on December twenty-second that she and her husband expected to leave Clayton that evening. I didn't see their home that night or the next, but on Christmas Eve it gave every evidence that no one was inside. Why then should you have been so angry and worried?"

"Bruno was in the garage. I could hear him, and I knew Dolores would never leave him."

"What kind of dog is Bruno?" Dan asked irrelevantly.

"A dachshund. And adorable. He loves Captain Billy and the captain loves him. They're together every minute the captain's awake."

Dan returned to his chair, to fix inscrutable eyes on the fire. Barbara watched him with increasing misgiving. "Say it," she urged finally. "You don't believe in Bruno either."

"No." He turned round. "For several reasons. Want them all?"

"Every one."

"All right. One: in the Elway garage were neither bed nor water nor any sign of any kind that a dog had spent five minutes there. Two: during all those thirteen days no neighbor heard a dog barking or whining; none of them knew of a dog belonging to the Elways. The police heard and saw nothing of a dog. Carston never mentioned a dog. And you've said he visited Penndale several nights. Why didn't he report it? You are the only one who heard the dog in the garage, Barbara, and the only one who telephoned the police. Ergo, no dog."

"It doesn't matter anyway," she said calmly. "My mythical beast served his purpose."

"I do believe this, Barbara. You saw or heard something at 355 Penndale that alarmed you, made you suspect foul play. So you concocted the barking dog—"

"Because I knew no one would believe what I actually did—and heard."

"Try me."

"I heard it Monday night, the night of December twenty-second. All day I'd tried to do as Dolores said: stay home, wait for word from her. And I did go straight home from the library that night. But I couldn't settle down to anything and I knew I wouldn't sleep. I don't know exactly

what time I left the steamboat, but it must have been close
to twelve-thirty. I walked down Fulton to Penndale, thinking what a fool I was. The house was dark when I reached
it, and I thought they'd gone. Then I heard a sound in
their garage. The sound of an engine running."

"Engine! You mean the engine of their car? You're sure?"

"Of course I'm sure. The garage doors aren't twenty
feet from the sidewalk. I could hear it clearly. Though it
wasn't loud. A low hum, more like a vibration. I thought
Dolores and Anthony were in there, just on the point of
leaving. It was frightfully cold, but if the street hadn't
been so open I'd have waited to see them go."

She stopped to look at him questioningly.

"Go on." There was no question of his interest and belief now.

"On the opposite side of the street, a short distance
beyond their house, a car was parked, facing me. A man
was sitting in it, behind the wheel, smoking a cigarette.
Waiting for someone, I thought. I was afraid if I stopped
I'd call attention to the house. So I walked on round to
Skyview, took the short cut across Fremont to Radisson
and back to the steamboat."

"What time was it when you got back?"

"After one."

"Then you must have reached your sister's home about
one o'clock or a few minutes before." Dan's anger rose
again. "How old are you?" he demanded.

"Twenty—twenty-four." She smiled. "Clayton's all you
say it is. Safe and decent. Shall I go on?"

"Don't tell me there's more!"

"I warned you, you wouldn't believe the truth. I can
hardly believe it myself. I'm not sure now why I did what
I did. I think I was numb with worry about Dolores to
begin with. And I was so helplessly alone. I didn't have
anyone to go to for help or advice. If I had had someone,

I couldn't have told about Dolores and Anthony. And then when I reached my cabin that night I was numb, too, with cold."

Barbara's voice, already dry with fatigue, grew tremulous. torn between interest and anger at the risk she'd taken, Dan remained silent.

"My mind seemed to thaw out with my body after I'd sat a few minutes in that warm cabin. I remembered then how dark all Penndale had been, except for the street lights on the corners, of course, and they're not too bright. I remembered that not more than one or two houses on the whole street were lighted; none at all in that 300 block. And there hadn't been a sound except the hum of that engine in the garage. . . .

"Then I remembered that car across the street and the man waiting in it. I thought it odd he should be waiting there, with every house dark. Remembering Dolores' fear of some man, I—I think I became a bit hysterical, sitting alone there. I was sure the man in the car was watching their house, waiting for them to come out. That that was why they sat in their car in the dark garage. That they knew he was there, that they were waiting too—"

She stopped again and her hands gripped the chair arms to still their trembling.

"You went back!" Dan accused.

"I went back. I couldn't help myself. The car across the street was gone. There wasn't a soul to be seen anywhere. Not a light anywhere either. But when I reached Dolores' home the—the engine in that garage was still running—"

"Good God! That was the time to have called the police."

"At half past two in the morning? No. If I'd only had brains enough—and courage—to telephone them on my way back to the steamboat the first time. But that second time—I couldn't have told them who I was, why I'd gone down to Penndale twice after midnight. They wouldn't have believed—"

"You're right about that," Dan said, grim again. "Who would? But go on."

"Besides, it was too late." She hesitated, moistened dry lips. "While I stood there, frozen with cold and—uncertainty, the engine stopped. It was then, in that first instant of silence, I think, that I felt—knew—Dolores was dead."

Her voice faded out. She lay back, her face eggshell white.

Dan sprang to his feet. "I'm a brute. Look here, young woman, when did you eat last?"

"I—this morning—I had coffee."

"Then all bets are off. You're going to bed and I'm going to tell Dora you're the gal who saved my life. She'll know just what to do for you."

It was not until he'd delivered Barbara into his mother's now doubly welcoming hands that he remembered Lisa. Wearily he started for the stairs, then raced down them to snatch up the receiver before the telephone's imperative demand could wake Marcus P.

"That you, Cumberland? Dan Cumberland?" a harsh, abrupt voice asked.

This time Dan answered promptly, "Yes, Chief."

"We've found Carston. Thorwaldson's on his way to get you."

"I'll make it snappy," Dan assured him. But as he heard the chief's receiver fall into place his smile faded. That call was too reminiscent of one he had answered before.

To forestall the whoop of the siren he was standing at the curb when the small police car slid to a stop before him.

"Where is he and how is he?" he asked as he folded himself into the empty half of the seat.

"At home. In bed." Thorwaldson's voice was none too pleasant. "Damn it to hell! Didn't the chief tell you? He's dead."

"Jack Carston!"

"Must of been lying there dead when you went out to his house this morning. God! After this, the first thing we do when we get a call is to break down a door somewhere!"

"Not gas—again!"

"Worse. Bad liquor. Plus canned heat. Well, this writes finish, I hope, to Water Street. Now maybe the City Council'll quit stalling. Tear it down."

The policeman's blue eyes turned on his wordless passenger. Dan was gazing straight ahead, his lips set in an ugly line.

In silence they arrived before the unpretentious gray house on Elk Street.

Chief Wilson met Dan in the small front hall, jerked a thumb toward the closed door to the bedroom on his left. "Want to see him?"

"No," Dan told him coldly. "I want to see you. Alone. For two minutes. Then I'm sending a wire to New York."

WEDNESDAY MORNING, JANUARY 14

But it was almost five o'clock before Dan again reached home. He stumbled up the steps, fumbled his way into the house. Too tired for further effort, he threw himself into the first wing chair in the living room, closed his eyes.

Two hours later, through seven o'clock darkness, two bulky shadows crossed the Cumberland porch to set the door chimes ringing.

Dan roused slowly, listened a moment, then groggily made his way to the hall. Before opening the front door he flashed on foyer and porch lights.

They revealed the sternly resolved figure of Professor McPhail. Behind him hovered a large and apprehensive police officer.

"I regret this action is necessary, Dan," the professor announced at once. "You and your father force me to it. This officer has a search warrant, issued by Judge Fleming. He will not use it if you will admit my wife is here and—"

"I can't admit that. Lisa isn't here."

"You force me then—"

"On your own responsibility. Your wife is not in this house."

At a nod from McPhail the policeman reluctantly produced a folded paper.

Dan accepted it, glanced at it, and stepped back to switch on lights in hall and living room. "The downstairs is open to immediate inspection. But my parents don't rise until eight. It would be most unfortunate if my father—"

"I have no desire to intrude on him or your mother. I know my wife is here. In your guest room. Don't attempt to deny it. Will you yourself lead us to that room, or must we find it?"

An anticipatory gleam lighted Dan's dull eyes. "Since you're in a position to insist, I'll lead the way."

He led the way. The professor and patrolman moved closely but silently at his heels. At the head of the stairs Dan turned right, tapped lightly on the first door.

To his surprise it opened at once. Barbara Sandys, fully clothed, even to her hat, stepped into the hall. She gave no sign of seeing Professor McPhail, but her eyes widened on the policeman, turned in startled question to Dan.

"It's all right," he assured her. "Professor McPhail merely wishes to search your room—for Mrs. McPhail." He thrust the door wide open, stepped aside.

Professor McPhail wished nothing of the sort. Against the astrakhan collar of his black topcoat his face was a mottled white. His erect figure appeared on the point of collapse. Uncertainly he lifted a gloved hand, motioned to the policeman to precede him down the stairs. Silently Dan, Barbara at his elbow, followed them.

In the lower hall the professor stopped. When he spoke his sonorous, measured tones had deserted him. "Apologies are futile, Dan. And explanations. I don't believe we have disturbed your parents. Could—may I rely on you to—"

"Keep your intrusion dark?" Dan completed. "If I can rely on you not to repeat it, yes."

The patrolman had already opened the outside door, permitting the wind, carrying small, hard grains of snow on its icy breath, to sweep in. Without another word Professor McPhail turned away.

For a moment Dan remained in the open doorway, watching his shaken retreat across the porch. At the steps, as if fearing his knees would fail him, the professor put out a hand, gripped the policeman's steadying arm.

"And now, young lady," Dan said as he closed the door, "why are you up at this ungodly hour?"

"Why are you?"

"I haven't been to bed."

"I'm worried about Captain Billy. I should never have left him alone. If anything happened—"

She had found her coat, was wrapping it about her as she spoke. "I must go back to the steamboat."

"What sinister influence has 7 a.m. to make everyone distrustful and determined?" Resignedly Dan found his own things. "All right. Let's go."

The green lamps still winked at ladder and doorways on the steamboat to guide them as they descended the path. On the bridge Captain Billy's windows still blazed with light. But as they drew closer they saw that the captain had abandoned his pacing.

Soon they could see him, motionless in a half-open window, overlooking the ship. Motionless in his steady hands, the long barrel of a shotgun caught the light.

"Someone's been on the bridge—or tried to go up there!" Barbara broke into a run.

"Wait! That gun—"

"It isn't loaded. And he can't see very far. But hurry!" Expertly she swung up the ladder, ran across the deck to unlock a door at the rear of the midship structure. Dan looked into a long dark room. Just inside, the green light revealed a heavy black triangle suspended from a chain. Picking up a short iron bar, Barbara tapped off eight bells.

"It's too early," she said breathlessly to Dan, now open-eyed in the doorway. "But perhaps he won't notice. What's he doing now?"

Dan looked up at the bridge. The gun had disappeared. The window was closing.

"Thank heaven! Now he'll get his breakfast, go to bed. But something's alarmed him—"

They sped along the deck to cabin number one. Its door opened readily. But the room was empty, the lamps still burning. On the bunk Lisa's black hat and gloves were the only evidence she had ever been there.

After one glance round Barbara turned and ran forward again, to disappear behind the square white base of the tower. Sick at heart, Dan followed.

From the little forward deck a stairway with handrails led up to the bridge. But they had no need to ascend it.

Lisa lay at its foot, a crumpled little black figure over which the wind had already spread a shimmer of snow crystals. Dan and Barbara had only to look at the twisted head to know she was dead. Overwhelmed with their own responsibility, they gazed at her speechlessly.

Barbara recovered first. "Pick her up," she commanded fiercely. "Take her back to my cabin."

Dan shook his head. "We'll have to leave her there. Call the police."

Ablaze with anger, Barbara turned on him. "And have Captain Billy accused of killing her? Taken away from his steamboat? When it's my fault this happened? I shouldn't have left him. He's sweet and gentle and absolutely harmless. He wouldn't hurt a—a moth."

"I'm to blame," Dan said in savage self-condemnation, "I'll make that clear to Chief Wilson."

Stooping, Barbara lifted Lisa's slight body, turned to carry her round the tower. "Get out of my way!"

"I'll carry her."

Silently they returned to the cabin, laid Lisa on the bunk. Only then did they notice the room was cold.

Barbara placed a hand on the radiator, lifted it quickly. "Why, it's hot—"

"Look!" Dan nodded to the window.

The inner window was shoved up as high as it would go. The storm window was closed but not caught into place by its hooks. As they looked the wind swung it out an inch or two, let it fall back.

"Why would she open that window?" Barbara wondered aloud. "These cold nights all the air she'd want comes in by the ventilator."

"Wait here."

Dan returned to the deck, followed the midship structure round to the window. Everywhere the middle of the deck was clear of snow, but along the rail and, along the house thin drifts were accumulating. The wind played with them, rearranging and smoothing them in new patterns. Nowhere was there anything to suggest why Lisa had opened the window or left the cabin.

Desperately hunting for any sign, Dan stooped to brush aside with his hand the surface snow beneath the window. For a moment he peered steadily at the more firmly packed snow beneath. Then suddenly he scooped it up in both hands to sift it back and forth, blow away the grains, fine and hard as sand.

As suddenly he stood erect, to hold his hands close to the window. A half-dozen grains, more perfectly rounded and larger than snow crystals, shimmered in the light. Seed pearls!

With long strides he returned to the cabin, leaned over the bunk. Gently he drew aside the soft fur collar of Lisa's coat to see, still caught at her throat, though crushed and broken now, the scimitar he had watched her open so dramatically in Mrs. Tolt's Tea-room.

Barbara, watching him silently, drew nearer. "What—why do you look like that?" Horror held her rigid, too, as she glimpsed the ugly bruises on the slender olive throat.

After a time Dan replaced the fur collar, turned away. "I don't know how to look," he said harshly, as if Barbara had just spoken. "How to explain what I know is true. Barbara, Captain Billy didn't throw or push Lisa off those stairs. No fall broke her neck. That open window did it. And human hands."

"Then someone was here! Bruno'd hear and bark. And Captain Billy—he wouldn't leave the bridge, but he'd—oh, why did it have to be last night!"

Dan didn't hear her. He turned to the window, to stand gazing, literally and figuratively, into darkness. Lisa was dead, killed by her own heedlessness and his stupidity, he knew. She'd listened in the car Monday night to every word Barbara had told him, repeated all she'd heard to her husband.

Yesterday afternoon in the restaurant Dan had suspected Lisa of having told or been forced to tell all she'd heard to McPhail; last night in this cabin he'd been sure she had. Yet in his anger—and in his certainty that Clayton wasn't Prague—he'd done nothing to protect her!

Wittingly or not, the professor must have passed on Lisa's tale—until it reached interested ears. And the owner of those ears—had moved to silence Barbara. On the one night she was absent from the steamboat.

Try as he would, he could find no other explanation. Yet no explanation could lighten his own feeling of guilt. Nor his responsibility now for Barbara.

He turned to look about the cabin. "Where's that key? We must get Chief Wilson down here. Don't worry," he said quickly at Barbara's alarm. "He's our only hope, and a good one. He'll know how to handle this. We'll lock this door. And we shouldn't be gone more than ten or fifteen minutes. Just long enough to reach a phone."

But they found no key, nor Lisa's purse, either in the cabin or on the deck.

"Go anyway," Barbara urged. "I'll stay here. It's almost eight. And Captain Billy will put Bruno out before he goes to sleep."

Reluctantly Dan left her. In less than fifteen minutes he was back, to find Barbara, dressed in a warm blue sailor suit and pea jacket, waiting for him at the ladder.

"I found the key and locked the cabin," she greeted him. "Come into the galley. I'll show you where I found it."

The room was brightly lighted now and warm. The long log table from the old steamboat galley still extended down the center of the floor. From many scrubbings, its wood was almost white. Shining pots and pans hung in rows on the rear wall beside a big black range where a coffeepot exuded a welcome fragrance.

But Barbara gave him no time to look. She led him to a small pantry, pointed to its little table. Over it were scattered the compacts, handkerchiefs, match packets, and other trifles he had glimpsed in Lisa's purse. The purse itself, lying on the floor, was recognizable only as a leather shadow. Near by were its torn-out lining and pockets.

The weight within Dan grew heavier as he remembered the long brown envelope he himself had removed from that purse. Slowly he drew it out of the inside pocket of his coat, hearing again Lisa's frightened words.

"For you," she had said. "To read—if anything happens to me."

Now Lisa was dead.

He was reading the four pages of loose writing for the third or fourth time when footsteps sounded on the deck. Barbara opened the galley door. Chief Wilson stepped in.

"For God's sake, Dan," he demanded, "can't you let me sleep, even if you don't need it?"

Dan didn't hear him.

"He just sits there, reading that letter over and over," Barbara murmured.

"What's he want me here for then?" Irascibly the chief walked over, shook Dan's shoulder.

Dan jumped, then, recognizing the chief, hastily thrust the pages into their envelope, the envelope into a pocket.

"You look like a man who's seen a ghost," the older man told him. "Snap out of it. What's wrong here?"

Dan turned for the door, and Chief Wilson, after a glance at Barbara, followed him. In a few minutes they were back, Pete Wilson as silent as Dan. But his eyes brightened on the coffeepot. "We can use that. Drink some," he ordered Dan, "then talk."

As if talking in his sleep, Dan told of his conversation with Lisa in the tea-room, of her determination to leave Clayton, of his idea that Lisa and Barbara change rooms when Lisa's presence in his own home was unwelcome, of the professor's appearance at the Cumberland home, of Barbara's insistence on returning to the steamboat, of what they found and how they explained what they found.

Almost incredulously the chief listened. "If you're trying to say McPhail followed his wife here, killed her, you're out of your mind, Dan. McPhail wouldn't have secured that warrant, invaded your home—to prove he knew nothing about this."

"I didn't say he killed her—or thought she was dead when he reached our house," Dan protested. "But the more I think of his departure now, the surer I feel he feared Lisa was dead when he left," He looked at Barbara. "I'll have to go back to Monday night, tell the chief what happened."

To his surprise she nodded. He told then of meeting Barbara in the library, driving her to the airport, of their talk while Lisa, in the tonneau, listened, of his certainty that later she repeated every word to her husband.

Barbara made no sound, but her face, as he spoke, grew still and her eyes dark with anger. The chief listened carefully, pulling his brows, interrupting frequently to make sure he extracted every detail.

When Dan finished, the two men exchanged a long look on some subject beyond Barbara's knowledge.

Chief Wilson sighed. "Looks as if this clinches it, boy. But it stumps me. We've never had anything like this in Clayton before."

He smoothed his corded hand back and forth over the smooth white wood of the table. "Way I see it," he said at last, "is that everything that's happened is all of one piece. We'll go through the routine, of course, but there ain't no reason to make a public investigation and scandal of Mrs. McPhail's death. When we find who killed the Elways and Carston—"

A smothered gasp from Barbara halted him. She had risen to look from him to Dan in mingled relief and disbelief.

"Sit down, Miss Sandys," the chief advised. "We've no time to talk about them now. What I'm saying is that when we find who killed your sister and Mr. Elway and Jack Carston we ought to know who tried to kill you."

"Me!"

"I think Dan's right. Mrs. McPhail told her husband who you were. He repeated what she'd said. God knows how far the tale went or what was added to it or who it finally reached. But that's the way I see it. No one'd have any reason to want that little Mrs. McPhail dead."

"No?" Dan looked up. "I thought as you do, Chief, when I phoned you. Since then I've read this." He drew the brown envelope again from his pocket. "Lisa herself wrote this yesterday. To save time I'd better read it aloud. Her writing isn't—"

"It'll have to wait." Chief Wilson rose. "Thorwaldson's in a police car up the hill. We'll leave him here with Miss Sandys. You and I, Dan, 'll take Mrs. McPhail home in your car. McPhail'll see the light, I'm sure. And Dr. Mollner will help. We'll explain her death as a household accident—women are always falling off ladders or down cellar stairs. And your part will be to see that the *News* does right by her."

WEDNESDAY AFTERNOON, JANUARY 14

A haggard Professor McPhail opened the door of his home, stood aside while Dan carried Lisa into the reception hall. After a few minutes alone with Chief Wilson he welcomed the opportunity to see what the chief called "the light." Dr. Mollner, arriving shortly, helped.

And the local page of the Clayton *News* featured the death of one of the city's most popular and active young matrons. The account of Lisa's fall down the basement stairs of her home that morning, with all the supplementary details of her social, Little Theatre, and sports activities, continued over on the women's page.

It completely overshadowed a brief, compact announcement of the passing of another citizen:

> John E. Carston, ex-manager of the Claytonian and Wayne River hotels, died at his home, 841 Elk Street, early this morning. Death resulted, according to Dr. H. T. Mollner, from an overstrained heart. Survivors include his wife, Clara Tennant Carston, and two children, Betty, 3, and Jack, Jr., 1.

By the time the evening edition reached the streets neither Chief Wilson nor Dan had time or interest to read it. From the McPhail home the chief had gone directly to police headquarters to supervise the investigations into both Carston's and Lisa's deaths. Dan, after dropping in at home to catch up on breakfast, had hurried to the News Building.

Hardly had he carried out Chief Wilson's instructions that the death of Mrs. McPhail should be featured when Toby found him to say that Marcus P. wished to see him in his private office.

Mr. Cumberland greeted his son with a gleam in his eye. "Since you and McPhail are now on such cordial terms, I've a special assignment for you."

He tossed two long mimeographed sheets across the desk. "That arrived in the morning mail. For release next Sunday morning. Dale's going to have a field day with it, of course, from the news angle. But for the editorial page we'll need your expert comment."

Dan shook out the clipped sheets. The first paragraph, however, brought him erect.

> In an effort to assist the people of his own state conquer a perennial enemy of their fields and lawns, a Minnesota professor of chemistry contributed notably to the conquest of Japan. The incendiary bombs which fired and gutted so many square miles of Tokyo, Osaka, and other Nipponese industrial centers in the closing weeks of the war derive directly, the chemical warfare service now reveals, from this Midwest scientist's experiments to find a solution to the quack grass pest.
>
> For many years Professor Terence Girard McPhail, head of the chemistry department at Clayton College, Clayton, Minnesota, has been conducting a personal war against quack

grass. He fought the plaguey weed with every known device and every inflammable material. When neither devices nor materials proved sufficiently effective and economical, as well as safe and simple for a layman to operate, Professor McPhail turned to a combination of his own. The result was a whitish, powder-like mixture that could be applied to a single plant or spread over wide areas.

Most ingenious feature of the mixture, from the point of view of farmer and home gardener, is the fact that the concoction responds to heat of any kind above a certain degree. Thus the farmer, after scattering the weed destroyer over infested acres, could lean back, assured that the first hot sun would complete his task for him.

Ignited, the mixture burns furiously for a few minutes. When the flames die away both the mixture and the quack grass, below and above ground, are consumed.

Samples of Professor McPhail's weed eradicator, submitted to the chemical warfare service shortly after the United States entered World War II, resulted in the development of a small incendiary bomb. Thousands of these bombs were released over strategic industrial and military areas in Japan. Men of the B-29s responsible for their distribution reported that after each mission they left their targets in a sea of flames.

There was more, much more, about the technical construction of the bombs and about Professor Terence Girard McPhail, but Dan stopped there.

"You'll get the editorial, Dad," he said gravely, "right now. But I'm afraid it won't mean much to McPhail. Lisa died this morning."

At two o'clock Chief Wilson and Dan climbed the ladder to the steamboat deck. From then on, while Captain Billy's sleek brown dachshund slept contentedly at Barbara's feet, they sat about the long table in the galley, pooling what they knew of the Elway deaths, of Carston's and Lisa's.

Yet two hours later they were no further ahead than when they began. Because of the thirteen-day time lapse in the Elway case and both Forester's and McPhail's unwillingness to state that death had occurred more than three or four days before discovery of the bodies, it was impossible to check alibis. Besides, as the chief pointed out, who were the suspects? Carston? He was dead. And obviously not by his own hand. But where he died and who had burned his mouth and throat, forcing jellied alcohol and raw liquor on him, remained to be discovered.

"Point out just one other person who has any connection with the Elways," he challenged. "The employees of the Claytonian and Wayne River hotels? They hardly knew Elway. They were responsible to Carston. Judson, owner of the house they rented for a year? The Mattesons, Bradys, Franklins, or any of the rest of the Elway neighbors? We've checked them all. None had more than a speaking acquaintance with them."

The chief dismissed that group with a gesture. "Who else? Only the witnesses at the inquest, the jury, the coroner and district attorney. Brierson, Brownell, McPhail, and Judson had met Elway, talked with him once or twice, no more. Forester, Thorwaldson, Mollner, and Moorehead didn't even know him. Of them all, only Judson had met Mrs. Elway. That brings us back to Carston. He knew them both, had known them for three years. Something could have occurred in that time to rouse his fear or hatred of Elway. But if he's the man we want, then who killed him?"

"How do you know he was killed?" Barbara asked with an edge in her voice. "You both say his death was no accident and expect me to believe you. Yet when I said the same thing about my sister's death, and Anthony's, you wanted me to prove it."

"We know Jack's death was no accident for several reasons," Dan informed her. "One is a copy of that invaluable newspaper, the *Morning News*. Another is a fingerprint—mine—on a hot-water faucet. That will have to satisfy you for the present."

"Let's get on," the chief interrupted. "Except for that fingerprint of yours, Dan, there isn't a sign of one—in the Elway home, or in Carston's, or here on the steamboat. My boys are trained to wear gloves when possible to keep from complicating matters with their prints. Yet someone always forgets. Does a murderer forget these days? Never!"

"But, Mr. Wilson, somewhere there must be something—" Barbara broke off, bit her lip.

The chief turned on her quickly. "Then why not tell us where the Elways came from, where he's lived during the past eight or ten years? The key to the Elway deaths may lie in your hands, Miss Sandys. And their deaths are the key to why Carston died and to the attempt on your own life that resulted in the murder of Mrs. McPhail."

Barbara shook her head stubbornly. "I can't tell you. Too many people who have nothing to do with Clayton and the death of my sister would suffer."

"I'll tell you who the murderer is," Dan said suddenly. "An amateur!"

"Amateur!" the chief scoffed.

"I know, I know. He's got away with four deaths. But the same technique was used in all of them. The Elways died in their own garage of carbon monoxide fumes from their own car, but they were found in their bedroom—"

"You're assuming that," Wilson reminded him.

"For the moment, yes, but the engine Barbara heard running for hours there the night of December twenty-second suggests that and one day we'll prove it. Carston died, heaven knows where, but was found dead at home in his own bed. Lisa McPhail died in Barbara's cabin but was found at the foot of the stairway to the bridge."

"That's true," the chief agreed.

"Whoever is the master mind behind all this has been lucky, that's all," Dan argued. "A man who's killed before—I'm thinking of your idea, Chief, that some Eastern gangster might have followed Elway here—wouldn't risk such complications. Too many chances of being caught between the scene of death and the scene of discovery." He turned to Barbara. "I agree with you. The man responsible for these deaths must be right here in Clayton. No outsider would have remained here a minute after—after he'd settled his score with the Elways."

Wilson dug out his watch. "It's almost five and we've been over everything again and again. If you believe the man responsible is an amateur right here in Clayton, my answer is that this is a town of amateurs when it comes to murder. Looks to me as if we're right back where we started."

Dan hesitated, said determinedly, "I hate to bring up Lisa's letter, again, sir, but I'm sure you're mistaken. One of the men concerned with the inquest not only knew Elway but knew his wife even better. McPhail!"

"Don't say that again," Barbara interrupted. "You've no proof."

"I had proof. You yourself saw me open Lisa's letter, read it not once but three or four times—"

"Produce it then."

"I believe that letter is still on this boat. If it were going to fall out of my pocket, it must have dropped when I put on my coat to carry Lisa—"

"We've searched the boat, the path to your car, and the car too," the chief reminded him wearily. "Only place that remains is the McPhail house. From what you say that letter contains, there's small chance of finding it there."

"Why bother about it?" Barbara asked. "Who'd believe anything she said?"

"Lisa went to the Elway home the morning of December twenty-third," Dan insisted. "I believe that. Her letter was too detailed, written under too great fear, not to be true. Not even Lisa, imaginative and romantic as she was, could have made up out of whole cloth—"

A twinkle appeared in Wilson's tired eyes. "I may swallow a gnat now and again," he said dryly, "but I draw the line at pianos."

"Someone playing Dolores' piano at ten o'clock that morning!" Barbara ridiculed, "Every word she said is unbelievable, but that—that is fantastic! How can you believe anything she'd write when you know she followed us Monday night, listened to what we said, repeated it? She had no scruples at all. And didn't even know she hadn't. All she wanted was adventure, sensation, excitement—and her own way. Oh, I could—for the first time I'm sorry she's dead. I could—"

In her anger Barbara rose to stand over the two men, her eyes blazing first on one, then the other.

"Why don't you take a little walk round the deck, Miss Sandys?" Chief Wilson suggested. "Then try to sleep. No sense in your working yourself up over what we say when there's nothing you can or will do to help us."

Barbara sat down. "I'm not going to leave and let Dan talk you into believing my sister and Professor McPhail were lovers. That they met in that dirty laboratory of his on the river. Dolores was devoted to Anthony, wouldn't leave him—"

"Oh, forget it, Barbara," Dan began irritably, changed his tone. "I'm trying to do what you insisted I do. Find out who killed your sister. And find out before he tries again—to kill you. You promised to help. Yet you refuse to tell us what you know and refuse to accept what Lisa knew—"

He turned back to the chief. "Remember the afternoon I asked to take my mother to the Elway home? Her impression corroborates Lisa. Dora said the house looked as if a stranger, a woman who'd never been in it before, had prepared it for strangers to see. I believe that woman was Lisa. The house was cleaned from bottom to top, and Lisa said she cleaned it, carried away everything, even the soap, that might reveal McPhail's fingerprints. Nothing was said in the *News* about the appearance of the house. Nothing was brought out concerning it at the inquest. McPhail wasn't in the house after the bodies were discovered. How could Lisa have written in such detail if she hadn't been there, cleaned it herself?"

The chief said uncomfortably, "Mrs. McPhail was a little thing. Didn't weigh much more'n a hundred pounds, if that. Would have been mighty hard for her to wade through that deep snow down the ridge, follow the river round to Penndale, and climb the ridge again to be in the Elway home a little after eight. She'd've had to leave her own home in the dark. Doesn't get light these days much before then. And she said she found the back door unlocked, left it that way when she went out. Yet when Thorwaldson got there the place was locked up front and back."

"Imagine her wading back through that, snow with a heavy bag or basket or something filled with all the stuff she said she took away!" Barbara contributed. "That's as impossible as her hearing someone at the piano."

"Not quite," Dan retorted. "She was small but not weak. You should have seen her at tennis or swimming—"

The chief got to his feet, stretched his cramped body, smiled at Dan and Barbara sitting side by side with faces averted. "This is hardly the time or place for—disagreements. We're all trying to accomplish the same thing."

"Why should I believe what he says?" Barbara demanded. "He won't believe what I say about the way he fell from that river bank."

Wilson's brows came together, but he asked quietly, "How did he fall?"

"On his face. And he didn't fall, really. He was hit on the back of the head. Someone threw a chunk of frozen snow and ice—"

"And you can't prove that," Dan accused angrily. "So why bring my tumble into the picture? It's complicated enough as it is."

"Let me judge that, will you, Dan?" Chief Wilson sat down again. "Begin at the beginning, Miss Sandys."

Dan pushed back his chair. "Then if you'll excuse me. I'll be around. . . ."

Barbara waited until he had gone, shutting the galley door behind him with a bang. Then while the chief twitched and pulled at his brows, listened without comment, she told of seeing Dan fall and of the figure she thought she'd seen on the bank above him.

When she finished, the old man sighed, rose again. "You two've stirred up a fine mess of suspicion and trouble—for me and Clayton."

"Don't you believe me either?"

"I'll tell you later." He picked up his heavy, sheepskin-lined coat, struggled into it. "I'm leaving Thorwaldson here with you. He'll see no one bothers you and Captain Billy tonight."

At the door he looked about the darkening deck. "Now where's Dan?"

Dan was not to be found.

Wednesday Night, January 14

In the Cumberland living room Dora made a pretense of reading the evening paper, but her eyes and ears were on her pacing son. Since he had arrived home about half past five he had pendulated back and forth in a straight line between fireplace and front windows. But his unrevealing face told nothing.

Somehow she'd have to stop him before Marcus P. arrived. If two such inflammable bodies as they both had become in the last few weeks met head on, the once serene Cumberland home would burst into flame. As Dan approached again she dropped her paper, put out a hand.

"Darling, sit down. You're ruining our best rug. And me. And if you're leaving tomorrow night we must talk about what you'll need."

"I'm not leaving," Dan informed her without pausing.

Relief and pleasure warmed her face, gave place to anxiety. Rising, she stepped in front of him to bring him to a halt with two firm hands on his arms. "Darling, it'll be wonderful to have you; you don't know how much I want you here. Unless—you're staying because Dr. Mollner thinks you—"

"Dr. Mollner? No, I haven't seen him. I'm not going, that's all. Not for a time, anyway. I wired the *Globe* this morning."

211

"Sit down, dear, please. Here." She drew him down beside her on a divan, her own anxiety submerged in his. "I know you're shocked at Lisa's death—and Jack's, darling. It's dreadful—all these tragic things happening—"

"Don't talk about them, Dora."

"I must, if you're foolish enough to feel you have any responsibility for either one." She added worriedly when he was silent, "Or are blaming Marc or me—"

"Of course not. I blame myself. No one else." He tried to rise but her hand through his arm held him beside her. "Damn this cracked head," he said instead. "I can see now—too late—my thinking's been cracked too. If I'd been thinking straight the other night I'd never have let Jack walk out of that library alone. And yesterday—I'd never have suggested that mad idea of Lisa changing rooms with Barbara—"

And yet, if I hadn't, he thought, not Lisa but Barbara might have been the woman lying at the foot of that stairway to the bridge. Might have been, he tried to assure himself. Barbara Sandys was entirely capable of taking care of herself. Too capable! He'd never met a young woman whose self-sufficiency was so complete and infuriating.

Dora, watching anger rise in him, said quietly, "I did all I could for the guests you brought in and out last night, Dan, but you haven't explained them. Nor about Jack. The paper says almost nothing."

His face closed against her quickly. "Don't ask me, Dora. And forget everything I've said or done lately—"

She racked her brains for something to interest and distract him. When she did hit on an idea her eyes lighted, but she restrained the words with firmly closed lips. Restrained them until she felt Dan's restless, unhappy urge to rise.

"Do you realize, darling," she asked then, "that we haven't been together like this since the afternoon you packed me off to gossip with Brownie? You've been too—absorbed with your own affairs to ask why she was so excited."

Contrite, Dan repressed his impatience, forced himself to respond to her effort for him. "Dora, I'm a heel! Why did you ever give birth to such a son? I'm no pleasure to you—or myself. To anyone." At her expression, he smiled. "All right, Mrs. Bones. Why was Brownie so excited?"

"That's better. Because she'd wangled the most amazing tale from Bob. He was nervous as a cat about having to testify that afternoon at the Elway inquest or he'd never have told her."

"Bob Brownell nervous!" A shadow of his old slow-breaking grin lightened Dan's face. "Nice try, Dora. If you hoped to shock me out of the mental fog I'm in you've certainly succeeded. Now tell me what in heaven made that solid citizen nervous? He talked the whole court into a coma of boredom. Thode diagnosed it as stage fright."

Dora laughed. "Yes, Brownie told me afterward Bob talked so much Thode finally let him go."

"And what brought on his nervous crisis?"

Too late, Dora's conscience woke. "Dan, Brownie swore me to secrecy. Bob would be furious if—"

"Mum's the word," Dan promised lightly.

"Well—one of their meter readers—his name was Everson, I think—was supposed to read the Elway meter before Christmas. And he said he did. He said he read it the morning of December twenty-third. He swore he not only read the meter in the basement but played the piano in the living room! He's—he's an odd character, Brownie said. Crazy about music, And he can play rather well by ear."

She stopped. Dan was gazing at her as if she had two or three heads. "Say that again—about the piano."

Dora's face lighted with pleasure at her success in diverting him. "It's just an impossible tale of course. Not a word of truth in it. But Everson told one of the gas company men he read the meter, then went upstairs and played the piano. And it's true, Brownie says, he did play pianos wherever he could. Some people were amused or interested and made no objection. Mrs. Elway not only let him play hers, he said, but when he came round in November she played for him. The boy wasn't offensive in any way, according to Brownie. He just wanted to play pianos, so he did."

"Did his tale include any mention of gas? That he smelled it?"

"No."

"O.K. And then?"

"Well, this is the really strange thing about it. While playing the piano at the Elways', he said he heard someone upstairs cleaning. He heard water running and swishing and supposed Mrs. Elway was up there. He even played a few minutes longer than usual, hoping she'd come down and play for him again. When she didn't, he went on to the next house."

"How'd he get in? Did he say?"

"Yes, he found the back door on the latch. He simply walked in, and when he went out, thinking that was the way Mrs. Elway wanted it, he left the door as he found it."

"When did he tell all this?"

"Sometime after Christmas, when he was accused of making a curbstone reading, of not going near the house at all. He told his supervisor to call Mrs. Elway, ask her if she hadn't heard him playing. . . . They did call, too, but no one answered, so they sent another reader down. The house was locked—"

"Now I've heard everything." Dan smiled but there was no smile in his concentrated eyes.

"Can you imagine a man like Bob, who takes himself and his work so seriously, being forced to explain that incredible story to a jury and a roomful of spectators?

Even the idea that the boy had played the piano had him paralyzed. He was terrified lest some question bring it out."

"So he testified there'd been no December reading of the Elway meter! That's not funny, Dora. That's perjury."

"No, no. The November reading he knew was correct. But by the time he heard about the piano playing the bodies and the gas had been discovered. He was sure this Everson had made the whole thing up."

"What became of Everson?"

"Oh, they had let him go of course. A week or so before Bob heard all this." Dora turned her head to listen. "Hush about it now. Here's Marc."

It was half past ten when Dan, at a window in his own room, saw the last car pull away from the McPhail home. All evening friends and faculty associates had been calling there.

No more arrived. At eleven he descended the stairs.

A few minutes later he himself stood on the McPhail porch, a firm finger on the bell. After a moment he pressed it again. And again. Then he tried the door. The bronze knob turned under his hand, the door swung inward, and he entered the reception hall, redolent now with the scent of flowers.

The long curtains in the living-room archway were thrown back. He passed between them to look through a series of rooms to another high archway, closed by paneled doors. But he was not interested tonight in harmoniously arranged furnishings. After a quick glance he returned to the reception hall, crossed to the stairs, mounted to the landing.

The door there was closed, but after only an instant's hesitation he opened it, stepped in, and shut it behind him.

He looked straight down the softly lighted room to the round baroque table and the man sitting behind it, chin on chest. Dan shed topcoat and hat on the first chair, was halfway down the room before his arrival was discovered.

The professor rose but did not speak until Dan stopped before the table. His heavy features were set like lead and suggested the color of lead. His brown eyes had a hard glaze.

"Sit down, Dan," he said without offering his hand. "I've been expecting you."

Dan sat down, his eyes veiled but wary. "Why?"

"Why? Who better than you understands the sorrow of losing Lisa?"

Deliberately Dan said, "Lisa meant no more to you than to me—these last years."

The iron-calm eyes became harder still. "You have a reason for being offensive, I suppose."

"I have a reason for speaking the truth. We'll accomplish nothing if you aren't willing to hear it and speak it."

McPhail's lips smiled. "I wasn't aware we were interested in accomplishing anything."

"No? Unless you tell me the truth, Professor, I'm afraid you're going to walk straight into a murder charge."

The professor studied him a moment, raised an eyebrow. "Murder? In Clayton?" When Dan moved to rise he added quickly, "I've heard you were using your talents on the Elway case. You know my connection with it. You know the verdict of the inquest."

Dan settled down again. "I also read Lisa's letter."

"Lisa's letter? She didn't write a hundred words a year."

"I won't debate that with you. It will save time to repeat what she said."

"Why?"

Dan's enameled surface cracked a little. "Because I'm going to complete—if I can—what Lisa tried to do."

"You have," McPhail stated, coldly. "She tried to leave me. You are responsible for her leaving me—all of us—forever."

"We'll discuss that later. Lisa's letter was written yesterday—"

"Why not permit me to read it for myself? I'm literate, if not credulous."

Dan shook his head. "No, I'll quote. Point number one—you and Mrs. Elway not only knew one another but had—"

McPhail smiled. "The incorrigibly romantic Lisa! She overestimated my susceptibilities, saw me falling before every coed who qualified for my chemistry seminars."

"Not so romantic," Dan assured him. "She did not picture you and Mrs. Elway in an aura of moonlight and roses. She named your rendezvous as that corrugated iron pen down on the river bank. That's pure realism, Professor."

"You've seen my laboratory down there?"

"The outside only."

"Then I doubt the existence of this piece of fiction you quote. The moonlight-and-roses atmosphere is—was—Lisa's style."

Dan went on steadily, "Late on the afternoon of December twenty-second you received a telephone call here at your home. You left hastily—for your river laboratory. Lisa, curious, followed you, saw Mrs. Elway hurrying along the old river road. Saw you meet her, talk with her for a few agitated minutes. Then Mrs. Elway hurried away. You returned home, much disturbed, though you made every effort to conceal it. You dressed and, with Lisa, attended the Faculty Club's Christmas party but insisted on leaving early. You arrived home shortly after eleven. Lisa came into the house, and you drove on to your garage. That was the last she saw or heard of you until after three in the morning. When you returned you didn't go to bed. You came here, to this room. At five Lisa, anxious—or curious—came too."

The professor was sitting upright in his chair, his eyes pinned on Dan. "Continue, please," he said as if Dan were a student, reciting.

"Lisa found you in a deplorable condition. Not only wet, cold, and, to use her very realistic word for it, drunk, but so terrified you were doubly incoherent. However, she understood enough to know you'd been in the Elway home, left it, with the Elways dead or dying there alone."

He stopped. McPhail had leaned back, was watching him with a curious concentration.

"Lisa's concern for the Elways was something less than nothing. But she was Mrs. Terence Girard McPhail, and as proud and ambitious for that name as you are yourself. She put you to bed with a sleeping powder or two in you. Then with a flashlight she went down the ridge herself and round to Penndale. She found the Elways' kitchen door unlocked, went in. And she found the Elways in their bedroom, on that morning of December twenty-third, just as Thorwaldson and Judson found them almost two weeks later. . . .

"But that bedroom—the entire house—was far from the orderly home Thorwaldson and Judson—several of us—were to see later. Someone had searched it thoroughly. Lisa was not concerned about that either. Her one idea was to make sure no sign of your presence there could be detected. Even if you hadn't told her she'd have known you'd been there. One of your cigarettes, bent in the middle as you crush them, was lying in an ash tray beside the divan in the living room."

McPhail's chestnut eyes lowered slowly to the tray of bent and dead cigarettes on the table beside him, lifted again to Dan. "That detail I suspect you of improvising since you entered this room. But continue."

"Lisa remained in that house until she had cleaned every surface, gathered up every soiled or perishable article to take away. Just what her reasoning was I don't know. But though she left that house in a condition that would suggest to any good housekeeper a stranger had cleaned it, she did manage to destroy or remove every clue that might have involved you. Or anyone else."

"She wrote all this—herself?" The professor's voice was dry, unrevealing.

"There isn't much more. Her luck was with her as usual. While upstairs, cleaning the bathroom, she heard someone moving about below. Someone who sat down and picked out popular music on the piano for ten minutes or more. She was paralyzed with fright but had the wit to go on making normal cleaning noises. The music stopped and the player left the house."

"That paragraph, I admit, is almost pure Lisa. But the pianist—surely he didn't play banal popular airs. Why not 'Afternoon of a Faun'—Lisa's favorite—or the 'Bolero,' by—" McPhail shifted impatiently. "Let that go. You left Lisa upstairs, with the mysterious musician departing. Naturally I'm all suspense."

"She left the house shortly herself, returned home. She'd made only two mistakes. Lisa must be credited, I'm afraid, with Mrs. Elway's torn nightclothes."

For the first time expression showed in the opaque brown eyes, vanished. McPhail asked, "And the second mistake?"

"It was noon or later when Lisa left the house. The sun was shining. She forgot her flashlight. When she discovered it was missing she was too tired and frightened to go back. You were home most of that afternoon and in the evening guests were here for dinner. But on the morning of the twenty-fourth, when she was preparing for your Christmas Eve party, she opened a drawer in the dining-room buffet. The flashlight she had taken to the Elways' was there! She knew then you had returned to the Elway home, found it. She was terrified herself then, not only for you but of you. That afternoon she telephoned me. That night she begged me to help her leave you and Clayton."

"Yes," Professor McPhail said, "I heard her."

"That's why you watched her so closely, isn't it? And yesterday when she did leave this house you searched till—"

"I found and silenced her?" McPhail leaned forward to say coolly. "I suspected that would be your defense."

WEDNESDAY NIGHT, JANUARY 14

Dan's foot pressed the floor as if braking a car on the brink of collision, but no muscle in his face moved. "My defense? Against what?"

The firm jaw thrust out at him. "Certainly, your defense. Do you think me a fool, Dan, a fatuous fool, blind to the way you and Lisa were together—here in my own home—every time I left Clayton? Do you think I haven't known, almost since the day of your return, that when you left for New York Lisa hoped to go with you? Could anyone who knew her be ignorant of that?"

"Yes."

"Yes! Is that all you can say? You come here tonight to repeat to me this ludicrous statement you say my wife prepared. And expect me to credit your lies as if I were a schoolboy. I have no such statement to quote to you. But I can give you the evidence of the eyes and ears of others who will testify to the truth of what I say."

"Testify?"

"I use the word advisedly. You were not so circumspect as you believed. I might be silent now, however, if you had kept your word with Lisa. You said a moment ago that for the past few years she has meant little to me. That is as false as the rest of your claims. I was devoted to Lisa. My deepest unhappiness has been that she was not similarly devoted to me. That she loved you. But I wanted her to be happy. If not with me, then with you. And I'd reconciled myself to losing her. . . .

"But, like Lisa, I'm proud of my name, the place I hold in Clayton, throughout this state. I'd have agreed to a divorce. I'd have done everything possible to—simplify arrangements for you both. If you'd been willing to cooperate with me in a dignified, adult manner. You not only didn't come to me, you didn't keep your word to Lisa. You fell like the simplest fool for this unknown blonde who, to claim a half million or more in property from the Elway estate, now finds it convenient to reveal she was Mrs. Elway's sister! I won't go into that at this moment. It's sufficient to say that from the hour you met this dubious young woman you no longer wanted Lisa."

"That half-million-dollar angle had escaped me," Dan murmured.

"It did not escape me—and others. And we are simple men, less experienced in opportunism than Mr. Dan Cumberland. Unfortunately you counted your half million or more—without Lisa. And when Lisa wanted something— or thought she did—she never gave up till she had it. She wanted you. And you couldn't talk yourself out of your promise to her. You tried to do it in this room Christmas Eve. You went directly from this room to meet your new infatuation, tell her you'd failed. And to tell her on the very doorstep of the house where the Elways lay dead!"

Though Dan made no move to speak, the professor raised a stern hand. "No, you listen to me now. Do you think no one observed you Monday night in the library, heard you humiliate Lisa, turn openly from her to this woman who calls herself Barbara Sandys? Do you think a dozen eyes weren't on you yesterday in Mrs. Tolt's Tea-Room? Didn't see Lisa in tears as a result of your brutal attempt to rid yourself of her?"

McPhail paused significantly. "And where was I at that very hour? Flying back from Minneapolis. I must have arrived in Clayton shortly after you took Lisa to your home to secure your parents' co-operation in convincing her she could never become a welcome member of the Cumberland hierarchy. Your own father admitted to me—apologized to me—at eight-thirty last night for having denied Lisa was there. . . .

"Lisa left that inhospitable roof with you. Where you took her I don't know. I didn't see her from Tuesday morning when I left for the airport until this morning when you and Chief Wilson brought her back to me, with a tale of finding her dead on Captain Billy's steamboat!"

"Chief Wilson—"

The professor's voice rose sternly in a new accusation. "Do you think to save your own skin by dragging Chief Wilson into this? When all Clayton knows he remains chief of police solely because of the support he receives from your father and the Clayton *News?*"

Dan sat as motionless and inscrutable as the professor had remained while listening to him.

"And where was I yesterday evening, all night long?" McPhail continued. "A dozen people can testify I returned on the six-thirty plane. I drove directly home to find my wife gone—and sufficient clothing missing from her wardrobe to indicate she had left my house deliberately. A dozen others can testify to my inquiries for her at Union Station, the airport, the Harrison Hotel, at the homes of various friends. . . .

"I watched your home, saw you return about ten-thirty with a woman in black in your car. I thought you were bringing Lisa back, perhaps to me. And I waited till midnight for that—happy event. She didn't return. Finally I routed out Brierson, convinced him you again had her secreted under your roof. He in turn persuaded Judge

Fleming to issue a warrant. By that time it was almost three in the morning, but out of consideration for your family I waited for a more seasonable hour to use it. . . .

"What did I find? That I'd been tricked. And Lisa subjected to further humiliation. Your parents wouldn't extend hospitality to my wife. But they accepted this questionable adventuress for whose person and fortune you had formed so quickly so strong an attachment. I trembled then for Lisa's safety. And I had reason. Four hours later you brought me her broken little body and asked me to connive in a lie—to save yourself."

The voice, sonorous now and dramatic, paused. Dan's lips twisted wryly. "You connived," he said.

The professor nodded gravely. "I connived. Yes. And I can continue to connive—if you are reasonable. We're both men of the world, Dan. And, I'm glad to add, as of tonight, both men of standing and honor in this community. I suggest we continue to maintain what you as a journalist I'm sure would call the status quo."

"In short—engage in a horse trade," Dan observed.

"I suggest we reach an agreement. In a few days the first announcements of the service my invention rendered our military forces in Japan will be released to the press. That publicity, I hope, may lead to larger opportunities for a man of my experience and background. It would be most unfortunate if—at that time—there were any shadow on my name. I speak frankly, Dan. For both of us. And may I point out that you have twice as much to lose as I? I alone would suffer under any accusations you might bring against me. Under the more telling ones I can present against you, your father and mother, too, would be involved."

The measured voice mellowed persuasively. "I do not believe for one moment you secured the fairy tale you've retailed to me tonight from any statement Lisa ever wrote.

And I swear I know no more than you how the Elways died. But I cannot disprove—and I know you would not have confronted me with the information if you did not have proof—that I knew both Mr. and Mrs. Elway. I met him—through a service my laboratories were able to render him. I met her through him and found her a most intelligent and charming woman. . . .

"She was lonely—had neither friends nor interest in Clayton. By chance last spring on one of her first walks along the river we met near my laboratory down there. After that she came frequently to watch, sometimes assist in my experiments. But nothing I know of either Mr. or Mrs. Elway would have clarified the mystery of their tragic deaths. Therefore I remained silent. In that silence I ask you—to connive. In return I shall continue to cooperate with you and Chief Wilson on Lisa's death. And her funeral will take place Friday afternoon, as scheduled."

"And if I refuse?"

Professor McPhail shook his head. "You won't refuse. Because in that event I shall charge you, through my lawyer, with the death of my wife."

"Your lawyer, I assume, is Thode Brierson."

"Thode Brierson, one of the cleverest and most resourceful young lawyers in the Middle West. And your equally good enemy, Dan, as I'm sure you realize. He has never forgotten or forgiven the injury you did him twelve years ago."

Dan was silent, turning over in his mind this incredible conversation. It was not so incredible as it appeared, he knew, if Brierson were part of the picture. Big Thode's resourcefulness, never too scrupulous, would know no limit if he could injure Dan Cumberland.

Yet the professor's threat did not impress him as much as the offer to trade silences. McPhail had spoken the truth about one thing: his expectation of higher posts when word of his invention was made public. As it would be throughout the United States on Sunday. And in Clayton specifically, with a page 1 story and supplementary features, pictures, and Dan's own editorial. Silence was vital to the professor's ambition, pride, and prestige.

What was the matter with his own wits? Dan wondered suddenly. Lack of sleep? That blow on the head? Or had his six months of soft living at home loosened his grasp of men and situations? Why hadn't he realized the significance of that chemical warfare release the moment he read it this noon? Knowing McPhail's colossal pride and love of publicity, he should have seen immediately what a weapon it placed in his hands.

He could have avoided this past hour's exchange of accusations, secured whatever information the professor had about the Elway deaths, and by now, perhaps, have been on his way to Chief Wilson.

It wouldn't be so simple now. Not with that threat of Brierson in the background. The last thing he'd ever do would be to give Big Thode any impression that he would yield under pressure.

He looked up. Professor McPhail's eyes were on his wrist watch. Dan glanced at his own. Midnight, lacking a minute or two. Unaccountably the skin on the back of his neck tightened.

The professor looked up, too, to listen. A bell was ringing somewhere. In an instant he was on his feet. "Here's Brierson now," he said, and hurried round the table.

But the footsteps Dan heard shortly on the stairs were neither Brierson's nor one man's. He turned to see Chief Wilson entering the room, two policemen behind him. All three looked cold and weary. From the hand of one of the officers dangled a clumsy, soiled white bundle. At a nod from Wilson he placed it on the floor beside the door.

McPhail surveyed them indignantly. "What does this intrusion mean at this hour, Chief?"

Wilson looked round the room, spied Dan standing beside his chair. "Oh, here you are. I was going to send for you." He nodded to the men. "Wait downstairs. In that hall. Don't let anyone up here."

"And take that filthy thing with you." With displeasure McPhail indicated the bundle.

"It'll be all right where it is," the chief said.

When the police had gone, closing the door behind them, he paused to rid himself of his cumbersome coat, shake free his wet, clinging trouser legs. "Been plowing around in the snow for hours," was his only explanation.

Uninvited, he marched down the room, swung a third chair round to face the table. "Sit down, Dan. Sit down, Professor."

They sat down, but before the chief could speak the bell rang again. A moment later a policeman thrust his head into the room.

"The D.A.'s downstairs, Chief. Wants to come up."

Wilson nodded.

Brierson made an angry entrance. "What's going on here? Why are those policemen downstairs?"

"They came in with me," the chief told him. "I just dropped in to have a talk with the professor here."

Brierson took the chair McPhail had placed beside his own. "I hope you know what you're doing."

"No harm in asking a few questions, is there?"

"At this hour? Well, get them over. As Professor McPhail's attorney, I'd like to hear them too."

Without haste Chief Wilson produced a small, flat tin box from a pocket, placed it on the table. Leisurely he patted his pockets till he found his knife, opened it, and began to pry up the top, which had already been cut part way around.

Motionless, the professor and Brierson watched him. The chief hadn't counted on Brierson's presence, Dan deduced, was stalling for time while he rearranged his plan in coming. Leisurely, too, he drew cigarettes and matches from a pocket.

Suddenly, on the knife tip, the chief lifted out a few grains of grayish white powder, extended the knife toward the professor. "Recognize this stuff?"

McPhail's face turned the color of the powder. "How—where did you get that?"

"So—you know what it is!"

"Nonsense," Brierson broke in sharply. "How can he tell by looking at a few grains across a table this size? Might be anything. Fine ashes, soap powder, dirty flour."

In the silence that followed the scratch of Dan's match crackled.

McPhail leaped to his feet. The chief dropped the knife, turned angrily, blew out the match.

"That stuff's inflammable, I gather." Dan smiled but returned cigarettes and matches to his pocket.

"Guess that answers your questions, Mr. Brierson," Wilson said. "Professor McPhail recognized this stuff all right. Anyway, it won't be a secret much longer. Dan tells me the story of the professor's concoction is to be released in next Sunday's *News.*"

Brierson leaned forward with lively interest. "Congratulations, Professor. It's high time Clayton knew the value of what you've done."

"I'm waiting to hear where Chief Wilson secured that powder," McPhail said coldly.

"Oh, there's plenty more where this came from. Some of it in surprising places. One of 'em's a box Jack Carston left for safety in Chinese Charlie's icebox."

"Carston! How would he get it?" Brierson wanted to know.

"That's what I'm coming to—in a minute." The chief closed his knife, returned it to his pocket, pressed down the raised bit of tin to close the can. "Also in Carston's box was a chunk of plaster, with a clipping from the *News* attached. That clipping describes the Claytonian fire a year ago. And another piece of plaster, with a clipping from the *News* of December twenty-second, telling about the Wayne River fire."

McPhail moved to speak, but Brierson stopped him. "I suggest we hear what the chief has to say, Professor."

"I'm trying to discover how Carston got this powder," the chief told him promptly. "And why he tied it up with bits of plaster from the two burned hotels. No, I'm not interested in hearing about that exactly. I know why he put powder and plaster together. The plaster contains some of this powder. That's why the hotels burned like tinder. No stopping 'em. That's why I was even afraid of Dan's match. This stuff ain't safe near heat or even in a very warm place. Behind that radiator for example, if it was turned on full."

While his listeners sat mesmerized, the chief rose. "I'll just have one of the boys see it don't get too warm now."

No one spoke until he returned, and Wilson gave them no time to speak then.

He said immediately, "You say you don't know how Carston got the stuff, Professor. But your invention's tied up with the destruction of those hotels. And those hotels were owned by Anthony Elway. You supplied the mixture to Elway, Professor."

"Are you prepared to prove that, Chief?" Brierson asked.

"Can the professor disprove it?" the old man countered. They all turned in question. Professor McPhail had sagged in his chair, that strange white look on his face.

A minute passed, perhaps two. When the professor looked up he put out one hand uncertainly to Brierson, but his eyes went straight to the chief's.

"Yes," he said.

WEDNESDAY NIGHT, JANUARY 14

"This has gone far enough." Angrily Brierson shoved back his chair. "You've pulled some funny ones, Chief, but to barge in at midnight on a man who's suffered the shock and loss Professor McPhail has today . . ." He jumped up to lean furiously across the table. "Since he's too courteous to ask you to leave, I'll speak for him. Get out!"

"No, no, T.B.," McPhail protested. "I'm at your service, Chief. That is, if it's necessary to talk further tonight. If not—I am tired."

"Excuse me, Professor." Chief Wilson rose, all apology. "I guess this was a bad time to drop in. It just occurred to me as I came up the ridge, saw your lights—"

"Came up the ridge! From the river?" Brierson exclaimed. "At midnight?"

"Yep. An old man like me." The chief turned to McPhail, who was also gazing at him with unbelieving eyes. "Good night, sir. And if you'll heed my advice, you'll take something to make you sleep. You've had a bad forty-eight hours." He hesitated, asked, "You all alone in this house?"

"Why, yes. That is, at night. During the day we—a man and his wife are here, take care of—the house and me."

"How'd it be then if I left Ben Schurz here, to handle phone calls, anything that might come up while you're asleep?"

McPhail started to protest, then smiled with understanding of the old man's effort to make amends. "If it
wouldn't place too great a strain on the taxpayers, I'd appreciate that immensely, Chief. I—I've been dreading the
night. And the house—without my wife—"

He turned to Brierson, held out his hand. "Thanks for
coming in, T.B. Let me call you tomorrow. . . ."

Brierson glanced irritably from Chief Wilson to Dan,
waiting politely at one side to leave with him. "Good
night," he said abruptly, gripped the professor's hand, and
turned for the door.

The professor offered his hand to Dan. "Good night,
my boy. We'll finish our—chat to our mutual advantage
soon, I hope."

At the door to the landing Dan and the chief caught up
with Brierson. He was examining with puzzled disapproval
the now wet as well as soiled sheet-wrapped bundle on the
floor. When the chief picked it up he asked, "What the
devil've you got there?"

"I don't know yet. But I had the devil of a time finding
it." Without further explanation the chief stepped out on
the landing.

Brierson followed, to brush past him, run down the
stairs. Dan paused to glance back. The professor still stood
behind his table, held erect apparently by hands braced on
its dark surface.

In the reception hall Brierson, already at the door, said,
"Be seein' ya," and was gone. While Wilson talked briefly
somewhere with Ben Schurz, Dan watched the remaining
policeman tighten the knotted corners of the bundle.

"Guess I'd better get this out to the car," the officer
said. "Now it's thawing out, it ain't perfume. Tell the
chief, will you?"

"Good," Wilson said when Dan told him. "I'll have
Foster take it along to headquarters. Then how about me
going home with you for a pot of good strong coffee?"

"Ye gods! Don't you ever sleep?"

"It's just the shank of the evening, boy. And you and I've got to have a talk."

Dan groaned. "O.K. But I can easily restrain my curiosity about why you arrived at McPhail's with that box of fire powder."

"Had to do something to get you out of that house. And I didn't want to talk about that bundle of Mrs. McPhail's we'd found tonight. Only other thing I had was that can."

"Get me out? Why?"

"Lord, do I need coffee," the chief said, and would say no more.

But when they sat before the Cumberland fire, coffee in big cups in hand, coffeepot and man-sized sandwiches on the low table between them, he was in no hurry to begin.

"After our telephone talk—sorry I called you just at dinnertime—I got to thinking about your idea of telling the professor what was in his wife's letter," he began finally. "Seemed to me it was too early for that. We didn't have the proof to back it up. But when I had a chance to call you back you'd already gone. Anything come of your talk with McPhail?"

"A counterattack," Dan admitted, and told of his extraordinary hour with the professor.

"As bad as that, eh?"

Dan shrugged. "Of course the idea that he and Brierson could rig a nasty case against me—if they wanted to go through with it—is grotesque. I didn't take it seriously. The fact that he wanted to bargain proved he didn't have much confidence, either, in getting away with it."

"I wouldn't be too sure of that. The prof's a smart man, and Brierson's smarter. He'd pull every trick he knows, and he knows plenty, if he saw a chance to get both you and me with one shot. Mind telling me what he's really got against you?"

"You know that old story, Chief. Dates back to Thode's senior year at Clayton, my junior year."

"All I remember is you had something to do with his not being able to graduate out there."

"That's part of it. I was business manager of the football team that year and all ablaze while in that exalted position to have Clayton College win the Midwest Conference championship. We had a good chance, too, with Thode—an All-American possibility—at fullback. Came within one game of doing it. Lost that game because Thode didn't play. Just two days before, the sports editor on the *News* nosed out a plot that Thode'd agreed to throw the game for three thousand dollars, offered him by a Twin City betting outfit. That represented only a fraction of what they'd win, but it was enough to put him through law school. . . .

"The sports ed didn't dare print the story—you know Dad's attitude on that sort of thing—so he told me. And I talked out loud. Thode never again donned a suit and had a hard time getting a degree anywhere. He never forgave me, and I still find it difficult to forget the agony I went through to decide which way to lose that championship."

"No, Brierson don't forgive or forget easy."

"So I've heard. What's he got against you?"

The chief demurred, finally confessed, "Guess I walked into that, asking you the same thing. And he's against me for much the same reason. I talked out loud too. But not because I thought I had anything on him. A few years ago in California I learned just by chance our D.A. owned some very good properties there. Wasn't anything wrong with that so far's I could see. So when I came back I opened my fool mouth and congratulated him. Wasn't anyone round, fortunately, for he blew up. Ever since he's been gunning for me—because I'm too old for my job."

"How long ago were you in California?"

"Oh, three, four years ago."

Dan whistled softly. "We'll make a mental note of that, Chief. Now what about Lisa's bundle?"

Wilson sighed gustily. "Finding a white bundle at night in snow is something I don't want to have to do again. Even though I suspected she wouldn't tote it any further than she had to, it took us more'n an hour to locate it. Don't know whether we'll turn up any prints on the stuff or how we're going to prove Mrs. McPhail carted those things out of the Elway house. But anyway we've got 'em. Dawson's packing 'em up now, I guess, to take to Carter in St. Paul. Between 'em, if there's anything to find, they'll find it."

He smiled and his brows smoothed out. "We got one piece of corroboration right there at McPhail's tonight. That is, Ben Schurz found it. While we was all in that study of the professor's Ben went through the house. The prof evidently gets everything ready at night for the next day. And there on a chest of drawers in his room, just like in the Elway bedroom, was spread the same things, and in the same way. If Mrs. McPhail cleaned up that house like she said, then she laid those things out just as she'd seen McPhail do, or as she'd done for him."

"That reminds me, you were a very humble man, Chief, when you left him tonight."

Wilson nodded. "Wasn't I? Left Ben there because I didn't want any more shenanigans tonight."

"Shenanigans?"

"Well, McPhail's got the jitters if you ask me. I thought a night alone, meditating on that box of fire powder, might be too much for him. If he supplied the stuff to Elway and Elway used it to wreck two hotels for their insurance, he's in a bad spot, the professor. Might try to—escape it one way or another."

Dan's eyes on the chief's face grew more and more specu-
lative. "You're pretty cagey for a man who wants to talk
to me," he prodded. "Aren't you going to loosen up? At least
about how you found that box at Chinese Charlie's."

"Owe it to what you said this afternoon about your
own excursion to Water Street and Charlie's friendship for
Carston. I thought your hunch might be right—that Carston was faking his down-and-out condition to make some
sort of hunt of his own. But if he'd found anything there
was nothing in his house or office to prove it. Nothing in
his safety deposit box at the Wayne River Bank, either. So
I moseyed down and had a talk with Charlie after I left
the steamboat."

"And he dug out the box? Just like that?"

"Well, no." Wilson winked. "But Charlie's a reasonable
man. Up to a point. I don't think I dug all he knows out
of him. But I did get the box and sent samples of the stuff
in it to St. Paul on the six-thirty plane, got a preliminary
report on it long distance just about ten minutes before
I arrived at McPhail's. It suggests that Carston was stum-
bling around, too close for comfort, to the truth about
those fires. And about how the Elways died. I didn't mention that last item to McPhail and Brierson. But in Carston's box was a complete story of the Elway case as it
appeared in the *News* from January 5 on. He'd linked up
fires and deaths in his own mind."

"And Jack was right, or he'd be alive today."

Again the chief was silent. Dan prodded again. "Come
on, Chief, what do you really want to talk about?"

The dark eyes searched his face a moment. "That girl.
Young woman, I mean. Barbara Sandys."

"What about—Barbara Sandys?"

"What about her—and you?"

"Nothing about her and me," Dan assured him quickly.
Too quickly. "She saved my life. You know that. And she

demanded payment. Demanded. She didn't ask. She demanded I find the man who killed her sister and Elway.
I wasn't willing to make that payment—at first. Not until
Carston died. Then to her suspicions I added a few of my
own that the Elways didn't die by accident. And I know Jack
died because the Elways died. So now I'm doing what I can
to help find the man Barbara's looking for. That's all."

"Well—if that's all," the chief said dubiously, "I'd like
to talk a little about her then. Don't it strike you as odd
how hell-bent she is to find the murderer of a sister she
don't seem to know much about? We've only got her word
for it that they were sisters, that they met along that river
bank dozens of times. She won't say a word about where
or how the Elways lived before they came to Clayton. She
don't say much of anything but *Find the man who killed
my sister.*' It sort of strikes me she ought to be more—more
concerned about her sister. She ain't shed a tear that I've
seen, expressed a single regret or kind word about this
sister she's so anxious to avenge. What she wants and all
she wants, apparently, is to *find the man.*"

"Oh, that's just a way of speaking. Man or men, man
or woman—"

"That ain't what I mean, and you know it. She's a
mighty resourceful young woman. Comes into a strange
town, lives here since last spring without anyone discovering who she is. And she manages to live in the one place no
one'd be liable to go. What's more, that steamboat's within
easy—almost secret—reach by the river of the Elway home
on Penndale. And she managed to get an evening job, too,
at the library, within two blocks of Elway's hotels."

Dan lighted a cigarette before answering. "You've read
her wrong, Chief. I'm sure of that. She's not had an easy
life, I'd say, has had to learn the hard way how to hide
what she feels and to depend on herself. I don't blame her
for not wanting to reveal who her family is—"

He stopped. The chief was digging an envelope out of a pocket to shake something onto the palm of his hand.

"But she not only don't help us," Wilson pointed out. "She hinders us." He thrust out his hand to Dan's startled gaze. "Ain't that a piece of Mrs. McPhail's letter? Certainly looks like it to me."

Dan picked up the fragment of charred brown paper, nodded slowly, turned it over. "Either of the letter—or the envelope."

"Same thing. Thorwaldson gave that to me tonight. Said after he'd delivered Miss Sandys safely at the library he went back to the boat, took a good look around. In the grate of the big cooking stove in the galley he found it."

"But why?" Dan asked, stymied. "What possible reason—"

"Two possible reasons, I can see. Either Mrs. McPhail wrote something that don't fit in with Miss Sandys' own plans. Or"—the chief rolled a knowing eye at Dan—"or she's jealous."

"Jealous! Of what?" Dan stopped, then grinned. "Wake up, Chief. You're dreaming."

"You're the dreamer, boy." Wilson placed his coffee cup on the table, settled back in his chair. "Now, take a real nap if you like. I'm betting we have a telephone call soon. In the meantime I've got work to do."

From one of his capacious pockets he extracted a small notebook, from another a stubby pencil. As if he were alone, he began to prepare a list of some kind. Two lists.

Dan watched with amused wonder for a moment, then settled back himself, half closed his eyes.

He roused to find a bright-eyed chief shaking his arm. "Wake up, Dan. You've slept more'n an hour. Ben Schurz's just called. McPhail's ready to talk."

WEDNESDAY NIGHT, JANUARY 14

Dan's grogginess left him when, close on Wilson's heels, he again entered the McPhail home. Ben Schurz closed the door behind them, nodded his head warningly toward the stairs. "He was almost ready for bed, Chief, when some guy called him on the phone. Since then he's been in a dither if I ever saw one. Finally asked if I could get you back here."

In the study the chief and Dan found a very changed professor waiting for them. Though now comfortable in dressing gown and slippers, he slumped behind his table, neither dignified, comfortable, nor calm. His eyes, blood-shot in a flushed face, flickered back and forth from Wilson to Dan in a curious sort of desperation. He did not rise. Nor speak. That in itself was significant.

"Well, Professor," the chief prompted when he and Dan were seated, "here we are."

McPhail ran the tip of his tongue about his lips. "I had to see you before I could sleep," he began apologetically. "I'm—I need more than a sedative, Chief. I need help—advice."

"At three o'clock in the morning?" Dan asked. "From us? When your attorney is one of the cleverest, most re-sourceful—"

"Yes. From you both." The professor's flush deepened. "At three o'clock in the morning. I believe this is the hour of the day when a man's physical vitality sags to its lowest point. I know it's the hour when my entire life has reached its nadir."

"You mean it's touched bottom?" Chief Wilson asked soberly.

"Touched bottom, on the very eve of success. I wasn't aware until this afternoon when I agreed to give the *News* an interview tomorrow that word of my invention is to be released Sunday. The chemical warfare service had not informed me. I—I'm much troubled to learn the announcement is to appear at this time."

"Why?" Dan wanted to know.

"I'm a scientist, unversed in the ways of business, totally inexperienced." After making that obscure answer McPhail picked up a cigarette, shredded it nervously as he continued. "I must be realistic about myself. And that will be difficult—for me. As a scientist, a chemist, I am average, no more, perhaps less. But I have a small ability as a showman. And a great and foolish vanity. With my showmanship, I was able to—to create for myself a wider reputation than men of much greater achievement in my field."

"No need to tear yourself apart, Professor," Wilson advised. "We've all got our failings. And as Dan says, it's three o'clock—"

McPhail smiled faintly. "No need to tell you what you both know as well or better than I. The painful fact is that until tonight I did not see myself as you and Dan have seen me, Chief. As a vain and inept man who—whose vanity and ineptitude have led him into abysmal folly."

When his listeners remained impassive he buried his face in his hands. "God help me," he murmured, over and over.

Dan moved impatiently in his chair. The professor dropped his hands, raised his head. "Even my despair is suspect now?"

"Something like that," Dan retorted. "I suggest you get on with whatever you have to say."

McPhail's head jerked back, his whole face flamed. "Very well, I'll get on with it. But I must start with my arrival in Clayton eleven years ago: Still an instructor in chemistry though I was then almost thirty-seven years old. For the twelve years before I came here I'd been an instructor in chemistry. At half a dozen Eastern colleges. But my—my ambition and arrogance always worked against me. I knew when I secured this appointment it was now or never for my future as a scientist, for my life also. . . .

"Clayton College gave me my opportunity. And I worked as I'd never worked before, on my science and myself. In seven years I advanced to head the department. In three years I won my first—social victory. At your expense, Dan, I'm sorry, in one way, to say. But you didn't need Lisa. I did. Part of the bitter cup I drink tonight is that I never acknowledged what I owe to her. . . .

"It was Lisa's efforts to have a garden and lawn at our first small home and her incessant teasing for some chemical to destroy the weeds that started my experiments. As I worked on her problem, and with some success, I became interested in the larger problem of the quack grass pest. Four years ago I hit on a solution—a mixture of various chemicals. As I had worked on it privately, in a little shed at the rear of our garden, I considered the mixture my personal property. So did Lisa. It was her idea to submit samples to the chemical warfare service. The more I ridiculed her the more she insisted. With the results you know."

He leaned back to observe the reaction of his listeners. It was all he could have desired. With growing confidence he continued.

"Chemical warfare took over the formula and of course, as its ingredients were essential to many war materials, it was impossible to secure priorities for the mixture's private manufacture. I had, however, a small quantity on hand, in tins similar to the one you brought here tonight, Chief. I had had it packed in that way to supply various farmers and large-scale gardeners who tested the stuff for me. . . .

"Two or three months later I—I received through an agent an offer for all the mixture I had remaining—about seventy-five cans. The offer was out of all proportion to the stuff's value, and my country was at war. Suspicious, I refused to part with a grain. For that you must accept my word. At the moment I have no other proof."

Again he paused; when no one spoke, went on reluctantly. "I reckoned without Lisa. She had her heart set on owning a home on Skyview. Two weeks later she told me this house was ours. She had begun its purchase with the money offered for my remaining tins of the mixture."

"Mrs. McPhail sold those seventy-five cans without you knowing it?" Wilson asked incredulously.

McPhail nodded. "I admit my carelessness. The cans were locked and padlocked in an old iron chest in the little shed. But to me my refusal to sell ended the matter. It did not occur to me to take further steps to safeguard them. Lisa, however—and quite rightly—considered herself a partner in the enterprise. . . .

"When she told me what she had done I was tremendously distressed, but it was too late then. Again I was negligent, criminally so, perhaps. I did nothing. Until you produced that tin here, Chief, I had not seen one since the day four years ago when I refused that offer."

He stopped, waiting for their comment. But both the chief and Dan continued to look at him expectantly.

Under that pressure the professor added, as if in conclusion, "I wanted to make my position clear—before Sunday."

"And you brought us here at this hour to hear that!" Dan jumped to his feet. "Come on, Chief. We're keeping Professor McPhail from the sleep he can now enjoy with a clear conscience."

Chief Wilson did not move. His black eyes, sharp as needles, bored into the professor's. "You told us just two hours ago you yourself could prove you hadn't supplied that stuff to Elway."

"I give you my word—I did not supply it."

"That ain't good enough. Professor. Who was this—this agent who wanted to buy it?"

"I don't know. I'd never seen the man before. I never saw him again. He said his name was White. Martin White."

"Martin White, eh?" the chief repeated and turned his eyes for a brief moment to meet Dan's. "That ain't good enough either."

"I can tell you nothing more."

"Can't—or won't."

"Believe me, I cannot."

"You mean you've changed your mind? Looks to me like someone's changed it for you, Professor. Someone talk with you since we saw you last?"

"Certainly not." McPhail's indignation was synthetic. "I thought my word would be sufficient—proof."

"You know better than that." Abruptly anger left the chief's harsh voice. He couldn't soften its tones, but he could choose softer words. "You said you wanted our help, Professor. Before we can give it—if we can—we've got to know a lot more'n you've told us. When did you discover Elway was the man who'd bought what was left of your mixture?"

The chestnut eyes fixed on a point above the chief's head. "December twenty-second."

Out of the suddenly tense silence the chief asked carefully, "How'd you find out?"

"From Dol— Mrs. Elway—told me."

"Why?"

"She'd just learned of it herself. She thought I should know."

With each question the chief had leaned further forward. Now he aimed a warning finger at the professor. "Don't make me pull things out of you one question at a time. We want the whole story. Here—or at headquarters."

The assurance McPhail had regained collapsed. "I'll tell you all I know. Though it's all incomprehensible to me now. Like a dream that turned suddenly into a nightmare. Everything was going so well. The incendiary bomb developed from my mixture meant much more than financial wealth to me. I—"

Despairingly he rolled his forehead back and forth in the palm of a braced hand. "I don't know where to begin, how to make you understand—"

"Begin with the Elways."

"I didn't meet them until last March when Mr. Elway was preparing to remodel the Wayne River Hotel. He brought samples of various materials to me at the college laboratories, asked me to make, personally, a comparative analysis of their dyes. The idea interested me and when the tests were completed I took my findings to him myself. To his home on Penndale. There I met his wife."

Realizing the climactic value he'd given that last sentence, McPhail broke off, studied his hands while he made a decision.

When he looked up he said frankly, "I think I loved Dolores from that moment. I'd never seen a woman like her. So striking in appearance, so completely detached and cold in manner and so—so utterly lonely. It was not difficult to understand why. Even in those few minutes—the first and only time I ever saw her and Elway together—I was conscious of an almost visible wall between them. . . .

"I did not see her again until late April, when we met by chance near my laboratory on the river. After that we met there frequently. At first she came merely as a friend. But slowly I learned to know her, and I found her anything but the cold, remote woman she appeared. She never spoke of her life before she came to Clayton, but little by little I discovered she'd developed that iced manner as a protection. . . .

"She loved Elway, God knows why. He was a strange, hard, completely self-contained man. Dolores' tragedy was that he had become involved in some activity she could not countenance. He was one of the ablest hotel managers in the country, she told me, but he preferred to manage—later I learned he actually owned—small hotels in more or less remote sections of the country as a facade for some illegitimate enterprise in which he was engaged with others."

Small drops of perspiration on the professor's forehead gave the only sign, except for an occasional waver in his voice, of the emotion he was repressing as he talked.

"By last October," he went on again, "Dolores'—loyalty to her husband was weakening. She was more willing to listen to my persuasions to leave him. For one reason, because I expected news of my invention to be released any day and by January to have made a most advantageous connection with an industrial laboratory in the East."

Apologetically he looked from the chief to Dan. "I'm taking much too long with my explanation, I realize. I'll do better. Dolores and I agreed to make a new start with the New Year. If by January first Elway would not give up this activity that distressed her so much, she agreed to leave him, return home, secure a divorce."

"What about Lisa?" Dan heard himself ask sharply.

McPhail answered almost as sharply. "As you should know better than anyone else, Dan, Lisa really was wedded to Clayton. I knew she'd leave me the minute I told her I was moving East. And I was prepared to make it possible for her to secure her divorce, remain here comfortably and happily . . ."

His voice faded out. After a moment he said half to himself, "All we had of one another, Dolores and I, were those fugitive hours in my river laboratory."

The chief broke roughly into the professor's reverie. "Mrs. Elway never told you what this crooked sideline of her husband's was?"

McPhail came back reluctantly from his thoughts. "Not until those last minutes I had with her the day after the Wayne River fire, that final day of her life. She telephoned me late that afternoon. She'd never called me before, nor I her. We met when we could. Knowing from that call and her voice that something more than the fire was agitating her, I hastened down the ridge to meet her. She told me then what Elway's real work was. . . .

"He bought small, comparatively new hotels, raised their value with impressive-looking but inexpensive re-modeling, then destroyed them for their insurance. But she told me that merely by the way. She was in deep dis-tress because Elway had promised her when he returned home from the Wayne River fire at five that morning that he was through with the racket—"

"Wasn't that what she wanted?" the chief asked.

"One moment. Elway was through with his 'racket,' as he called it, but not with Clayton. If she'd remain here with him, he swore he'd rebuild both hotels, run them legitimately."

Dan was impatient too. "Then why was she so upset?" he interrupted.

"Because later in the morning Elway saw his partner or partners, told them his decision, and was informed he

couldn't withdraw from their agreement. They even threatened—"

"She say who the partner was—or partners?"

McPhail shook his head. "She—and I—weren't concerned with all that. All I could think or feel was. that
our own plans, all that Dolores and I had visioned for our
future, were lost, that she was leaving me—"

"Leaving?" Chief Wilson repeated. "Aren't you skipping
something?

"Yes. Dolores had come to say good-by. She and Elway
were leaving Clayton that night, she told me. She was going to remain with him. And I would never see her again.
I—there wasn't much time to talk, and she wouldn't listen
to me. She was almost hysterical with happiness and fear,
both at the same time. I—I knew then I'd meant little to
her really. It—it was almost as if she'd never known me.
Elway was all that mattered, his happiness and—safety.
She hardly understood my feeling— at losing her—in her
concern for his life."

Hastily the chief prompted before McPhail could slip
again into reverie, "But you said she told you Elway had
used your mixture, Professor."

"Yes," McPhail said as if the words had traveled a long
way to reach him. "Dolores suggested—warned me really
—to go away, too, for a time. Until the excitement over
the Wayne River died down. Though she said I was—safe.
She said my mixture had been used in the Claytonian re-
modeling and the Wayne River's, but that it was impossible to prove that either fire had been set. . . .

"It's difficult to explain," he said helplessly. "We
weren't talking about hotels and fires and mixtures. Only
about ourselves. And she—in those last moments I had
with her—she seemed to hold me responsible in some way
for the trouble Elway was having with his partner. It was

because my mixture made detection impossible that this man insisted on using it in a new hotel Elway'd bought in Iowa somewhere. I—I didn't comprehend fully all she'd said until she was gone. Gone! The last time I saw Dolores she was hurrying away from me—back to Elway."

"You saw her again that night," Wilson stated flatly. "We know you were in the Elway house."

"I saw her again that night," McPhail parroted dully, "but she was dead—beside her husband."

"Where?" Dan asked.

"In their car—in their garage."

WEDNESDAY NIGHT, JANUARY 14

"Wait a minute," the chief interrupted. "You want a drink or anything, Professor? Talking's dry work. And I want you to tell what you saw and did in the Elway home from the beginning."

"Thank you, no." McPhail's voice rasped but he shook his head. "I'm as anxious as you are, Chief, to tell my sorry tale, end the suspense that has tortured me."

"Wasn't necessary to torture yourself. If you'd told me all this three weeks ago you'd've saved us all a lot of grief. Saved your own wife's life, maybe."

"Saved acting the clown at that inquest, saved making a mockery of Dolores . . ." The professor's bitterness sprayed over them for a moment, then he raised a shaking hand. "Don't. . . . I can't go on if I think about what I've done to my own life and others."

"Start talking," Dan said savagely, thinking of Jack Carston. And Lisa.

The professor looked at him, began quickly. "I was out of my mind with grief and worry for Dolores' going. But I had to return home, attend with Lisa the Faculty Club's Christmas dinner party. It was eleven o'clock before I could get her home. Then just as I was, in dinner clothes, I went down the ridge and round to Penndale. I don't know what I intended to do. Simply verify, I think, that Dolores had gone. . . .

"I came up the ridge behind their house. I could see no lights; I thought they'd gone. But as I moved closer, keeping in the shadow of the hedge, I heard a motor running. In the garage. I stood there, thinking to hear Dolores go even if I could not see her. But the motor continued to run. That was all I could hear. . . .

"It seemed to me I'd listened to it for an hour though it may have been only a few minutes, I grew uneasy, alarmed—remembering Dolores' fear that some man might try to prevent their departure. I—I am not a brave man. I didn't know what to do. But I did move closer until I could turn my flashlight for a moment on the house. The rear garage door was closed, of course, but when my light moved on I saw that the kitchen door was open. Wide open. Then I knew something was wrong."

"You went in?" the chief prodded.

"I went in. Into the kitchen. I turned on the lights. I could hear the engine throbbing on my left. I opened the door there—into the garage. Elway's sedan was there, the motor running and—"

"And?" Wilson prodded again.

"In the front seat were Dolores—and her husband. Dead."

"Carbon monoxide?"

"Yes. Though they had used chloroform first. A can lay at Elway's feet, as it had dropped from his hand."

The chief started to speak, stopped, said instead, "Go back. What did you do first?"

"I'd left the back door open and the house door to the garage. I raised the rear door of the garage then. And opened the car door—beside Dolores—"

In the silence a clock somewhere struck four. As if that were a signal, a softer sound came from the windows. The tick-tick of wind-driven snow. Subtly the atmosphere of the study changed. Quieted. Even quieted the professor's forced, rasping tones.

"I don't know how to explain what I did then. I'm sure I had already accepted Dolores' decision as final. That she was dead did not overwhelm me as much as the horror I felt that she should be dead—like that—in that dark garage. Wearing a fur coat and hat. With bags behind her in the tonneau. I knew I should leave her—them—there, call the police. But that meant nothing to me.

"I am not a strong man physically, but at that moment I acquired strength. I lifted Dolores from the car and carried her into the house. I placed her on a couch in the living room, removed her hat and coat. It was then I saw the bruise on her forehead. It—it maddened me. I—I thought Elway had struck her when she discovered what he intended to do. And I determined that if she had never known peace and understanding with him she should have them in these last minutes with me. . . .

"I had no thought of danger, took no precautions against observation. All I desired was to save Dolores from the degradation of suicide or—murder. I carried her upstairs, laid her on a bed. Not till then did I realize she could not be found like that. Nor Elway in the garage. I went back—for him."

McPhail's voice broke completely. Oblivious of his listeners, he turned away, perhaps to relive in his mind those tragic hours in the Elway home.

Chief Wilson and Dan remained silent, too, carefully silent, lest they rouse him to awareness of them. When the professor turned back he picked up his explanation far in advance of his final words.

"I made her as beautiful as I could, placed her like a queen in that chair. Elway I—I threw on the floor at her feet, prone—where he deserved to be. After a time—I turned out the lights."

He looked up. Consciousness of his listeners returned to his eyes. "I remember going downstairs, sitting in the darkness of the living room, listening, I think, to the throb of that engine in the garage. In my haste or confusion I had forgotten to shut it off. But I could do no more. I was exhausted—of strength, thought, emotion. How long I sat there I don't know. Or how I left that house, returned to my own. I have no memory of coming in here, but Lisa found me here—"

"You knew your wife went to the Elway house after she had helped you to bed?" Chief Wilson asked, gently for him.

"I didn't know that day. I didn't know anything till evening. Lisa had given me something to make me sleep. When I woke, I woke from more than sleep. I remembered how Dolores had died—and Elway. And I was terrified that they had already been discovered. I knew then I had done the worst possible thing. The most superficial examination would reveal they had died of carbon monoxide poisoning, and no evidence of gas would be found in that house, in their bedroom. . . .

"But there was no word of their discovery in the evening paper or on the radio. Again I waited until midnight. Then I went back. The kitchen door was closed but not locked. The rear garage door was still raised. I had thought to turn on the gas in the kitchen range, but remembered then that Dolores had mentioned one day that their water heater was out of order. That Elway would do nothing about it. I went down to the basement, turned on both pilot light and main burner. . . .

"I hadn't intended to do anything else, but in spite of myself I—I went upstairs. My eyes would not believe what I saw there. The room rearranged, Elway's linen just as I arrange mine, on his chest. The beds ripped open. Elway's sleeve . . . Dolores' lovely . . ."

He made a small hopeless gesture. "I understood when I saw a flashlight on the floor beside Dolores' chair. Lisa's! I believed then I had failed in what I'd tried to do for Dolores. I darkened the room, went quickly downstairs. I locked the kitchen door, left the key in the lock, and went out through the garage. I pulled down its rear door, locking it into place too. Then I returned home, by the river road. Out of habit, I suppose, I replaced Lisa's flashlight in a drawer kept for such things. I didn't know what she was going to do, and I felt no concern. I thought then to go to Brierson, take him with me to you, Chief, and tell you all I knew. But—it was late; I decided to wait till morning. . . .

"In the morning Lisa was preparing for our Christmas Eve party as if nothing had happened. I decided again to wait. She did nothing, said nothing. After Christmas I had to fly East for some conferences. I returned January third for the reopening of college, expecting to hear the—the bodies had been found. They had not, and I resolved then to let events take their course. When discovery finally came the next night, I knew how successful I had been. Guilt was placed then on the defective heater. And nothing had been found in the entire house to reveal my presence there. That, I knew, I owed to Lisa."

"You said nothing to her at any time about what she'd done?" the chief asked.

McPhail shook his head. "She had not acted entirely out of concern for me. She was thinking of herself, her own safety. When Dan entered this house Christmas Eve I knew she had sent for him, had some plan. When I listened to her in this room, imploring him to take her away from Clayton, I knew what she intended to do. If Dan had—co-operated, she would have used her knowledge to force me to give her a divorce and almost every dollar I had or ever would have. In return for her silence.

"But I couldn't permit her to leave me. My own position and safety now depended on her remaining my wife, living with me here as—as usual. And I might have succeeded in winning her acceptance, had I not insisted on her accompanying me to the library Monday night. I was afraid to permit her out of my sight. You both know what happened there. You know my alarm when I learned she and Dan had met in the reading room, as if by arrangement. . . .

"She arrived home sometime after one that morning, hysterical with anger against me for involving her in the Elway deaths, and fear of this Barbara Sandys who had appeared so mysteriously as the—avenger of her sister. I had no difficulty in learning what had happened, what she had overheard. We talked almost all night before I could convince her—or thought I had—that our security depended in remaining together. But unfortunately I had to leave yesterday for Chicago. By the time I reached Minneapolis I was so agitated over what she might do, I left my plane, returned home. . . .

"Lisa was gone, but she had left a note. She had written down, she said, all she knew about the Elway deaths. If I tried to force her to return to me—what she said in her melodramatic way was 'if anything happened to her'—she had placed her letter where it could easily be found. I could accept neither her decision nor her threat. I made every effort to find her. Failing, I went to Brierson, told him everything. He agreed we must find Lisa before all else. He sent me home to wait for the warrant and police officer who would accompany me to the Cumberland home."

McPhail sagged back in his chair, gray with fatigue and strain. "The rest you know."

"I wish we did," the chief said grimly. "There seems no bottom to this thing. We'll have to go over your story again and again, Professor."

"My story!" McPhail's voice rose in bitter mockery. "For me—that story ended a month ago. On that December afternoon when Dolores came to say good-by."

Wilson's shaggy black brows came together in a straight line. He glanced at Dan, lowering silently beside him, shook his head, rose stiffly.

"Get some sleep now, Professor. There ain't any help anyone can give you tonight. Except Ben Schurz. He'd see no one bothers you."

He could have saved his breath. McPhail was as unaware of their presence as of their departure.

In the reception hall the chief turned bright, sleepless eyes on Dan. "Think you could stay awake another hour or two, son? It's almost closing time for Chinese Charlie. I'd like to have a final talk with him before his anger at Carston's death wears off and he forgets to remember."

"Sleep?" Dan repeated. "What's that? Wait here. I'll get our car."

A few minutes later, when he opened the house door to the Cumberland garage, he thought he must be walking in his sleep, dreaming of what he saw. The outside doors were open and the car occupied. As he gazed, the engine started and the little light on the board revealed the occupant to be his father.

Alarmed, he raced round the rear of the car, opened the door, and flung himself into the front seat just as the car moved forward.

"What's the matter, Dad? Dora isn't—"

Marcus P. stepped on the brake, turned furiously. "So—here you are! Dora's not had a wink of sleep all night, worrying about you. You left the house without a word of explanation, didn't come back, didn't phone. I was just starting out to look for you."

"The chief and I've had quite a night, with more to come," Dan assured him. "Dad, we've broken the Elway case—or will have in another few hours. We're going down now to Chinese Charlie's. I'm glad you're up. It's time you got in on it."

"Broken the Elway case! What're you talking about? And what's Charlie got to do with it?"

"Plenty. Come along. We'll explain on the way. Wait, I'll tell Dora."

"No. Don't disturb her. I finally persuaded her to take a sleeping capsule."

Dan grinned. "So you're the worry bird, Marcus P. All right. Let's go. We pick up the chief at McPhail's."

But when Marcus P. stopped the car at the end of the long row of parked cars on Radisson he refused to descend the hill with them. "The whole thing's preposterous. Sounds like an old dime novel. I don't want anything to do with it—"

"Park here," Wilson told him calmly. "I need you, Marc. We've been together on too many cases for you to let me down now. The way I feel, this'll be my last one. Clayton's getting too big and complicated for an old man like me."

"Come on, Dad," Dan urged. "I'll buy you one of Charlie's best steaks. This'll be my last chance if this stop winds things up. I'll take the train tonight."

Under their combined persuasions Marcus P. yielded. With the chief still talking of their interview with McPhail, his father still scoffing, Dan slipped and slid beside them through the heavily falling snow to the glare of lights and cacophony of juke boxes and tinny pianos that was Water Street at night.

Chinese Charlie's was crowded with men and women drawn indiscriminately from Clayton's bottom to top drawers. As Charlie bowed and smiled them down the long room, they glimpsed mink coats and trailing skirts, lumber

boots and jackets, overalls and reefers, and every variety of
working and business dress in the cubicles to either side.
Over the entire room hung the rich fragrance of Charlie's
specialties—tenderloin steaks and subgums.

"You my guests, please," the Chinese said, throwing
back the curtain to his own private booth. He stopped a
moment in its doorway to talk with words and gestures to
one of his boys, then entered himself, drew the limp green
curtain, and sat down opposite the chief and Marcus P.

Dan, on the short cross bench at the end of the table,
watched with increasing apprehension. In the glare of the
booth lights both the chief and his father appeared very
old and tired. There was nothing he could have done to
spare Wilson, he knew, but he could have saved his father
this night's anxiety.

He turned as he heard the Chinese repeating, "You my
guests, please. Maybe last time. I think Charlie go home
soon. China need plenty men and money now. You think
good idea, Chief?"

With Chief Wilson he exchanged a long, bargaining
look.

"Very good," Wilson assured him, finally.

"O.K." Charlie's white teeth flashed in a smile. "I tell
you now what you ask last night. Talk no good with food."

In his completely R-less English he told slowly, carefully, of his ten years in Anthony Elway's employ. Lest some
question of theirs stem that flow, his listeners made no
interruption.

Charlie had experienced fourteen fires during those ten
years, he said as impersonally as though mentioning fourteen movies he had witnessed. Until the burning of the
Claytonian all of them had been on a small scale. That
blaze had frightened him with its ferocity. Only after great
inducements had he been persuaded to move to the Wayne
River.

There one day in September he had picked up a bit of fallen plaster, no larger than a pea, in one of the private dining rooms, carried it back to the kitchen, and dropped it in the ash tray on the little table where he had his tea. Later when he smoked a cigarette there he had tossed the lighted match into the tray. Before he could withdraw his hand a flame seared it so deeply the scar still remained. When he looked in the tray the bit of plaster had vanished.

Up to that moment he had not considered Elway's fires any of his concern. Then, remembering the fierce Claytonian flames, he had gone to Carston, announced his intention of leaving at once and taking his boys with him. When Carston was convinced of his determination he had served as Charlie's guarantor for supplies and rent of the building on Water Street and in addition had started down the hill the trickle of town customers that shortly became a nightly stream.

After the Elway deaths were discovered Carston had hounded Charlie until he confessed his reason for leaving the Wayne River. It was then that Carston had adopted the vagabond appearance that enabled him to prowl the ruins of the two hotels and haunt the cheap hostels, restaurants, and, bars on Water Street. Looking for a man named White. Martin White.

"He find him. So he die. But he no die on Watah St'eet," Charlie was declaring solemnly when with a clash of brass hooks the green curtain shoved back.

Wilson and Dan looked up, annoyed, expecting to see Chinese boys with laden trays. Charlie turned with open displeasure to reprimand their rude arrival.

But no Chinese boys filled the narrow doorway. Thode Brierson did. Over his shoulder brash blue eyes smiled into Dan's. James M. Blythe, representing the American Protective Association of Insurance Companies, again had arrived at a strategic moment.

THURSDAY MORNING, JANUARY 15

"Well, gentlemen!" Brierson's smile was humorless. "Sounds as though we should get together. We all appear to be discussing the same subject." Uninvited, he stepped into the booth that Blythe might enter.

"You know Chief Wilson and Dan Cumberland, I believe, Mr. Blythe. And of course you've heard about our famous Chinese Charlie." He stopped as he recognized Marcus P., silent and withdrawn in the far corner. "I'm sorry, Mr. Cumberland. I didn't see you." He introduced Blythe, then slid into the long seat Charlie, after one oblique glance at the newcomers, had vacated.

"Thought you'd departed long ago," Blythe told Dan as they shook hands. "Only learned last night you were still here."

"What brings you back to Clayton?" Dan asked.

"The Chicago office got word of Carston's sudden death. Thought it worth looking into—on my way West." He inserted himself into the seat beside Brierson before adding, "How right they were!"

"Mr. Blythe looked me up when he arrived last night," Brierson explained after a moment's pause. "I brought him up to date on the Elway deaths, Chief, but of course until I listened in on your talk with McPhail last night I knew nothing of their relation to the hotel fires. What I heard sent me back downtown to rout Blythe out of his bed at the Harrison. We've talked ever since. Hungry work. So we came down here for steaks and were just finishing our coffee in the next booth when Charlie's enlightening monologue began in here. We were reluctant to interrupt until he approached a period. I won't apologize, Chief. Our eavesdropping saved you the trouble of repeating all he said."

"That's one way of looking at it," the chief told him gruffly. "You bring Mr. Blythe up to date, too, on McPhail's activities—and his wife's—in the Elway home the nights of December twenty-second and twenty-third?"

Brierson's hooded eyes lifted. "How'd you hear about that? I thought I'd give McPhail a little peace until after his wife's funeral."

"Oh, we went back by request. Heard the whole story. Unless you're holding out on something else, I guess we're all up to date." Wilson fixed his eyes on Blythe. "What do you make of it all?"

"I'm staggered," Blythe confessed. "One of our best men checked that Claytonian fire. I came out myself on the Wayne River, as you know. Couldn't find a thing to question. Neither could your fire chief. Nor one of your most astute minds."

He gave Dan a small, ironic bow. "We paid off on the Claytonian. Were just about to—on the Wayne River. Now—this! And in Clayton of all places. My guess is that when this story breaks it's going to empty some of your best schools."

"It hasn't broken yet," Marcus P. reminded him.

"Thanks to the chief's smart work, Mr. Cumberland. And Brierson's here. You can count on my discretion, of course. If there's anything I can do. And I think I can."

He looked from Marcus P. to Brierson, then leaned toward the chief with a confidential air. "Mr. Brierson's been telling me about this woman who ca.ls herself Barbara Sandys, claims to be Mrs. Elway's sister. Sounds to me as if you had something there, Mr. Wilson. That woman's a rank impostor."

Suddenly Dan found himself disliking the ingratiating Mr. Blythe with an intensity that made him grit his teeth. Through them he challenged, "You know that?"

Blythe's shrewd eyes grew shrewder still. "Well, well, the silent county heard from! Yes, I know that. Dolores Elway had no sisters. I am her only brother."

"Your name Sandys?"

"No, and I'll gamble this woman's isn't either."

Pete Wilson's eyes turned darkly on Brierson. "You knew of Mr. Blythe's relationship to the Elways and didn't produce him for the inquest?"

"Certainly not," Blythe informed him. "Mr. Brierson didn't know until I told him last night. And if you're going to ask next why I didn't show up of my own accord I'll answer that too. The day after Christmas I went South on a new assignment. Last I heard of Dolores and Anthony, they were in the East somewhere."

"You were saying you could prove you and Mrs. Elway were brother and sister," Dan said pointedly.

"Did I say that? I can, of course, though not with anything I have on me. Oh yes, wait. I may have something."

Although the restaurant outside was noisy with the chatter of departing breakfasters, silence in the booth fairly rang while Blythe dug out a tooled leather billfold from a pocket, opened it on the table. From beneath its glassine square he drew out two snapshots, exposing a small square card.

"My family," he said proudly, passing around the first print. "I could expatiate on my wife, Mary, my three boys, *and* the cocker spaniel. But all you need notice now is my wife and the bushes behind her—bridal wreath, I think.

Now look at this one, taken that same day at that same spot. Mary, my honorable self, Dolores beside me, Anthony beside her. These snaps were taken last July fourth when they stopped off in Milwaukee on their way to Wilmington."

When the pictures were returned to him he picked up the billfold, held it out. "Dolores gave me this a year ago. That card was in it and I left it there." He read aloud, "'Merry Christmas and all that to my one and only brother, from Dolores.'"

"That's not conclusive proof of course," Brierson pointed out. "But it's sufficient, I think, Chief, to suggest our next move. A session with this so-called Barbara Sandys."

Dan jumped to his feet. "You take the words out of my mouth."

But Chief Wilson shook his head. "Sit down, Dan. It ain't six o'clock yet. Why don't we eat first? I'll call the station, send someone to bring Miss Sandys and Thorwaldson down here—"

The protest on Dan's lips died as the chief's foot, under cover of the table, made sharp contact with his shin.

A little after seven Barbara appeared in the narrow doorway. Dan jumped up, his eyes approving. The chief rose, too, left the booth, saying, "I'll send Thorwaldson back to headquarters."

In a heavy, dark blue cape, a blue beret tilted over her shining hair, Barbara looked young and alive and fresh even at that dreary hour. As Dan stood back for her to seat herself beside him he tried to force his sleepless eyes to smile reassurance.

Apparently Barbara needed no fortifying. Composedly she opened her cape, crushed her large black purse in her lap, looked questioningly round the table. As neither Brierson, Blythe, nor his father had risen on her entrance,

Dan, angry, made no introductions. They sat in silence until Chief Wilson returned, drew the curtain across the doorway, seated himself beside Blythe.

Although his voice revealed nothing of it, Blythe's eyes appreciated Barbara too. "Looks like it's up to me," he told her, "to begin the fireworks. Miss—er—Sandys, my name's Blythe. James M. Blythe, of the American Protective Association of Insurance Companies. The gentleman on my right is Mr. Thode Brierson, district attorney of Clayton County. I assume you know the others."

Her gray eyes moved gravely from face to face. "All but Mr. Cumberland, and I know who he is of course."

Dan's glance followed hers to pause on his father. Marcus P. might have been asleep for all the interest he evinced in either the people about him or what they were saying. Impatiently Dan turned back to Blythe. Marcus P., he thought, would have to face this thing, publish the facts, no matter how it damned Clayton's spotless reputation.

"Difficult as it is," Blythe was saying, "we suspect, Miss—uh—Sandys, you're not the charming young woman you appear to be. We're all very much interested to hear why you came to Clayton, remained incognito and practically invisible until Mr. and Mrs. Elway died, then suddenly came forward to claim Mrs. Elway as a sister."

If Barbara were disconcerted she concealed it admirably. "It is not true that I came forward—in the sense of making that knowledge public, Mr. Blythe. I told Mr. Cumberland—Dan Cumberland—in confidence that Mrs. Elway was my sister. I told no one else, did not intend to tell anyone else. And I told him because I wanted to secure his aid in discovering the murderer of the Elways. As for Mrs. Elway, I never knew her, though I had seen her often."

As both Dan and the chief moved to speak she said quickly, "You're thinking about my conversations with her? I had none. The only one I ever quoted accurately was the last one. That wasn't with me. I'm afraid I listened in on her last meeting with Professor McPhail. I followed her round the river on my skis. They stood just above me on the river bank—"

She turned back to Blythe. "My name is Barbara Emmett. If you require credentials I have them in my purse."

Mr. Blythe required no credentials. He sat rigid in his place, his eyes wide open and blank with shock.

"Why are you here?" he managed finally.

"You know why."

"How long have you—known?"

"Since the Claytonian burned."

"What goes on, Blythe?" Brierson demanded. "Who is this woman?"

"I'll answer that, Mr. Brierson," Barbara said. "I'm a confidential assistant to Mr. Jerome Payne, president of the American Protective Association."

"What's that mean? A detective?"

"A confidential investigator for Mr. Payne. When our regular investigators need special assistance. Or—succumb to the richer if less orthodox opportunities the insurance field offers."

Brierson turned on Blythe. "And you accept her unconfirmed claim as Cumberland accepted her claim to be Mrs. Elway's sister?" When Blythe remained voiceless he held out his hand. "I'd like to see those credentials."

He studied the card in the small black leather case she produced at once, compared, feature by feature, her face with that of the young woman in the photograph. Then, after reading carefully the descriptive details beside it, passed the folder across the table to Chief Wilson.

Dan leaned over to look and read, too, turning a wicked eye on Barbara. "'Age: 32,'" he quoted.

Her color rose quickly. "I told you twenty-four—that was as low as I dared go—to account for—explain—some of the very strange things I said and did. I hoped you'd think I was just a young thing, in need of aid. But I've been with Mr. Payne since I was twenty-four, the last five years as one of his assistants."

"We'll check further, naturally," Brierson informed her. "In the meantime, Miss Emmett, we'd like to hear what you have to say."

"What I have to say is very simple, really. For some years Mr. Payne's been concerned about fires on small hotel properties, insured with our companies, in different parts of the Midwest and South. Careful investigation revealed no evidence that any of them had been inspired. And until the Claytonian burned the amounts were small, usually covering partial damage only. . . .

"The Claytonian's total destruction and the value of its insurance showed no resemblance to this series of suspect fires, but the circumstances under which it occurred had the same—plausibility. Accidental fires, Mr. Brierson, don't take such complete advantage of every physical and personal condition, in their communities."

"You sound like a textbook," Dan commented. "What's that mean?"

"It means that fire can break out right next door to a fully equipped and manned fire station. Or at any hour of the day or night. At any season, in any temperature. The Claytonian and Wayne River fires took advantage of every condition. Twenty-below-zero weather. Inadequate fire equipment and reduced and inexperienced forces. Frozen hydrants. Many other things. Their betraying factors—as in all the suspect fires—were their perfection and logic."

"And Clayton isn't Prague!" Dan murmured for the benefit of Marcus P., but when Barbara look puzzled he said quickly, "Do go on, Miss Emmett."

Her color showed again, but she went on. "The Clay-tonian fire was so successful and on such a tremendously enlarged scale—from the point of view of the beneficia-ries—that Mr. Payne felt sure it would be repeated. Per-haps in Clayton, perhaps elsewhere in this somewhat iso-lated valley. I was sent here last spring to learn all I could about a great many things and people. To anticipate if possible, if not, to be on hand for the next one. I was on hand when the Wayne River burned."

"Very interesting," Brierson commented. "And you have been reporting regularly to Mr. Payne?"

"Certainly."

Dan's eyes narrowed. He knew now where Lisa's letter had gone!

"What do you intend to do now?" Brierson asked.

"First I'm going to ask Chief Wilson to send for Char-lie Wong."

"You know him?"

"Charlie himself, no. Who does? But I know what he knows about these fires."

Fortunately the Chinese appeared almost at once. The pressure within the small booth threatened to burst its walls.

Charlie halted in the doorway, his long eyes flickering darkly from one intent face to the other, paused on Bar-bara's.

"Come in, Mr. Wong," she invited. "You know Chief Wilson, Mr. Cumberland, Mr. Dan Cumberland, and Mr. Brierson by those names, don't you?"

He nodded.

"By what name do you know the fifth man in this booth?"

Charlie smiled politely at the tall man leaning back in his corner, smoking. "Mistuh White. Mah-tin White."

"You've seen him before?"

"Many times. Many cities."

"And here in Clayton?"

"In Clayton sometimes he live on Watah St'eet. Last two weeks he live on Watah St'eet. Big Joe's Place."

Blythe smiled. "You'll have to do better than that, Charlie. Mr. Brierson here knows I arrived last night—by train."

Barbara's hand emerged from her purse, holding several snapshots. "Who is the man in these pictures, Mr. Wong?"

He glanced at each one with sliding eyes. "Mistah White. That way he look when he live on Watah St'eet. I take those pictuahs."

Dan glanced at the uppermost print as Barbara passed them to Chief Wilson, turned to Charlie. "Is this the tall thin man who followed me, watched me, the day I came down here looking for Carston?"

"All same man." Charlie hesitated, added, "He d'ess difflunt, walk difflunt, but all same man."

"That's all for now, Mr. Wong." Barbara smiled her thanks and Charlie, relieved, vanished.

Brierson held out his hand for the snapshots, studied them expressionlessly, returned them without comment. Blythe, pinned in his corner, remained silent, motionless, expressionless, too.

Barbara turned to Chief Wilson. "You know that Martin White, with Mr. and Mrs. Elway, formed the Midwest Hotel Syndicate. With Anthony Elway, Martin White was responsible for the destruction of the Claytonian and Wayne River hotels in this city. And as James M. Blythe he can be charged with the deaths of Mr. and Mrs. Elway. For one reason, because he is their sole beneficary."

For a moment the five men stared, speechless. Barbara Emmett faced them calmly. Brierson was the first to find his voice.

"Do I understand you are charging Mr. Blythe with arson?"

"I am. Though no one actually set a match to either hotel. No one actually knew when the fires would occur. The combination of twenty-below weather and concentrated heat served as the match. Anthony Elway and James M. Blythe made that combination possible."

"Very clever assuming, Miss Emmett. The catch is, I'm afraid, that the Claytonian didn't burn until its second year under Elway's management."

"Because two years ago Wayne River Valley had a very mild winter. The temperature never fell below zero."

"Let that wait." Brierson shifted impatiently. "You've also charged Mr. Blythe with the deaths of his own sister and her husband. His motive, you say, was his desire to inherit their estates—"

"Mr. Elway's decision to abandon his career of arson was Mr. Blythe's immediate motive. The other followed."

As he listened to this extraordinary conversation Dan watched the faces about the table. Brierson's square brown planes were set like granite. The chief's, brightly flushed, tense. Marcus P.'s, pale and weary. Only Blythe remained at ease, his eyes, like hard blue marbles, fixed on Barbara.

"You are prepared to prove your charges, Miss Emmett?" Brierson asked.

"I shall say no more until Mr. Blythe is arrested—"

"Arrested!" Blythe sat up. "Arrest me, and I'll blow this town wide open."

"Begin blowing," Chief Wilson advised curtly. "I'm arresting you now for the murders of Anthony Elway and his wife."

Blythe laughed, winked at Brierson. "Listen to the hick policeman. Thinks he can arrest me on the unsupported word of a Chink and a—"

Unexpectedly Marcus P.'s hoarse voice spoke from the corner. "You can be arrested without prejudice to yourself, Mr. Blythe. Go along with the chief. If Miss Emmett's charges aren't supported—and I admit from what I've heard this morning they appear groundless to me—Mr. Brierson will have you released within twenty-four hours."

"Twenty-four hours! He'll do better than that or—" Under Brierson's stony glance Blythe shrugged angrily, rose.

"Come along with us yourself, Mr. Brierson," Wilson invited amiably. "You too, Marc. No one knows the law better'n Judge Fleming. He'll be in his office by the time we get there."

"Fair enough." Brierson rose, too, left to retrieve his coat and Blythe's from the next booth.

Dan and Barbara looked at the rising men, then at one another. They might have been members of any belated steak party breaking up on friendly terms. But when they left the booth Dan understood the chief's amiability.

Thorwaldson was nowhere to be seen. Except for the chattering voices of Chinese boys in the kitchen and the clink of dishes and silver, the now dimly lighted restaurant appeared deserted. And Blythe for all his contemptuous confidence had not agreed to accept either the chief's or Brierson's orders.

Not even the chief was armed, Dan knew. Uneasily he drew Barbara back to permit the others to precede them. As he watched Marcus P. slowly buttoning his coat he knew the same thought harried his father.

Blythe, talking with Brierson, moved steadily toward the door. A step or two behind them the chief and Marcus P. walked, apparently undisturbed. Reassured, Dan, with Barbara beside him, started forward.

After a few steps he stopped short. Everyone stopped. Blythe had whirled to face them coolly, a revolver's round eye fixed on them from his hand.

"We part here," he said. "So sorry. Brierson, open the door and give me the key. Then get back—"

Marcus P. went right on walking. "Don't be a fool, Blythe. You'll get a fair hearing."

"You heard me, Brierson," Blythe snapped. "Open that door. Wide."

Warily Brierson moved round him, opened the narrow door, thrust it back as far as it would go, extracted the key from its lock. Warily he dropped it into Blythe's outstretched left hand, joined the chief and Marcus P.

"I have been a fool," Blythe told them as he backed toward the door. "But I'm wise now."

The gun fell from his hand. He plunged forward, almost knocking over like so many ninepins the silent trio nearest him.

Fist still extended, Thorwaldson leaped into the room, seized the limp figure from the floor, roughly threw it onto a seat in the neighboring booth.

"Got him!" he panted. "And got them, Chief. Charlie just brought them. Carter sent the prints down this

morning. And Foster found prints too. On the cups. Good
ones, he says."

Oblivious of his stunned listeners, he produced two
square brown envelopes from a pocket, gave them to the
chief. Then, turning, he picked up Blythe's revolver, thrust
it into a pocket, closed the door. Face flushed, eyes sparkling, he remained in front of it, unconcernedly dusting
snow from his shoulders.

"What goes on, Wilson?" Brierson demanded.

Wilson didn't hear him. He had walked to a serving
table, was laying out, aligning, and comparing the square
slips, dark with finger smudges, he had shaken out of their
envelopes.

Thorwaldson answered. Nodding his head toward the
still unconscious Blythe, he said, pleased, "The chief's got
ferret eyes. Spotted his gun. He sent Wong with the cups
and a note to Foster, told me to stand by outside. I guess
he figured if Blythe thought he had the only weapon he
might pull it—"

Marcus P. and Brierson looked from Thorwaldson to
the chief, then silently moved over to inspect Blythe. Dan
turned to Barbara. She had lost nothing of her composure
apparently, yet as he walked with her to a booth across the
room he felt her tenseness.

In the quiet of the dim room his own nerves tightened.
The telltale skin on the back of his neck gave additional
warning. Uneasily he rose to his feet to watch the chief.
Barbara slipped from the booth to stand beside him.

Wilson had completed his manipulation of the slips.
Now he stood gazing at them as if mesmerized.

Gradually the stillness affected everyone. Marcus P.
and Brierson turned also to watch the chief. He seemed
unable to tear his eyes away from what he saw.

Mr. Cumberland took a step forward. "What's up,
Pete?"

The chief gripped the table, thrust himself erect, turned slowly. "Marc!" he said unbelievingly. "Marc!"

His hand wavered unsteadily toward the slips. "Marc! Carter found prints on a cake of soap Mrs. McPhail carried away from the Elway bathroom, the morning of December twenty-third. Two of them match exactly prints Foster took from the coffee cup you used here this morning!"

Dazedly he turned to Dan. "There's no mistake. You can see for yourself. Charlie didn't know which cup was which so took all five of them to Foster. Look—I already had Brierson's prints, Blythe's—that is, Martin White's—yours, and mine. These are Marc's—from his cup. And these are from the soap—a perfect right forefinger and middle—"

As the chief talked Dan strode over to look at the two aligned squares. Now he whirled round.

Marcus P. had advanced no farther. He stood rigid, gazing back at his stricken son while his already pale, triangular face drained to a blue white. His hat dropped from his nerveless hand. He moved his lips but no sound came.

"Marc!" the chief repeated, his harsh voice shaking. "Don't stand there like that. Explain, man!"

"You tricked me! " Marcus P. said almost inaudibly to Dan. "My own son!"

"Tricked you? Dan?" Wilson walked incredulously toward him. "Marc, think what you're saying. Unless you can explain how your prints got there I—I'll have to arrest you—"

Moment after moment crept away as the two men, lifelong friends and associates, faced one another. At last Marcus P. shook his head. "I can't explain, Pete," he, said woodenly. "Go ahead. I'll—be glad to get it over."

"Dad, wait!" Dan sprang toward him. "You're ill, you don't know what you're saying. There must be some explanation—"

"No. If you hadn't tricked me with your talk of McPhail I'd have been in Winnipeg by noon. You'll find my bags in the trunk of the car."

"And left Brierson and me to face the music!" a thick voice shouted. Unobserved except by Thorwaldson, Blythe had propped himself up in the booth, one hand nursing his jaw. Over it his blue eyes blazed at Marcus P.

"Stay here. Face it out. That's what you advised us to do, isn't it? No one could prove anything! You with the *News* and Brierson as D.A. could handle everything! And you sat there in that booth, you old crow, telling me to march off to jail like a good little boy scout! While all the time—well, talk now, damn you, or I will!"

"You fools!" Brierson shotted him down. "You fools! Shut up, both of you." He stood a moment glaring from Blythe to Marcus P., his vast shoulders thrust back, his head high. Suddenly, as he read capitulation in their faces, he flung himself into the booth beside Blythe, buried his head in his hands.

In shattering silence the chief took Marcus P. by the arm, guided him to the booth, helped him into it before sitting down himself.

Dan felt a hand on his arm, looked down. Wordlessly, under Barbara's light pressure, he crossed to the booth, seated himself beside her.

Blythe's bold blue gaze moved contemptuously from Brierson, face still hidden, to Marcus P., a small, shaken figure in the corner, then to Barbara and Dan. "One way or another, you get 'em, don't you, sister? A very nice day's work. Brierson, Cumberland—and son."

"And you, Mr. Blythe," she reminded him smoothly. "Fortunately, I'm sure you'll talk in Minnesota. There's no death sentence here. You'd find it more difficult, say, in New York State, wouldn't you?"

For a moment electricity charged the air between them. Blythe's arrogance expired. "Sure, I'll talk—under those conditions. Why not? Seven years ago Mr. Marcus P. Cumberland had a fire in his old rattletrap News Building. Not a bad one, at that, and one hundred per cent bona fide. But that fire almost finished him. He needed everything. New building, new equipment, new financing. And by that time I'd had three profitable years with Elway, he staging the fires—under different names of course—me staging the claims and taking my percentage of the insurance. I showed this small-town publisher how to get almost total-claim payment. And I got my cut and that was that—until four years ago. . . ."

"Then McPhail came through with his mixture for burning out weeds. Cumberland learned of it from Brierson, who'd got the patents on it and was going to join forces with the professor for its manufacture. I'd done Cumberland a good turn and now he saw a chance to do me and himself a better one. He sent for me and when I heard his idea I sent for Elway. But by that time it was too late. The chemical warfare service had taken over McPhail's formula, and when I tried to buy the stuff he had on hand he took me for an enemy agent of some kind, turned me down. . . .

"But it was too good an idea to pass up, so through Cumberland we interested Mr. District Attorney here in our little problem. In no time at all he'd wangled the mixture, all neatly canned, from Mrs. McPhail. Elway tried it out on a small scale in Arkansas. It was a dream, foolproof. So we formed a little company. On the cuff, of course, since both Cumberland and Brierson were honorable gentlemen. We bought the Claytonian. It tied us up for eighteen months but when it came through at last it proved McPhail's mixture to be a gold mine. That is, when combined with other conditions like those in Clayton, and they could be duplicated almost anywhere as long as the war lasted and perhaps for years afterward, all over the country. . . .

"And that's just where our honorable partners wanted Elway and me to take the stuff. Anywhere, as long as it was far from Clayton! We'd run all the risks while they'd cash the checks we'd send 'em! Elway's pigheaded answer to that was to buy the Wayne River. That fire would've been foolproof, too, if Dan Cumberland hadn't stuck his oar in. The *Morning News* saw nothing strange in another hotel fire in twenty-below weather, but the evening edition immediately linked the Wayne River with the Claytonian. That woke up Carston—"

"Wait a minute," the chief interrupted. "Go back to the Elways. We'll talk about Carston later."

Blythe's face darkened. "You're right," he admitted, "Dolores comes first. She'd been against us all along but after the Claytonian burned she gave Elway no peace. The night the Wayne River burned she told him to choose between her and us. That decided him. He'd already figured he could do as well for himself without fires as with the four of us sharing his profits from the insurance. When I reached Clayton, December twenty-second, Elway told me he was through. . . .

"But Cumberland, Brierson, and I weren't, and we'd just bought a new hotel in Waterloo, Iowa. About seven o'clock that night we went down to talk turkey to Elway. Found him and Dolores putting bags in their car, all set to leave us flat. When she threatened to go to the police herself, tell all she knew if we didn't let them go, I lost my head, struck her—and the fat was in the fire. Elway went berserk. He'd have killed us all if he could. . . .

"We knew then that none of us was safe as long as Dolores lived. And there was no way of silencing her and not Elway. Brierson came up with an idea. Elway'd put on a very good act over the loss of the Claytonian. Seeing him after the Wayne River burned, anyone would have thought him a broken man. And Dolores, though she was tough as a knot, looked as if a breath of wind could do for her. A double suicide, because of the fires and her health, seemed to Brierson a logical solution for all their troubles. And by coincidence—or shall we call it premeditation?—though I had a gun, your D.A. had a better weapon—chloroform. . . .

"I agreed with Brierson, but Cumberland reminded us of the number of people in the valley who'd been killed or narrowly escaped death while warming up their motors in closed garages. And Dolores and Elway had everything set for just such an accident, even to the suitcases in their car. Brierson and Cumberland almost came to blows over their suicide versus accident theories. But Brierson won because we couldn't stay there for hours. We used the chloroform, removed the gags and ropes we'd made from torn sheets to leave no bruises, and started the motor. . . .

"About ten o'clock we were ready to leave when we missed Cumberland. Found him in the kitchen, sick—too weak to move. Brierson took him home while I went up to the Harrison to interview Carston on all he knew about the fires and Elway. The poor dope knew nothing—fortunately for him and us! At midnight I met Brierson and we drove around, checking each other on every detail. We'd left the back door unlocked—just in case. We couldn't think of a slip we'd made, but to be sure we went back. Before one o'clock, sometime. Penndale was deserted and dark. While Brierson waited in the car I returned to the house."

Blythe stopped to look from one to another of his silent listeners. The chief, Dan, and Barbara, alert and intent, returned his gaze. Marcus P. and Brierson, submerged in their own despair, appeared unaware of him.

"Maybe they think they're in a tough spot now," he said with a cynical nod toward publisher and attorney. "They should have been with me when I found the garage doors open, the motor still running, Elway and Dolores gone! I was sure they'd escaped or that someone had been there, freed them—"

At the memory, moisture beaded his forehead. "We know now what happened, but all I knew then was that our idea the Elways would be found, chloroformed and gassed in their own car as if by their own choice, had blown up in our faces. I almost went nuts when I discovered them— upstairs—dead—dressed for bed! Brierson's horn outside warned me to hurry so I had no time to do anything but tumble the beds as if they'd slept in them. I did try to lift Elway, but I was in a panic, let him fall. That's how he got the ripped sleeve there's been so much talk about. I never thought of killing the car engine, turning on gas in the house. . . .

"Brierson did. He nearly went wild when I told him, but he wouldn't go back into that house and neither would I. We called Cumberland and he advised us to forget it, sit tight, and go on as usual. He couldn't face it himself, though, stayed in bed until those *Evening News* stories began to get under all our skins. When he couldn't stop them without making Dan's nose sharper than it was he sent me over to talk with Master Mind, Jr." Blythe's straight lips curled in a smile for Dan. "Boy! How you fell. And what a report you turned in to bolster my own."

"Don't mention it," Dan said wryly. "But we digress. When did you learn who upset your applecart?"

"Christmas Day. I'd hardly left Clayton when Brierson at a party at the McPhails' found the professor drunk and babbling, learned he'd moved the bodies. Brierson wired me. . . .

"We didn't know, however, until Cumberland arrived in Chicago the day after the Elways had been found that he had drunk a glass of water in their kitchen, washed his hands there. The strain of waiting for that discovery and fear that prints of his might be found had been almost too much for Marcus P.! I interned him in a Chicago hotel while I flew back here to see what Brierson and I could, do. . . .

"Again it was too late. Mrs. McPhail had had a busy day in that house. Carried away God knows what, including the soap, and had washed or taken away the glass. We didn't know that, of course. We suspected Dan Cumberland of taking them. He was asking pertinent questions up and down the town, obviously meant trouble. When he slipped round the Elway house on his way to the river the very hour Brierson and I were inside hunting that damned soap and glass, Brierson inveigled him in, delayed him while I went down the ridge—"

Barbara said quietly, "You were the man I saw. You threw—"

Blythe's eyes turned on her, hardened. "You were the crazy Norsk female that came skiing round the bend!"

Angrily Brierson sat up. "Shut up, Blythe. What can you hope to gain by this monologue?"

"His life," Barbara informed him. "He'll either talk here or in New York, and New York State, as you know, Mr. Brierson, has capital punishment. Blythe and Elway staged their first fire there. In that fire a woman died. That's why they've operated ever since in the West and South."

"You—! To save your own neck, you—" Speechless with rage, Big Thode turned on Blythe, turned back, said hopelessly, "All right, Wilson. Now you know—"

"Not everything. What about Carston?"

"Carston! He died in his bed, I suppose. Looked as if he were going to the last time I saw him."

"When was that?"

"Monday night. He stumbled up to my office about nine o'clock, almost had a stroke right there because he'd begun to suspect Elway of firing his own hotels. He was so drunk and incoherent I drove him home to sleep it off."

"He was in the library Monday night from eight o'clock until almost ten," Dan corrected. "He went straight from there to the Harrison bar, left shortly before one. He didn't go home. I searched every room in his house Tuesday morning. He wasn't there, hadn't been there all night. But he was there dead at midnight Tuesday when Thorwaldson finally went out to his house, had been dead almost twenty-four hours."

When Brierson protested he added savagely, "You lie! You or you and Blythe killed Jack. And Lisa."

"Lisa!" Brierson shouted. "Are you crazy? Lisa died at home—this morning."

"Lisa died on Captain Billy's steamboat last night. The chief and I found her there this morning."

Brierson whirled on Blythe. Marcus P. moaned, shrank farther back in his corner. Blythe challenged them both defiantly.

"How was I to know the woman there was Mrs. McPhail? You said she was Barbara Sandys, claimed to be Dolores' sister. You sent me down to find out what her racket was. But she wouldn't let me in, told me to go round to the window. It was so dark she couldn't see me until I was right beside her, then she screamed, tried to close it. Wasn't quick enough—"

"Don't go on," Wilson advised him. "We know the rest. You've admitted you murdered the Elways and Mrs. McPhail. We know you killed Carston with bad liquor and—"

"Stop talking yourself, then," Blythe suggested. "We won't live any longer whether we get one sentence or three.

Sure, Brierson and I killed Carston. What're you going to do about it?"

"Don't be so sure you're talked yourself into the Minnesota State Penitentiary for life," Chief Wilson warned. "If New York wants you it can have you—and welcome."

When that threat obliterated Blythe's arrogance the chief turned to Brierson but his words were chosen for Marcus P. "You know the law, and you know what this thing's going to do to Clayton if it's made a nine days' wonder. With what we've got and what Blythe'll tell to save his neck, you and—and Marc don't stand a chance with a jury, Brierson. But it's up to you."

Brierson said with stiff lips, "Not entirely. You forget Miss Emmett and the American Protective Association—"

Barbara spoke quickly. "What is the choice, Mr. Wilson? The APA is no more interested than you in nine-day wonders. Our sole concern is to end these fires—"

The chief's knotted brows smoothed out. "These men'll be charged before Judge Fleming of the district court, Miss Emmett. If they decide to plead not guilty they must stand trial. Perhaps months from now. If they plead guilty the judge can sentence them today, commit them to the penitentiary for life. And before anyone in town knows what's happened I can have them on their way to Stillwater."

Marcus P. opened his eyes, spoke two words. "Guilty, Pete."

Brierson nodded. Blythe shrugged.

Wilson drew a long, gusty breath. "Then it's up to you, Dan, to see that the *News*—"

"No." Dan looked at his father. "It's time Clayton grew up, knew the truth about what goes on here. If the responsibility is mine the *News* tonight will carry the whole story."

Mr. Cumberland looked at his son for a long moment. "The responsibility is yours, Dan. First for Dora. Then the *News*. You'll stay?"

His decision to remain in Clayton already made, but powerless to voice it, Dan held out his hand.

"Not now. One day—perhaps," Marcus P. murmured and, when Dan did not withdraw his hand, turned away.

Over his old friend's shoulder Wilson shook his head at Dan, with his eyes indicated the door.

Brierson and Blythe sat stolidly, side by side, gazing into space.

At the top of the hill Dan sat motionless in the car, his hands gripped on the wheel. After a time he knew he was not alone there. He looked round. Barbara sat beside him.

Her heavy cape was folded round her; her hands, enclosed in the fuzzy white mittens, were folded too. Obviously she had been sitting there some time, had every intention of continuing. But she neither turned nor spoke.

In the mirror he saw why. Her clear gray eyes, brimming with tears, met his.

His frozen grip on the wheel relaxed. Carefully he started the car before he asked then, "Coming?"

"Coming."

"Always?"

"Always."

ABOUT THE AUTHOR

Vera Kelsey (1892-1961) was the daughter of an American couple, born in Winnipeg, Ontario. She grew up in Grand Forks, North Dakota. She was a reporter for the *Fargo Forum*, and graduated from the University of North Dakota. Her early writing career included working for the *North China Daily News,* which allowed her to travel extensively in Asia, and then she spent almost five years in South America, particularly Brazil, before making her home in New York. She wrote mystery novels, travel books, and historical and regional nonfiction. She spent her last years in Minneapolis, and owned a cottage on Lake Minnetonka.

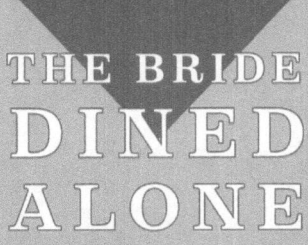

THE BRIDE
DINED
ALONE

VERA KELSEY

COACHWHIP
PUBLICATIONS

SATAN
HAS SIX
FINGERS

VERA KELSEY

COACHWHIPBOOKS.COM

COACHWHIP
PUBLICATIONS

COACHWHIPBOOKS.COM

*Death Has
Seven Faces*

HUGH AUSTIN

COACHWHIP
PUBLICATIONS

NARROW
GAUGE TO
MURDER

CAROLYN THOMAS

COACHWHIPBOOKS.COM

COACHWHIP
PUBLICATIONS

COACHWHIPBOOKS.COM

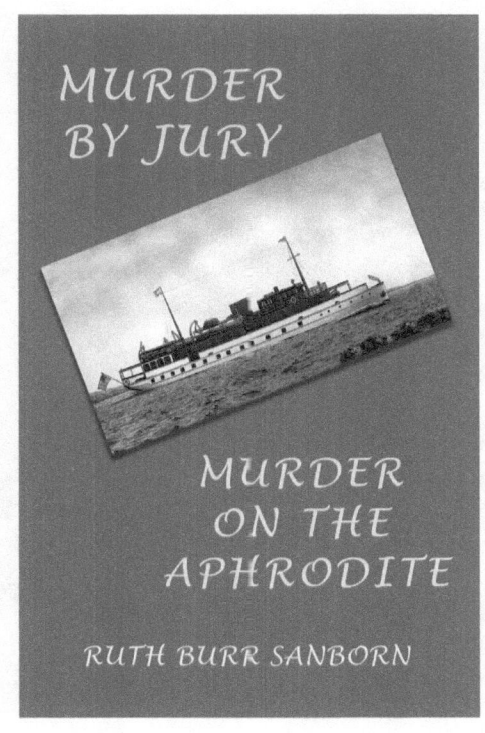

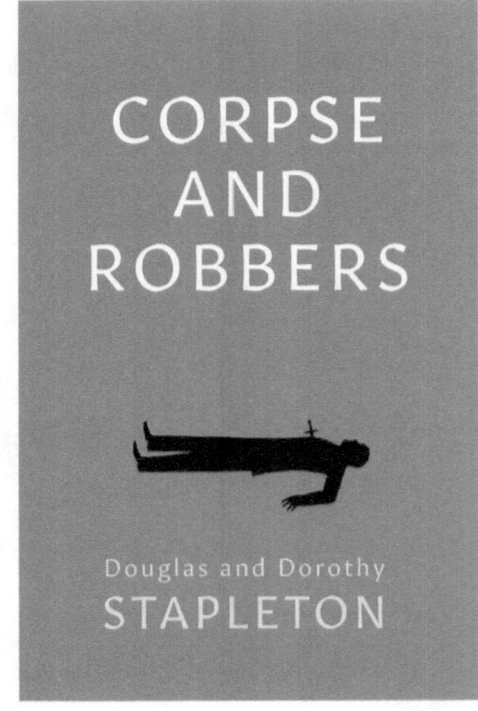

HELEN BURNHAM

THE MURDER OF
LALLA LEE

THE TELLTALE
TELEGRAM

COACHWHIP
PUBLICATIONS

Scarecrow

EATON K. GOLDTHWAITE

COACHWHIPBOOKS.COM

www.ingramcontent.com/pod-product-compliance
Lightning Source LLC
Chambersburg PA
CBHW031000260626
47169CB00002B/627